NOT A
RAT RACE

Dr Arpita Sen has completed her bachelor's degree in dental surgery (BDS) from YMT Dental College and Hospital, Navi Mumbai, and has completed her MBA in human resources (HR) from Narsee Monjee Institute of Management Studies (NMIMS), Mumbai. During her MBA, she was awarded gold medal for securing the first rank as well as Chancellor's gold medal for all-round student performance. In her spare time, she loves travelling, reading novels, singing and performing classical dance. Follow her on Twitter @SenArpita25.

Abhirup Bhattacharya is a graduate in fashion technology from the National Institute of Fashion Technology (NIFT), Kolkata, and has completed his MBA in finance from Narsee Monjee Institute of Management Studies (NMIMS), Mumbai. He is also the author of *Nirvana for Gen X: Re-Discover Your Inner Zen* (2019), *Decoding Gita: Algorithms for Personal Success* (2019), *Winning Like Sourav: Think & Succeed Like Ganguly* (2018) and *Winning Like Virat: Think & Succeed Like Kohli* (2017). Apart from being an author, he has nearly a decade of experience in financial services and consulting. Follow him on Twitter, Instagram and Facebook @abhirupbh.

NOT A RAT RACE
SUCCESS MANTRAS OF WORLD ATHLETES

ARPITA SEN *and*
ABHIRUP BHATTACHARYA

Published by
Rupa Publications India Pvt. Ltd 2023
7/16, Ansari Road, Daryaganj
New Delhi 110002

Sales centres:
Allahabad Bengaluru Chennai
Hyderabad Jaipur Kathmandu
Kolkata Mumbai

Copyright © Arpita Sen and Abhirup Bhattacharya 2023

The views and opinions expressed in this book are the authors' own and the facts are as reported by them which have been verified to the extent possible, and the publishers are not in any way liable for the same.

All rights reserved.
No part of this publication may be reproduced, transmitted, or stored in a retrieval system, in any form or by any means, electronic, mechanical, photocopying, recording or otherwise, without the prior permission of the publisher.

P-ISBN: 978-93-5702-010-7
E-ISBN: 978-93-5702-014-5

First impression 2023

10 9 8 7 6 5 4 3 2 1

The moral right of the authors has been asserted.

Printed in India

This book is sold subject to the condition that it shall not, by way of trade or otherwise, be lent, resold, hired out, or otherwise circulated, without the publisher's prior consent, in any form of binding or cover other than that in which it is published.

Contents

Introduction: Combining Sports and Management   vii

1. Speed and Combativeness: LIONEL MESSI   1
2. Creating Benchmarks: CARL LEWIS   16
3. Self-Motivation: VIRAT KOHLI   30
4. Consistency Has No Age: MARTINA NAVRATILOVA   45
5. Fighting Adversity: MARY KOM   60
6. Giving Controversies a Big Punch: MUHAMMAD ALI   73
7. Reaching the Success Shore: MICHAEL PHELPS   86
8. Kicking Poverty to the Curb: PELÉ   95
9. Breaking Stereotypes: LEWIS HAMILTON   105
10. Serving with Perfection: P.V. SINDHU   116
11. Quest for Perfection: SACHIN TENDULKAR   128
12. Defying Critics: CRISTIANO RONALDO   138
13. Shattering the Glass Ceiling: SERENA WILLIAMS   147
14. Combatting the Enemy Within: TIGER WOODS   159
15. Racing Ahead with Passion: MICHAEL SCHUMACHER   170
16. Charging Ahead: USAIN BOLT   181
17. Nurturing Mental Toughness: ROGER FEDERER   190
18. Understanding the Mind of a Strategist: VISWANATHAN ANAND   198

19. Facing Challenges Head-On: NADIA COMĂNECI   208
20. Competing against Oneself: SERGEY BUBKA   219
21. Leading from the Front: M.S. DHONI   232
22. Master of the Trade: RAFAEL NADAL   247

Acknowledgements   259

Introduction

Combining Sports and Management

Sports and management are almost like reflections of each other separated by a mirror. Qualities such as passion and hard work are as common and relevant in a sportsperson's life as they are in an entrepreneur's. The success principles that apply to famous sports personalities, such as Sachin Tendulkar, can also be attributed to the likes of Mark Zuckerberg and Elon Musk. This book dissects the qualities of 22 athletes across sports and analyses one major attribute that separates them from the rest. These sports personalities hail from different backgrounds but have one thing in common—their hunger for success. Despite the odds, they have managed to be successful and have aimed to win every single time.

The life of a corporate professional is not much different from that of a sportsperson; both are driven by the same principle of excellence. When a captain like M.S. Dhoni makes decisions on the cricket field, it is not different from a chief executive officer deciding his next strategy for increasing sales. If we consider the moves a grand master like Viswanathan Anand makes in a rapid chess tournament, his ability to think faster than anyone else—a core skill needed to make quick and correct decisions in any profession—makes all the difference. Many of these professionals have also built very strong personal brands and ventured away from their primary professions. Just like corporate workers focus on enhancing the performance of their products and building a strong brand recall, our champion sportspersons too aim to better their performance each time they take the field. During our research for the book, we found that there are several areas and aspects where we can easily draw a parallel between their career trajectories and how companies operate to deliver their promise.

As management professionals, we found an uncanny similarity in the success principles of these champion athletes and our own professional and personal lives. We strongly feel the challenges faced by these athletes in achieving greatness are no less than what any of us also encounter in our lives. Sports are as much an application of skills and strength as they are mind games. In a similar manner, we have experienced that success in the corporate boardroom, too, is dependent on the same principles. Often, we feel that our daily challenges are unique and have no resemblance to anyone else. It is actually quite the contrary. There are parallels that can be drawn from our journey by finding common areas to look into and improving upon the same. Our main objective while writing this book was threefold: dissecting the path of these athletes—their journey and challenges, take away key lessons from their decision-making process and showing how we can relate them to the corporate and personal lives of our readers.

Being successful or famous is an end result of excellence—whether in sports, corporate or student life. Our key idea was to identify the ingredients behind the success of these athletes, so that we can apply them in our professional and personal lives. Often, it is believed that talent leads to success. Yet, during the course of writing this book, we found that talent was only a small fraction of the attributable reason behind the incredible journey of these champions. In fact, in the case of most of these athletes, we found that they were disadvantaged through either deformities, genetic disorders, family issues or economic challenges. Yet, each of them overcame those hurdles by their sheer hard work, perseverance and determination to achieve their dreams. Leadership in sports is also another aspect that is covered in depth in this book. Succeeding in a sports field in a team sport is no different from winning a corporate battle against stronger brands. Whether you are leading a team on a soccer field or driving a sales team to augment your market share, the key principles for winning remain the same.

Our focus has been to undertake an in-depth analysis of one key ingredient behind the success of each athlete. We feel that each of these qualities is deeply rooted and relatable. During the course of reading, we suggest you to go slow, make notes and try to analyse the lessons that you can draw from the book, which is also replete with tips for a quick recap of the success principles.

As a reader, you can begin reading from any chapter, as each one focusses on a particular athlete. The purpose of the book is to inspire young minds and professionals in developing the outlook of a champion in their daily lives. Happy reading!

1

Speed and Combativeness

Lionel Messi

You have to fight to reach your dream. You have to sacrifice and work hard for it.[1]

LIONEL MESSI

Years ago, a little boy from Argentina named Leo harboured a strong desire to play football. Seeing his love for the sport, his grandmother convinced his mother to buy him a pair of cleats. Thus, a star was born. At the tender age of four, young Leo joined Grandoli Club, where his father coached him. This is the story of Lionel Andrés Messi Cuccittini, winner of seven Ballon d'Or awards and six European Golden Shoes. He plays as a forward and is the captain of the Argentinian national football team. This prolific goal scorer holds the record for over 700 senior career goals for club and country.

EARLY LIFE

Born in 1987, in Rosario, Argentina, Messi played soccer with his two older brothers and their friends from an early age.

---

[1] Brandon, Roy, *Lionel Messi: The Rise to Stardom*, CreateSpace Independent Publishing Platform, 2016.

He was never intimidated by the appearance and age of the bigger players and was as quick as a rabbit in throwing goals. He joined the Newell's Old Boys, a Rosario-based club, at the age of six. He played for Newell's for six years, scoring about 500 goals as a member of La Maquina del '87' (The Machine of '87'). He used to regularly do ball tricks during his team's games to entertain the crowd.

GROWTH HORMONE DEFICIENCY

At the age of 11, Messi was just 4 feet 4 inches in height. Being shorter than the rest of the boys his age, he was eventually diagnosed with GHD (growth hormone disorder),[2] also known as idiopathic short stature.[3] As a result, he did not gain as much height as required for the game of soccer. GHD as a condition is noticeable only a little later in life, when there is physical manifestation like delay in maturation and short height. This is how Messi's condition remained undiagnosed till the age of 11. In an interview to *The Telegraph*, he said, 'I was so small, that they said that when I went to the pitch, or when I went to the school, I was always the smallest of all. It was like this until I finished the treatment and I then started to grow properly.'[4]

The treatments for idiopathic short stature were expensive, costing about $1,000 a month. Messi's modest family found

---

[2] Growth hormone deficiency is a medical condition where a pea-sized gland situated in the brain, known as pituitary gland, produces less growth hormone, which not only promotes growth but also helps in maturation.

[3] Ayyagari, Saketh, 'What Disease Does Lionel Messi Have?' Sportskeeda, 22 July 2022, https://bit.ly/3J4Xwvk. Accessed on 26 July 2022.

[4] Balague, Guillem, 'Lionel Messi's Improbable Progression from Struggling Youngster to World Super Star', *The Telegraph*, 2 December 2013, https://bit.ly/3zxNX4U. Accessed on 26 July 2022.

it quite difficult to arrange such money for his treatment. At this juncture, it was Newell's Old Boys who promised to cover his medical expenses. However, they eventually discontined the help. He was later scouted by Buenos Aires Club, Club Atlético River Plate, but they were unwilling to pay for his medical treatment. It was only later, when he was signed by FC Barcelona that his contract included medical coverage. It was only owing to proper treatment that Messi could become one of the legends of the game. His perseverance and decision to leave Argentina and move to Barcelona paved the way for his career ahead.

By the time Messi turned 13, he was already being compared to the Argentinian football stalwart, Diego Maradona. It was surprising for a boy of Messi's age to possess similar skill sets as a seasoned player. When these stories reached the ears of FC Barcelona, its then director, Carles Rexach i Cerdà, invited Messi's family for a trial. They were told that if he was selected to the team and following that shifted base to Spain, they would cover his medical expenses. Messi was initially reluctant to make this move, but thinking of his bright future, the family took up this life-changing step in September 2000.

When Cerdà pitched Messi to his board of directors, they were initially sceptical to sign him for two reasons: first, he was a foreigner, and second, he was too young for the game. However, his skills and passion for the game mesmerized them all. Owing to the fact that Messi was reserved by nature, barely speaking to anyone, his teammates initially thought he was mute. He took some time mixing up with his teammates due to his introversion. However, when they saw him scoring goals, they were left speechless. After just spending two minutes on the pitch, he proved that he meant serious business with the ball. Coach Cerdà was so impressed that he offered the contract straight away on a paper napkin, the only thing he had at that time. Messi's life thus changed that very moment.

After some time, however, Messi started feeling homesick, as his mother and siblings shifted back to Rosario and he had to stay in Spain with his father. In an interview, he said, 'I made a lot of sacrifices by leaving Argentina, leaving my family to start a new life. But everything I did, I did for football, to achieve my dream. That's why I didn't go out partying, or do a lot of other things.'[5]

CONTROVERSY AROUND TREATMENT

Messi could not play many matches in the beginning due to a transfer conflict with Newell's. In February 2002, he was finally enrolled in the Royal Spanish Football Federation. He used to follow an arduous routine. He practised all day, stopped having fizzy drinks and chocolates to prevent vomiting while playing, and injected growth hormones in his legs at night. By the age of 14, his treatment was complete as he reached the height of 5 feet 7 inches.

> **Learning Tip:** Do not let a physical disability or weakness come in the path of achieving success. Opportunities come to those who do not use their weakness as an excuse for giving up.

Messi's treatment received much criticism from rivals who accused him of using the growth hormone injection for enhancing his performance. Messi's condition was, however, serious. If untreated, he would have had a fragile body with a

---

[5]'Lionel Messi Biography', *Biography Online,* https://bit.ly/2zIVONX. Accessed on 28 October 2022.

low bone density and would not have been able to play football at all. He used the medication but only in therapeutic dosage. Nevertheless, he was questioned about this repeatedly in his entire career. In an interview, he said, 'I injected my legs once every night. I started at 12 years old. It was not something that left an impression on me.'[6]

> Learning Tip: If you believe in yourself, no physical shortcoming can stop you from achieving your goals and fulfilling your dreams.

COMPENSATING FOR HIS WEAKNESS WITH SPEED

At the height of 5 feet 7 inches, Messi retained a very low centre of gravity, which enabled him to have a perfect combination of balance, speed and agility. His short stature was initially considered a weakness by his rivals, but with the help of neat footwork and speed, he was able to compensate for that weakness.

Every player uses his speed—an integral aspect in football—to get ahead of the other to score a goal. Speed was the real contributor behind Messi's excellent ball control. He lacked great height and muscles, unlike his peers. He knew that dribbling was the only aspect of the game he could master. A footballer's muscles have lactic acid accumulation after high speed dribbling, which may cause a burning sensation in the muscles. He overcame this with his amazing speed and was able to endure more due to his short stature. He was also excellent at reading the game before his rivals could and that

---

[6]Terrell, Alex, 'Leo's Needle' Mare Barcelona Star Lionel Messi Reveals Brutal Details of Childhood Hormone Injection Hell Aged 12', *The Sun*, 20 March 2018, https://bit.ly/3zAwusA. Accessed on 27 July 2022.

contributed to his great dribbling abilities. In the 2014 FIFA World Cup, Messi was reported to be the best dribbler of the tournament.

At the start of his career, Messi started as a right winger who used to either dribble or cut inside with his dominant left foot and used to either shoot or play a defence splitting pass through the middle. Eventually, he started interlinking with his midfielders operating as a false-9[7]. He was apt for this role, as he had a strong sense of awareness, great speed, excellent dribbling skills, ability to give a killer pass and was deft with long- and short-range finishing skills. Today, he can operate from anywhere. He strikes his signature deceptive move, where he performs a shimmy to shift the ball to the other leg. The opponent often misjudges this sudden shift and stumbles under his own inertia.

One of the many leading reasons for Messi's mastery over his football and incredible balance even when he does ball tricks and swiftly shifts the ball between his legs is him having a low centre of gravity, which implies greater balance. Centre of gravity is believed to be a point where all the gravity of the body is concentrated. It is believed to be lower for shorter bodies and higher for taller bodies. Even if he falls, Messi's flexible body allows him to spring back every time and charge for the goal. His instincts are superfast. It seems as if his mind and body both are supercharged at the same time. His inexhaustible stamina and ability to tire others has been instrumental in him scoring goals till the end of match.

---

[7]False-9 is one of the toughest roles in a football field. In this role, the player usually plays between where a traditional number 9 centre forward and a playmaker number 10 would usually play. A false-9 digs deeper into the field to receive the ball. Without a striker in front of him, he draws all the central defenders towards himself. This is a decoy, as it forces the defending team to have a high back line.

Learning Tip: Develop your strengths to a level that they compensate for your weakness.

FOCUSSING ON MENTAL STRENGTHS

Messi has amazing situational awareness. His mind is more dominant than his body. He is an excellent controller of the ball. His mind automatically calculates how much force is needed and how many touches are required. People say he runs even faster with his ball than without. He is not just a master of penalty shots but also of long passes, dribbling, assisting and crucial defence moves.

He moves towards the goal like an eagle chasing its prey. By the time someone is able to react to his move, he has already made his second move. He has the ability to make split-second decisions. It is difficult to catch up to him. The way he cuts through defences, opening spaces behind him, is like a rocket launching in space.

Learning Tip: It is not just physical ability but mental ability as well that make you stand out.

DISPLAYING SPORTSMANSHIP

In his entire career, Messi has never spoken ill of any player nor has he knowingly landed himself in any controversy. He has willingly steered away from negative conversations. Messi has been known to always keep a calm demeanour and has a very pleasant and charming personality.

In his entire soccer career, he has received only three red cards, two of which were the subject of debate. On 15 August 2005, Messi was playing his first international game in

Budapest, a friendly match with Hungary. He was only 18 and representing his country for the first time. He was a substitute player and came to the ground at the 64th minute, replacing Lisandro López. However, in just 44 seconds, he was shown a red card and a way out of the field. The referee thought Messi had hit his opponent's face with his elbow, but Messi denied any intention of doing so, explaining that he was only trying to free himself from his opponent's firm grip. Nevertheless, he respectfully accepted the referee's decision and left the field.[8]

His second red card came 14 years later while playing in the 2019 Copa América tournament against Chile. In the 37th minute of the match, Chilean player Gary Medel thought Messi deliberately pushed him back while chasing the ball. Medel then pushed himself towards Messi. Because of the body contact, both the players were given red cards. Messi received a $1,500 fine and a game suspension.[9]

> **Learning Tip:** It is important to ignore detractors and keep calm during negative criticism. This is true sportsmanship.

PLAYING FAIR

Messi has been a devoted player; he has never cheated to win. According to him, 'There are more important things in life than winning or losing a game.' For him, the experience of playing is more enjoyable than simply winning or losing. No one has ever doubted his fair play because of the way he carries himself both on and off the field. In 2018, he received the Barca

---

[8] Lionel Messi | Red Card in 40 Second.(First Match of His Career), Youtube, https://bit.ly/3fT6BgQ. Accessed on 28 July 2022.
[9] 'Messi Rails Against "Corruption" After Red Card in Win Over Chile', *Sportstar*, https://bit.ly/3S9ept6. Accessed on 28 July 2022.

Players Association's Fair Play Award for fair performance in the 2015–16 season.

Messi has never disrespected anyone on the field—may it be a co-player, opponent, coach, referee or the media. In 2019, while playing against Rayo Vallecano, Messi fell on the pitch. The referee suspected foul and consulted the video referee, but Messi displayed sportsmanship by stating that Vallecano hadn't fouled. In 2016, while playing against Club Atlético Osasuna, or simply Osasuna, he fell down while marching towards a goal and his opponent suddenly approached him. He immediately got up and informed the referee that the opponent had not committed a foul.

ANALYSING MISSED OPPORTUNITIES

In his remarkable career, Messi had also tasted a fair share of misses, some of which the team paid for with a loss. In the 2014 World Cup Final, Messi had a wonderful opportunity to score when he received the ball from the midfield. He raced towards the post, leaving behind the German defenders, but shot the ball too wide from the goalpost. In the 2016 Copa América, Chile and Argentina both failed to score in the 120-minute football match and were given penalty shoot-outs. Messi missed the golden chance to score, as he skied the ball over the goal. He was so traumatized by this penalty miss that he made a decision to retire from the Argentinian team. However, after taking a few weeks off, he analysed his misses, worked on his shortcomings and returned to play with Argentina. In his own words, he described his disappointment of not being a world champion as follows, 'I would've loved to be a world champion. But I don't think I would change anything else in my career to be one. This is what I was given, what God gave me. It is what it is. I couldn't dream of everything that I experienced after. It was far bigger than anything I could've imagined.'[10]

Messi had pretty good capability of hitting free kicks with great aim and precision, but some of those kicks often lacked power. Every free kick that Messi has scored has come from within 25 yards and he has failed to kick powerfully on those coming farther away. In due course of time, he has overcome this and mastered his free kicks. He initially used to rely on placement over power, but with time, he learnt to analyse his misses and has worked immensely on his power.

> **Learning Tip:** It is imperative for one to analyse the 'why' behind the failures and work on 'how' to overcome them.

COMBATIVENESS

Messi is a natural with the football, but that alone would not have sufficed without putting in enough hard work. While many believed he was an overnight success, Messi rightfully summarized his success thus: 'It took me 17 years and 114 days to become an overnight success.'[11] He trained day in, day out to excel at what he does best and supersede his colleagues by a huge margin. Being blessed with speed was an advantage, but using that speed to achieve success is known as combativeness—a quality Messi had displayed in every walk of his life. He was a leader who led by example. He has been

---

[10] Marsden, Rory, 'Lionel Messi Wouldn't Trade His Accomplishments for Argentina to Win World Cup', *Bleacher Report*, 26 October 2019, https://bit.ly/3bc6Q49. Accessed on 28 July 2022.

[11] 'Leo Messi: This Is My Training Formula', Soccer Training Info, https://bit.ly/3cMvSaD. Accessed on 28 July 2022.

committed to constantly improving himself. He is his own teacher. In his own words, 'I have many years to get better and better, and that has to be my ambition. The day you think there are no improvements to be made is a sad one for any player.'[12]

The difference between being 'ordinary' and being 'extraordinary' is that little 'extra'. Messi has extraordinary speed and agility, he kicks with extraordinary aim and precision, he glides through the defenders with extraordinary dribbling. All the milestones he has achieved in his life are due to the extra willpower and ambition he has and the dedication and hard work he puts in the game. To succeed in any field, we need preparation to be ahead of our competitors.

Messi's approach towards football is comparable with that of Jack Welch's towards business. John (Jack) Francis Welch Jr was the chairman and CEO of General Electric from 1981 to 2001. As Messi uses his speed and combativeness to move towards the goal, Welch used his innovative thinking and was the first person to take action on ideas before anyone else. He said the people who can grab ideas are heroes. Unlike other CEOs, Welch used to be a part of his company's hiring process, as he wanted to surround himself with people who can recognize and focus on incredible ideas before anyone else. As Messi has immense control over his ball, Welch had control over innovation.

Welch always supported the constant search for new ideas. He loved to take risks. He rewarded people for thinking out of the box and daring to take risks. In a similar fashion, Messi has always brought innovation in his style at all levels. He honed and refined his own style of play with each match. He knew

---

[12]'5 Traits of Lionel Messy which Proves Why He Is the Best Athlete World Will Ever Have ....', 3 AM Thinker, https://bit.ly/3r1ovQd. Accessed on 20 September 2022.

he could not 'muscle' his way through the defenders of the opponent's team, so he devised ways of 'gliding' through them. Messi is known to have reinvented his own game several times. He was often placed in different domains of the football field, which had a different set of expectations from him.

In the 2004–05 season, he started off from the right flank, eventually cutting to the centre field and shooting with his dominant left foot. In 2005, on his 18th birthday, he was offered the contract to be a senior player in Barcelona. He was then inducted in the starting 11 of the team. After acquiring his Spanish citizenship, he got the Number 19 t-shirt and became the most natural choice for a right winger.

Between 2009 and 2011, he assumed the role of a false winger, with the freedom to cut inside and roam in the centre. He sometimes also played as a false-9, positioned initially as a centre forward but would also cut deep into the midfield to link up with other players. Through his games, he even developed himself into a combination of numbers 8 (creator), 9 (scorer) and 10 (assistant).

Messi rose to captaincy after the departure of former captain Andrés Iniesta Luján in May 2018. Though Messi did not differentiate between players based on their performance, he was a strong advocate of meritocracy. In 2016, in the match between Barcelona and Celta Vigo, Messi took the penalty and passed on the ball to striker Luis Suárez to score the goal. Had Messi scored the goal himself, he would have reached his landmark 300 goals. Four days later, he scored two goals and crossed his landmark and one of the players who assisted him was Suárez. There were several instances where he took the decision of passing the ball to another player who was in a more advantageous position than him. In situations where multiple defenders cover him, he finds an open teammate to pass the ball to. So far, he has shared the dressing room with 110 players. So, he knows the strengths and weakness of each of his players in depth.

> **Learning Tip:** When you play a team game and the victory of the team is of paramount importance, it is mandatory to know the strengths and weaknesses of people working with you.

CANCELLING OUT THE NOISE

Messi never pays attention to what others say or think about him. Neither is he concerned about hogging all the goals himself. He has always remembered that when he is in the field, there will be thousands of people in the stadium either cheering him or hooting at him; there will be media people around him, either praising him or defaming him; there will be opponents trying to pull him down professionally as well psychologically and there will be people trying to get into his head, excite him or cheat him. However, all he needs to remember is why he is there: to play the game.

LIFE BEYOND FOOTBALL

Messi has been compared to great footballers such as Christiano Ronaldo and Diego Maradona. He was proclaimed by the latter as his successor. 'I've seen the player who will inherit my place in Argentinian football and his name is Messi,' Maradona had once said.[13] Messi was the highest-paid footballer for five years out of six from 2009 to 2014. In 2019, *Forbes* ranked Messi

---

[13] Adams, Tom, 'Maradona: Messi Is My Successor', *Sky Sports*, https://bit.ly/3OUruUp. Accessed on 28 July 2022.

the world's highest-paid athlete. Taking inspiration from the medical difficulties he faced during his childhood, he opened the Leo Messi Foundation, which supports healthcare, education and sports for children. He has also served as a UNICEF goodwill ambassador. He financially supports Sarmiento, a football club based in Rosario, his birthplace. In 2017, Messi married his childhood sweetheart Antonella Roccuzzo; the couple has been blessed with three sons.

Messi's Performance in Various Clubs over the Years (till 31 July 2022)

Club	Season	Total	
		Appearances	Goals
Barcelona C	2003-04	10	5
Barcelona B	2003-04	5	0
	2004-05	17	6
Barcelona	2004-05	9	1
	2005-06	25	8
	2006-07	36	17
	2007-08	40	16
	2008-09	51	38
	2009-10	53	47
	2010-11	55	53
	2011-12	60	73
	2012-13	50	60
	2013-14	46	41
	2014-15	57	58
	2015-16	49	41
	2016-17	52	54
	2017-18	54	45

Club	Season	Total	
		Appearances	Goals
	2018-19	50	51
	2019-20	44	31
	2020-21	47	38
Paris Saint-Germain	2021-22	34	11
	2022-23	1	1
		845	695

2

Creating Benchmarks

Carl Lewis

Every New Year's Eve, I have a pact to do something I never thought I'd do. So, I created this list. You have to free your mind to do things you wouldn't think of doing. Don't ever say no.

CARL LEWIS

Frederick Carlton Lewis, popularly known as Carl Lewis, is regarded as one of the greatest athletes of all time. His tally includes nine Olympic gold medals, one silver Olympic medal and 10 world championship medals in an international career spanning nearly two decades. During the course of his brilliant athletic career, he set several world records in 100 metre, 4x100 metre and 4x200 metre relays as well as in indoor long jump which still stands today. In 1999, Lewis was voted the 'Sportsman of the Century' by the International Olympic Committee and elected the 'World Athlete of the Century' by the International Association of Athletics Federations of the Century.

A remarkable athlete and a fierce competitor, Lewis believed that if we can control our mind, we can achieve anything. His mental belief in his abilities propelled him to create new benchmarks in the world of sports. Also, his diversified interests post-retirement are an example to emulate. Let us decode the various factors behind his success story.

EARLY LIFE

Lewis was born in Alabama, US, in 1961 to William and Evelyn Lewis. His mother was a hurdler in the Pan American Games team in 1951 and missed being part of the 1952 Olympic team owing to an injury. His brother Cleveland played professional soccer for Memphis Rogues in the North American Soccer League, while his sister Carol also represented US in the 1984 Olympics as a long jumper. He was coached by his father in his initial years and his parents ran an athletic club, which was an important influence in shaping him.

Hailing from a family with sports lineage definitely played a significant role in shaping his thought process. His parents were activists and were friends with Martin Luther King Jr. They encouraged Lewis to be an independent thinker, which helped shape his self-belief. In the athletics club, his parents treated him like any other child and this helped him become more self-reliant early on in life. There is an important lesson to be learnt, especially for parents. Often, as parents, we tend to be overprotective about our kids which, in turn, prevents their growth as individuals. The example set by Lewis's parents should be followed by others as well.

> **Learning Tip:** Explore the outside world with an open mind to observe and learn from experiences. This helps in becoming self-reliant in life and gaining invaluable life skills.

Though the environment at home was conducive to his excelling in sports, Lewis considered himself the weakest link in his household. However, this did not prevent him from trying and replicating the success of his siblings in sports. He toiled hard at the long jump pit and spent most of his weekends at the track fields. His gait was also small for his age in his early life before his muscles developed and started to assume their full shape. In fact, most of his initial attempts to succeed in long jump failed, yet he continued to jump longer distances and run faster. With these repeated attempts, he was able to gain mastery over the fear of failure, which is one of the major reasons why we do not win challenges. Our minds become programmed in such a way that our fear of failing overcomes our desire to win. It works like this: let's say a student appears for his board exam. Instead of aiming to perform well, he starts to focus on not failing. In such a scenario, can he expect to succeed in the exam and reach his target?

A sport is no different. In fact, it is a mirror image of every aspect of our lives. Airbnb is today one of the largest players in tourism industry worldwide. However, very few people may be aware that in 2008 when it was founded, it was unable to find much investor interest. The founding team even had to design cereal boxes to meet their expenses![1] Yet, their perseverance with their idea paid off and created the company as we know it today. In a similar way, the perseverance of Lewis and his 'never-give-up' attitude helped him in overcoming adversity. He looked at failure as a mere stepping stone before he could taste success.

> **Learning Tip:** Never give up in the face of adversity and always try to learn from them.

From his early teens, Lewis was encouraged to make his own decisions. For instance, even though he loved growing up in

---

[1] Kenji Explains, 'How Airbnb Founders Sold Cereal to Keep Their Dream Alive', Entrepreneur's Handbook, 15 August 2020, https://bit.ly/3T5AtW7. Accessed on 16 August 2022.

Willingboro, he decided to pursue his studies at the University of Houston, which was away from his home. Even his parents supported his decision though they would have preferred their son being near them. During the early part of his career, he wasn't too successful as a runner. In fact, during one such race, he lost the lead and as a result, his teammates blamed him for the debacle. But this only made him prepare harder, become more competitive and increase his training schedule.

> **Learning Tip:** To build a strong foundation for the future, one must have confidence in one's decisions and abilities.

One of the reasons why his decision of moving to Houston was so important in his career was because it was there that he came under the influence of Coach Tom Tellez. The relationship of the duo lasted his entire career and was a major reason for his success. In fact, Coach Tellez was quick to spot the talent and explore various possibilities with his young prodigy. Even though Lewis initially aspired to be just a long jumper, it was the association with Tellez that helped him eventually prepare for four sprint events as well. He had always aspired to break the long jump world record of Bob Beamon of 29 feet 2.5 inches (1968 Mexico City Olympics) and at the age of 20, he was just 7 inch short of his aspiration. Yet, his magical moment came years later when he was finally able to reach 29 feet in the 1991 World Championship Games held in Tokyo.

There are a few important lessons to be learnt here. First, we should always try to have the right partnerships if we seek to succeed in our career. A significant portion of the credit for Lewis's success is owing to the influence of his coach. In a similar manner, in our work life too, we should seek the help of mentors and look for ample guidance. Billionaire Michael Bloomberg often attributes his success to his mentor

William R. Salomon and his learning from just observing the latter. In Bloomberg's own words, 'He [Salomon] was a good listener, but he didn't manage by consensus. He was his own man, he made his own decisions, and he didn't look back'.[2] A good mentor is someone who does not take away your freedom to make decisions but rather believes in your abilities and gives them the right direction.

Second, always set high goals for yourself. If we aim higher, we will practise and perform better. Lewis could have been content with achieving his target in long jump, yet he decided to focus on the sprint events. In a similar manner, all of us should aspire to chase new and challenging dreams. This will not only make our profiles more diverse for our career growth but also provide us additional skills. In many ways, in the fast-changing corporate world, the skills required for any role are no longer defined like a box—as whatever is in the box is your role and whatever is outside should not concern you.

Our third and most important learning is to have patience. Lewis definitely felt that he could create a benchmark in long jump in his initial years and break the world record. However, when success got delayed, he kept working harder till he achieved his goal. In a similar manner, instead of giving up in the face of adversity, we should use it as a stepping stone for achieving greater success in our lives.

THE INFLUENCE OF JESSE OWENS

It is extremely important to have the right role models in one's career. In the case of Lewis, the person on whom he wanted to model his career was Jesse Owens, who was an

---

[2]Trenchard, Richard, 'Five Business Leaders Who Have a Mentor to Thank for Their Success', Virgin, 8 July 2018, https://bit.ly/3AkXUmJ. Accessed on 16 August 2022.

American athlete who won four gold medals in the 1936 Summer Olympic Games, thereby breaking Hitler's myth of Aryan Supremacy.[3] He even set three world records and tied for another in a race spanning 45 minutes in the 1935 Big Ten Track Event—the period of 45 minutes is often regarded as the greatest 45 minutes ever in the world of sports.[4] In fact, as a kid Lewis had met Owens at a long jump event in Philadelphia that Lewis had won. The story of how Owens, as a Black American, was treated in a foreign land during the Olympics, and how he had to fight for his rights in the US was inspirational for Lewis. This further motivated Lewis and provided a sense of purpose to his career goals. He felt that because his parents were civil rights activists, his victory as a Black American would deliver a very powerful message. He too wanted to win four gold medals in all the events in which Owens had competed—a feat he achieved in the 1984 Olympics.

SPORTING CAREER

By 1981, Lewis was already regarded as the fastest sprinter in the world and was able to achieve the timing of 10 seconds, which stood as the low altitude record. The same year, he also achieved the world number one rank in long jump. In the 1983 World Championships, Lewis was able to achieve his first world record with a timing of 37.86 seconds in the 4x100 metre relay. During the same event, he also won the 100 metre race.

---

[3]Sen, Deeptesh, 'How with 4 Olympics Golds, Jesse Owens Ran Hitler Out of His Aryan Supremacy Theory', *The Indian Express*, 28 July 2021, https://bit.ly/3zWCf32. Accessed on 16 August 2022.

[4]'Jesse Owens and the Greatest 45 Minutes in Sport', International Olympic Committee, https://bit.ly/3QqVvMR. Accessed on 16 August 2022.

In the 1984 Summer Olympics in Los Angeles, he finally equalled Owens's feat of four medals, which he had won in the 1936 Berlin Olympics. After having won the 100 metre race, the next event for him was the long jump. In this event, he was able to jump 8.54 metres in his first attempt (which was sufficient for him to win), fouled in the second and then passed on the next four attempts. The crowd, on the other hand, felt that he should have tried to break Beamon's record of jumping 29 feet 2.25 inches in the 1968 Olympics and booed him.[5] Yet, he realized that winning the gold medals in the other two events was more important than risking injury. It was a strategic decision that helped him a great deal, as he was able to win the gold medal in both the 200 metre as well as the 4x100 metre event. Sometimes, in life, all of us are faced with a number of choices; in such a scenario, we must make our decisions based on priority and not on individual aspirations. Lewis could have tried to create the world record, but winning four gold medals was more important to him than breaking the record. This decision also ensured that he remained fit in the remaining two events in which he created an Olympic record of 19.80 seconds in the 200 metre relay and bettered his own previous world record with a time of 37.83 seconds in the 4x100 metre relay.[6]

The one thing that set Lewis apart from the rest was his ability to bounce back and create new benchmarks at times when most people questioned him. The year 1987, when he lost his father to cancer, was perhaps the most challenging for

---

[5]'Not a Day Like Any Other: Olympic Champion Carl Lewis Was Booed in 1984. Summer Games in Los Angeles', *KUC News*, 6 August 2022, https://bit.ly/3U2WIw1. Accessed on 12 September 2022.

[6]Solomon, George, 'Lewis Gets Record with His 4th Gold', *The Washington Post*, 12 August 1984, https://wapo.st/3xUWxtw. Accessed on 26 September 2022.

him. Lewis even wanted the gold medal that he had won in 1984 for 100 metres to be buried along with his father. 'Don't worry,' he had reassured his mother, 'I'll get another one.'[7] In the 1987 World Championships, he was defeated by Canadian sprinter Ben Johnson in the 100 metre event. Johnson created a new world record at 9.83 seconds compared to Lewis's 9.93 seconds in the same event.[8] This led to a major controversy and a fuelled rivalry after Lewis suggested that Johnson had a false start[9] and most likely took performance enhancement drugs.[10] In the midst of this, Lewis repeatedly referred to the demise of his father as the major motivating factor for the 1988 Olympics. In the 1988 Olympics, Johnson, once again, outran Lewis in the 100 metre relay at 9.79 seconds compared to Lewis's 9.92 seconds. However, Johnson later on tested positive for drugs and the gold medal was awarded to Lewis, who was also reinstated as the world record holder for 100 metres, which was broken by Leroy Burrell in 1990 at 9.90 seconds.

> **Learning Tip:** Play a fair game whether in the corporate world or in sports. If one seeks to improve performance, it should only be through sheer effort and perseverance.

However, the greatest challenge in Lewis's professional career came at the age of 30 in the 1991 World Championships in Tokyo. In the 100 metre race, he was up against Burrell and Raymond Stewart, who had been ranked as the world number

---

[7] Burnton, Simon, '50 Stunning Olympic Moments No44: Carl Lewis's Four Golds in 1984', *The Guardian*, 29 June 2012, https://bit.ly/3Pt7LLJ. Accessed on 16 August 2022.
[8] Smythe, Steve, 'IAAF World Championships History: Rome 1987', *Athletics Weekly*, 27 June 2017, https://bit.ly/3Pl0EF2. Accessed on 16 August 2022
[9] 'Track and Field Johnson Made False Start in Record Run, Lewis Says', *Sun Sentinal*, 13 September 1987, https://bit.ly/3dmWMGM. Accessed on 20 September 2022.
[10] 'Johnson Falls from Hero to Zero in 100m Disgrace', Olymics.com https://bit.ly/3BKwC8W. Accessed on 26 September 2022.

one in the previous two years. In the face of such competition, Lewis created the new world record at 9.86 seconds and clinched the gold medal. The true face of a champion can only be seen when the odds are stacked against him. The long jump finals in the event saw him up against Mike Powell. Lewis had won 65 consecutive meets, where he had participated in long jump, in the last decade. It was widely considered to be Lewis's final attempt to break the record held by Beamon. He did jump 29 feet and 2.75 inches finally acheiving his goal. However, as the jump was wind aided, it was not considered. Powell, however, broke the record with a jump of 29 feet 4.25 inches! The record was finally broken after a span of 23 years but not by Lewis. He acknowledged the feat of his opponent and even regarded the athletics meet as the best of his career.

It is important to respect your opponents and recognize new talent. Life, like sports, is a great leveller that will provide you an opportunity to bounce back if you continue your efforts. Hence, we must be gracious in defeat and humble in our victory.

True champions raise the level of their game when faced with more challenges. Instead of being buried under pressure, they strive harder to win. Yet, results are something that no one can control. A case in point is the 1988 Seoul Olympics 200 metre final event. Lewis had planned to run the race at a time below 19.8 seconds. He felt that no one else running the race had run faster than that, so it should be a safe bet for him to win. He managed to achieve that, clocking a time of 19.79 seconds only to have been outrun by fellow American Joe DeLoach, who clocked a time of 19.75 seconds! Thus, as can be seen from this example, in life and in any sphere of our work, every event can be broken down based on the two-factor rule—factors you can control and those you can't.

We should only focus on the factors that we can control. In this case, Lewis had done his best, but that wasn't the best performance of the day.

Such setbacks are quite common even in our lives. This can be as simple as a situation when an aspirant fails to crack the Indian Institute of Technology Joint Entrance Exams (III-JEE) exam or the common admissions test (CAT) exam to secure a seat in the prestigious institutes. With such cut-throat competition, it is understandable for students to have a mental breakdown. In such a scenario, it is their mental strength that comes to the rescue. It is as common to fail as it is to succeed. What really matters is what we learn from it. Lewis is a classic example of how, through persistence and consistent hard work, one can overcome any challenge. He wasn't the fastest runner in his childhood, but he worked hard and when it mattered the most, he was definitely the finest.

In 1996, he qualified for long jump in the Olympics for the fifth time in a row and also won the gold, taking his tally to nine. It was believed that he would also be considered for the 4x100 metre race. However, as he had skipped the mandatory relay training and demanded the anchor position for the race, the coach felt otherwise. The American team finished second in the event, behind Canada. Lewis subsequently retired from track and field events in 1997.

LIFE BEYOND SPORTS

Setbacks had a major role in shaping Lewis's career. In fact, the more he failed, the more he realized the importance of success, and such debacles only made him mentally stronger. In 1984, after winning four gold medals in the Olympics, it was believed that he would receive a significant number of brand endorsements. However, the controversy about his skipping four chances in long jump and the general perception that he lacked humility did not create a positive perception among the consumers. Coca-Cola, which had offered him a deal prior to the Olympics, backed off and Nike dropped him as its brand ambassador. In addition to this, there was a rumour of him being gay, which further created a negative image among the conservatives in the American society.[11] After the Nike deal fell apart, Lewis signed a deal with Japanese sports equipment maker Mizuno. Such controversies however did not deter him from his professional goals, as he was ranked numero uno in both 100- and 200-metre events for the year. The only way to silence one's critics is through sheer performance.

> **Learning Tip:** It is only through our performance that we can silence those who criticize us. Our focus should always be on creating a better version of ourselves.

Post retirement, Lewis has been working as the assistant track coach (2014–22) and was named the head coach for track and fields in July 2022 at his alma mater, the University of Houston. His coaching mantra has been to focus on building the mental strength of his students and creating a long-term vision for young athletes. This is critical, as it helps in overcoming setbacks. In fact, his mantra is simple: whether an athlete is successful or not, they should continue to focus on the journey and remain in control of their fate. In his early life, Lewis's mother always taught him to focus on doing his best and not worry about the result. As a result, even though he was not winning in the beginning, he was always trying wholeheartedly to improve and never felt discouraged by short-term failures.

---

[11]Myslenski, Skip, 'Carl Lewis Can't Outrun Controversy', *Chicago Tribune*, 22 July 1990, https://bit.ly/3hpGXk3. Accessed on 9 November 2022.

In a similar manner, to be successful in life, we must remember to start competing with our own self and aim to be better with every passing day. In fact, we can easily formulate and accept the step principle for succeeding in our lives. Each of the steps represents the various milestones that we encounter in our journey. Our continuous focus should be on taking the maximum number of positive steps and minimizing the negative steps in our journey. Once the first target is achieved, one must set the goal for the next target.

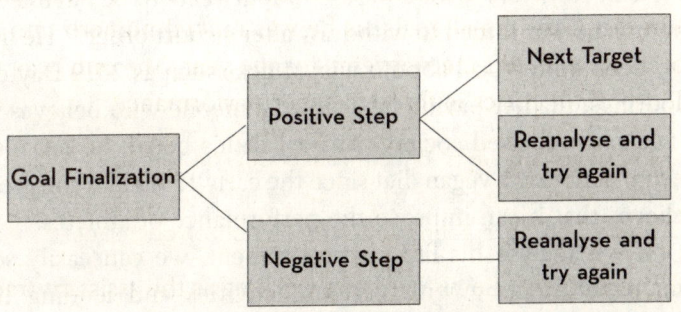

Step Model for Achieving Success

The one thing that set Lewis apart from other athletes was his conscious effort to continuously improve himself. Apart from the time spent on the tracks, he focussed his efforts on his reading skills and observing how celebrities would conduct themselves at award ceremonies such as the Grammys. His focus was on preparing himself for life beyond sports. Sportspersons have a limited timespan at the top of the game. Unlike professionals in other disciplines, who retire at the age of 60, sportspersons mostly retire in their mid-30s. Lewis was very quick to understand this and wanted to build a brand for himself. He holds nine gold medals and was the first athlete to qualify for the same event (long jump) in five consecutive Olympic Games (1980 to 1996).[12] Owing to the Soviet invasion of Afghanistan, the US team did not participate in the 1980 Moscow Games.

However, post-retirement, he was keen to break new grounds. He has appeared in cameo roles in several movies and series such as *Perfect Strangers* and *Material Girls*. In 2011, he even tried to run for elections for the New Jersey state senate as a Democratic candidate. However, owing to a rule that he had to live in New Jersey for a period of four years to be eligible to contest, he was forced to withdraw after a court order.[13] He has also been quite vocal about racist attacks such as 2019 Dayton shootings, further paving his role as someone who believes in a fair and unbiased society. As part of his belief, he has also been promoting a vegan diet since the early 1990s and sincerely believes that it can improve the performance of athletes.

If we analyse his life post-retirement, we can easily see him experimenting with various activities and lending his voice wherever needed. What really goes inside the mind of a champion athlete can best be understood by understanding the life of Lewis. He wasn't the strongest, nor the fastest and neither the strongest, but when it came to performing on the big stage of athletics, he delivered a stellar performance. We all have limitations in our lives. The key, therefore, is to attempt to overcome those and define a better life for ourselves.

In the 17 years of his athletic career, he has earned accolades and nicknames such as 'Olympian of the Century', 'King Carl', 'Sportsman of the Century' and 'the Son of

---

[12]'Carl Lewis-American Athlete', Britannica, https://bit.ly/3SB3wzJ. Accessed on 26 September 2022.

[13]Mulvihill, Geoff, 'Carl Lewis Quits NJ Senate Race after Court Ruling', *Seattle Times*, 23 September 2011, https://bit.ly/3AqzKHm. Accessed on 16 August 2022.

the Wind'. Even post-retirement from active sports, he is reinventing himself and setting new benchmarks for others to emulate. The question, therefore, is: can we emulate his life lessons to set our own benchmarks?

Lewis's Personal Best

- **100 metres:** 9.86 seconds (August 1991, Tokyo)
- **200 metres:** 19.75 seconds (June 1983, Indianapolis)
- **Long jump:** 8.87 metres (29 feet 1 inches) 1991, w 8.91 metres (29 feet 2¾ inches) 1991 (both in Tokyo)
- **4x100 metre relay:** 37.40 seconds (US team – Michael Marsh; Leroy Burrell; Dennis Mitchell; Carl Lewis – August 1992, Barcelona Olympics)
- **4x200 metre relay:** 1:18.68 minutes (Santa Monica Track Club, Mt. SAC Relays – Michael Marsh; Leroy Burrell; Floyd Heard; Carl Lewis – 1994; (former world record, presently held by Jamaica 2014 IAAF relays)

3

Self-Motivation

Virat Kohli

Cricket is the most important thing to me. So, the rest of it pales in comparison.

VIRAT KOHLI

Virat Kohli is arguably the best batter in world cricket and is also one of the most successful captains in the history of Indian cricket. His motivation towards succeeding each time has catapulted him in the world of cricket in a manner that he now has the world at his feet. His leadership skills and ability to keep himself at ease while handling the media are things to emulate. Kohli's success story is not just a matter of luck but a recognition of his hard work and dedicated focus to succeed. He understands his responsibilities and the importance of performing on the field.

Kohli looks at the cricketing ground like a gladiator who wishes to be the last man standing. He started his cricketing career in Delhi and represented his state team in the Ranji Trophy. He went on to lead the Under-19 Indian team to World Cup glory in 2008 and eventually became a part of the senior side. Was it luck? Or hard work?

If we take a look at his initial cricketing career, when he made his national debut, many people questioned his attitude and skills. However, he has already led his team as captain in major tournaments: winning the Under-19 cricket World Cup and reclaiming the number one ICC Test ranking for five consecutive years. What sets him apart from the rest of the squad is his ability to make batting look very simple and effortless. Kohli's cricketing exploits can also be compared with that of a CEO. Just like a CEO tries to lead his company towards achieving a profitable quarter, Kohli too aims for the ultimate glory of winning the game each time he plays for the team. Even if he wins a match, his motivation to win the next remains unmatched. Kohli is the only batter in the world to average around 50 in all three formats of international cricket: Test matches, One Day Internationals (ODIs) and Twenty20 Internationals. His ability to chase down seemingly difficult targets with ease is a model to behold. He is also the most successful captain in Indian Test cricket. What could be the reasons for his phenomenal success? How does he keep himself motivated under all circumstances? Let's read on and decode the success recipe for the consistency of Virat Kohli.

FINDING THE RIGHT MENTOR

As a young lad, Kohli was no different from any other nine-year-old when he first became part of the West Delhi Cricket Academy, under the guidance of Rajkumar Sharma. As a coach, Sharma not only shaped his student's destiny but produced a gem for world cricket at large. It is often easy to get swayed by the fame and success that is readily available in the world of cricket, but the teachings of his coach have kept Kohli's feet firmly planted on the ground. His coach and mentor always shielded him from such distractions off the field. During the Under-19 World Cup, advertisers had made a beeline to sign prospective India players. His coach was worried that Kohli might get distracted, but the latter convinced his coach when he said, 'You will not get damaging reports about me.'[1] The presence of a mentor is all the more important when one goes through a tough phase in life. When the Delhi & District Cricket Association did not select Kohli for the Under-14 team for reasons outside cricket, the young boy was completely heartbroken. His parents and coach consoled him, asking him to keep working towards his goal. Following their advice to a tee, Kohli worked very hard, and as a result, the following year, he was invited to be part of the Under-15 team. It is in such moments of despair that having someone to support you and believe in your skill sets makes all the difference to your future. Kohli is lucky in many ways that his coach also doubled up as his mentor, but a significant bit of it also has to be attributed to his hunger for learning with utmost humility.

DRIVE FOR PERFECTION

Malcom Gladwell, in his book *The Tipping Point*, talks about the 10,000 hour rule.[2] According to this rule, when someone puts 10,000 hours into doing a task, he becomes an expert at it. This logic can be applied to any professional in any field and Kohli seems to epitomize it. Whenever Kohli scores centuries on a consistent basis, many spectators start believing it is quite natural for a player of his calibre. An incident that actually showed Kohli's mettle was when he went to play cricket to save his side from defeat in the Ranji Trophy match, just a day

---

[1] Lokapally, Vijay, *Driven: The Virat Kohli Story*, Bloomsbury Publishing, New Delhi, 2019, p. xviii.
[2] Gladwell, Malcom, *The Tipping Point: How Little Things Can Make a Big Difference*, Back Bay Books, 2002.

after his father's demise. Kohli was batting unbeaten at 40 the previous night with his side staring at a follow-on. He lost his father at three o'clock that morning.

The following day, Virat resumed his innings and made a total score of 90, saved his side from a follow-on with his partner Puneet Bisht (who scored 156) and then went to his father's funeral. He had definitely chosen cricket as his life and was willing to go the distance to achieve his dreams. It is this determination that differentiates the best from the rest.

Imagine you have lost your dear one and have a make-or-break presentation to a client the following day. Will you have the resolve to execute the presentation with utmost skill the following day? Will you be willing to attend the presentation first and not the funeral? There can only be utmost respect for such an individual for his dedication towards the work at hand.

> **Learning Tip:** It is important to realize what is important in life and be mentally tough to achieve the same against all odds.

If we look at Kohli over the years, we would not say he has been the most talented cricketer to come up the ranks, but he is certainly someone who has learnt to improve with every game. The same cricketer who struggled with his batting in the Indian Premier League (IPL) 1 (batting average 15) was the highest run-getter in IPL 9 (batting average 81.08) with as many as four centuries to his credit. He feels that he has a responsibility of leading his side to victory and, hence, any gap in his technique needs to be eliminated as soon as possible.

In human resources (HR) management, there is a theory called the Peter Principle, which suggests that people get promoted to the level of their incompetence. This management principle, formulated by Lawrence J. Peter in 1969, implies that people get promoted based on their current skill sets and not on the basis of the skills required in the next role. The result: the higher you go up the corporate ladder, the less equipped you are.

Kohli, however, seems to be defy this law. So, how does he manage to achieve this? The answer lies in his ability to adapt quickly to a situation. For instance, when he played the Under-19 World Cup, he introduced himself as a right-arm fast bowler, but now when he plays for Team India, he bowls off-spins. If we are to plot the career curve of Kohli versus other cricketers, it would look something like this.

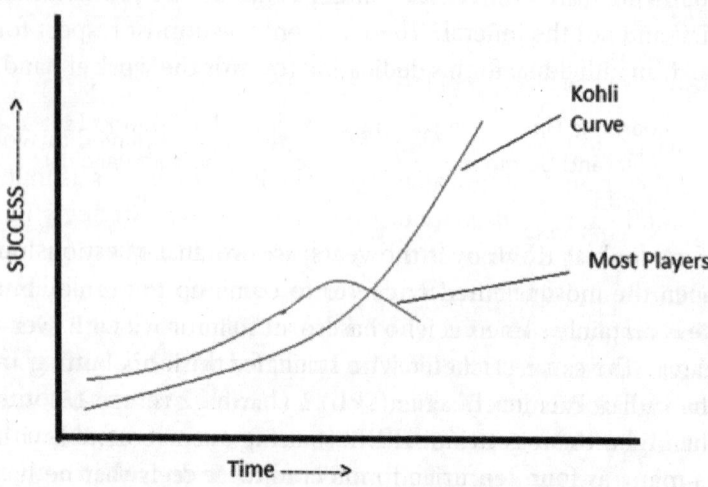

Virat Kohli's Career Trajectory as Compared to Other Cricketers

How do you think Kohli trains himself amidst such a tight schedule? He practises everything in his mind over and over again and then slogs it out in the nets. He analyses which delivery troubles him and then practises the same over and over again till he has mastered it. Passion is something that will not let an individual go to sleep, and Kohli exemplifies that passion.

Entrepreneurs also apply the same model while starting their ventures. They slog it out to perfect their business models. Just like in any project, the top performers are normally those who put in that extra 2 per cent effort in their work. In fact, the motivation to put the same effort can be anything; it might be a promotion or a salary hike, but only when it is in pursuit of excellence can the extra effort be made in a sustained manner. Now, add to that the expectations of a billion people and you will know the motivation that drives Kohli to success.

BUILDING STRONG SELF-BELIEF

If we try to look at the game of cricket, it is not played or won on the ground but in the mind of the individual. It is as much a mind game as it is about executing the right strategy. In a way, our mind consists of two selves: one that questions our abilities and the other that restores our faith in our abilities. For simplicity, let us refer to these as Self 1 and Self 2. Self 1 always poses questions like 'Am I right for the job?', 'Am I good enough at this level?', 'Can I do this?'. Self 2 is, on the other hand, a more reassuring self. This part of our self reminds us of our best performances and motivates us to do well in a given situation. It is our ability to regulate the two selves that makes the difference. In the case of Kohli, his Self 2 overpowers the anxiety and doubts imposed by Self 1.

According to Kohli, he did lose his way a bit immediately after winning the Under-19 World Cup. At that juncture, he engaged in a lot of self-introspection to understand what he really aimed to get in his life. As he once said, 'I couldn't handle what happened after we won the World Cup. People looking up at you and thinking that you were someone who could play for India and just giving you tags like "blue-eyed boy" and stuff like that. I couldn't take it, honestly. I made a lot of mistakes.'[3]

DEFINING THE RIGHT SET OF GOALS

What makes Kohli an invaluable asset of the Indian side is his ability to quickly adapt himself to the situation and change his game play to suit the team's requirements. New Zealand cricketer Kane Williamson, in an interview, had this to say about Kohli, 'His ability to adapt throughout all formats is certainly something to admire. And, it's also something to learn from.'[4]

Perhaps one can attribute Kohli's success to his hard work, tenacity and focus. He keeps his mind clutter free and focusses only on the work at hand. So, how does one achieve this? The answer lies in having clearly defined measurable goals. Even as he is planning his innings, he is equally clear in his mind about the next objective along with the time frame to achieve the same. The secret to this lies in adopting the SMART methodology of defining goals. This is an acronym that was originally coined by George T. Doran in the November 1981 issue of *Management Review*.[5] According to this methodology, while defining any goal, one should be:

---

[3] Ugra, Sharda, 'I Realised I Was on the Wrong Track', ESPN Cricinfo, 27 May 2011, https://es.pn/3psbbDT. Accessed on 17 August 2022.

[4] Mehta, Rutvick, '"Kohli's Ability to Adapt Throughout All Formats Is Certainly Something to Admire," says Kane Williamson', *DNA*, 30 September 2017, https://bit.ly/3ArJKQP. Accessed on 17 August 2022.

[5] Haughey, Duncan, 'A Brief History of SMART Goals', ProjectSmart, 13 December 2014, https://bit.ly/3SUc05O. Accessed on 17 August 2022

- **S**pecific: What is it you wish to achieve?
- **M**easurable: When was the last time you measured your goals?
- **A**ssignable: Are you sure you can do it or do you need some support?
- **R**ealistic: Can you achieve it?
- **T**ime-related: When are you going to achieve it?

SMART goals, when applied by an individual, will help them stay focussed on their work and achieve the goals within clearly defined timelines. Take a small piece of paper and define your goals using the SMART methodology. This will help you stay on track and focussed. Kohli has consistently performed better while chasing his SMART goals. The reason for his success is his ability to break down targets into manageable chunks, where he does not put additional pressure on himself. In fact, he averages more while chasing targets.

In case of working professionals, sometimes in office we feel bogged down by the amount of workload that we have at that point in time. The question is: how do we take care of the workload? The secret lies in the approach we adopt towards breaking down the work and prioritizing it. Basically, it involves segregating the work into three categories: unnecessary, necessary but can be delayed, and necessary and urgent. Breaking down the work in such categories helps us in achieving our goals in a much better manner.

LET YOUR PASSION DRIVE YOU

Ever heard of the phrase: 'the winner takes it all'? Why do you think this happens? It is largely because top performers in any field start playing for pride and with an incredible amount of passion and dedication towards their profession. We have all seen the aggressive Kohli on the field. We have also seen the teary-eyed and disappointed Kohli, who refuses to take off his pads if dismissed early. The look in his eyes and his body language define what passion truly is and how much he values success. Representing one's country and bringing glory to its people is the greatest motivation that any sportsperson can have.

If you speak with the sales head of a multinational firm, you will see the same passion and hunger to stay ahead of the competition and better the sales targets every quarter. Ask him any question about his product and he will be the first one to tell you why and how his products are a cut above the rest. At the end of the day, when he finally manages to bag the order from a client, his joy knows no bounds—his efforts have finally paid off.

Kohli is also an excellent fielder, as he always wants the ball to come to him. When he wears the pads and gets down to the batting crease, he wants to stay at the crease for as long as possible, so that he can lead his team to victory. When he captains his team and sees aggression from the opposition, he lets his performance answer the aggression. If we look at his earlier career, Kohli was never a six-hitter, but in the last couple of years, he has realigned his game to become a big shot player. Due to his sheer hard work, Kohli has been able to add another level to his game. That's what makes the difference.

> **Learning Tip:** Be passionate about whatever you are doing in life. It holds the key to success.

LEADING FROM THE FRONT: CAPTAIN KOHLI

In the case of Kohli, cricket is the centre of his existence and he understands that he has a role to execute and perform on the field. Kohli also analyses the strategy of his opponents on the field and then makes the next move. A CEO also approaches his role in a similar manner. He understands his competitors' products that exist in the market, their pricing strategy and a possible response to them.

Consider for instance, why are CEOs like Steve Jobs revered so much? It is largely because of the actions they took before emerging as the CEOs of their firms. Jobs, for instance, being a co-founder of the company, started it from scratch to build one of the largest technology giants in history. In a similar manner, Kohli too started from scratch by performing well at the Under-15 and Under-19 domestic circles before finally doing well in the international team as a player and now as its captain. His work ethic and dedication towards his game earn him respect from his fellow teammates, which makes it easier for him to implement the right strategy in an effective manner.

As a CEO, one often needs to take tough decisions like selling off a factory or laying off employees to cut costs. Kohli's life too involved a similar set of challenges. For instance, while deciding on the team, he may have had to occasionally drop players just to ensure balance in the side. This, in turn, might have spoiled the personal relations within the team. There may have been occasions when verbal abuse was hurled at him from the spectators as was the case in Australia in his first tour. Under these circumstances, he had to act in a calm manner and accept the challenge. Equally there were times when the umpire gave an unfair decision. As a player, Kohli had to accept the decision and move ahead in the innings. In these circumstances, just like a CEO, he had to create a vision and instil confidence in his team to win the match with the same vigour.

As a player and captain, Kohli has to analyse the situation real time. A single mistake can lead to the team losing the match. Now add to that the pressure of being active as a brilliant fielder in the field. His ability to break down targets into manageable chunks stands testimony to his data analysis skills. If we consider the fact that, often, his decision-making is based on a fraction of a second, we can make out the sheer accuracy with which his brain functions and calculates. Even though Kohli has now passed the baton of captaincy to Rohit Sharma, he remains the most successful Indian Test captain with a win percentage of 60 through 36 Test wins.

BUILDING A POWERFUL BRAND

Any brand is recognized by two things: its performance and consistency in improving the same performance over a period of time. Is Kohli a successful brand in the making? Or is he already at that stage? He surely knows how to manage his presence on social media. In a bid to stay connected with his fans, he occasionally shares videos and photos on social media. Needless to say, they go viral in a very short while. He understands that to connect with the youth, it is important to maintain and enhance one's presence on social media. Owing to his consistent performance in all three formats of the game, Kohli brings out a sense of fulfilment among the audience who come to the stadium to watch him play. He is probably the only cricketer who generates the same amount of enthusiasm that was once reserved only for the maestro Sachin Tendulkar. Just like a product earns trust for a brand with its consistent performance over the years, Kohli, with his unflinching dedication and hard work, has built a brand for himself.

Learning Tip: There are no shortcuts to brand building. Be consistent in whatever you are delivering.

SEIZE THE OPPORTUNITY

Carpe diem, or seize the day, is a Latin aphorism implying that it is extremely important to live in the current moment and try to do the best in it. Often, as individuals, we tend to feel that life has been unfair. In such moments, we overlook the opportunities that life has presented to us at that juncture. If we consider Kohli's debut in One Day cricket, it was the result of an injury to the regular opener. Opening was not his forte, but he did not let go of the opportunity. It is small incidents like these that make a difference in the long run.

There is a lot to learn from this approach towards life. Even in terms of the lives that professionals lead, living one day at a moment helps in focussing on the objectives in hand. This, in turn, leads to improved productivity at the workplace. If we carry baggage from the past, it will always hold us back and not let us perform.

MOTIVATION TOWARDS FITNESS

There is an age-old saying: when wealth is lost, nothing is lost, but when health is lost, something is lost. So, how does a professional sportsperson like Kohli manage his health? What kind of fitness regime does he follow? The prowess that he exhibits in the field is a result of the tough fitness routine that he follows to the tee. For sportspersons and cricketers, in particular, fitness is the most crucial aspect not just in terms of performance but also in terms of the sheer impact that it has on the career of the individual. Clearly, there are very few cricketers who are more agile on the field than Kohli today. He focusses more on lower-body exercises to stay fit. This, in turn, provides him the extra stamina while converting the ones to twos on the field. The fitness regime seems to have done wonders for this Delhi lad as he has gained strength to hit those massive sixes for which he is nowadays known.

MOTIVATION THROUGH LEADERSHIP

Leadership is a natural trait that has nothing to do with age, experience or authority. It is the social influence that one exercises to achieve a common goal. When an individual leads by example, others follow him even if he does not have any formal authority. Kohli has always shown himself to be a natural leader in the team. In 2003–04, when he was appointed the captain of the Delhi Under-15 team, he scored 50 as captain against Himachal Pradesh and followed it up with his first century against Jammu and Kashmir. Clearly, he found himself fit for the job and the challenges that lay ahead. Kohli also enjoys the glory of having captained the World Cup-winning Under-19 team. It is significant, as even at that age, he remembered to share the triumph with the rest of the team. Siddharth Kaul, Kohli's teammate, had once said, 'Virat was astonishingly aggressive and focussed. He hated losing. He simply talked about winning the final, and sometimes it would lead me to wonder if there was anything other than cricket that engaged his attention.'[6]

His stint of playing in the IPL and leading a side that comprised players like A.B. de Villiers speaks volumes of his skill sets. His ascent to captaincy for the Indian team happened in

---

[6] Lokapally, Vijay, *Driven: The Virat Kohli Story*, Bloomsbury Publishing, New Delhi, 2019, p. 34.

Self-Motivation

an unexpected manner when M.S. Dhoni decided to step down before the final Test in India's tour of Australia. Kohli grabbed the opportunity with both hands. Kohli always wishes to be in action whether it is shining the ball or aggressively responding to the opponent; it is extremely difficult to keep him out. On being appointed the captain in limited overs cricket, he had this to say: 'It's a very special moment in my life, it's a lot of responsibility and something I am really looking forward too. I didn't realise when the transition happened in my own head starting off as a player who just wanted to play for India and now having the responsibility to be captain in three formats...'[7]

The glory of winning the IPL and World Cup has eluded Kohli despite his very high success rate as captain. While critics can question his attitude as being overaggressive on the field, there is little to doubt about his passion for the game. While his records in T20Is and ODIs have been outstanding, his ability to play the seaming delivery in Test cricket will once again come under the scanner on overseas tours. Though he has scored a significant amount of runs from 2016–18 to 2022, one must also keep in mind that most of his runs have come on subcontinental pitches, which are known to be batting friendly. As Kohli ages further, his batting prowess is bound to decline. Even Tendulkar and Saurav Ganguly were a shadow of their former selves in the later years of their careers. Will Kohli be able to defy this? The good part about Kohli is that he is consistently evolving and learning all the way. He has been going through a lean patch of not scoring at will over the last 24 months (2020–22), however it is only a matter of time before he comes out with flying colours.

---

[7]FP Sports, 'MS Dhoni Will Always Be My Captain: Virat Kohli on Leadership, MSD the Batsman, and More', *Firstpost*, 10 January 2017, https://bit.ly/3AsI8Gu. Accessed on 17 August 2022

Kohli has an attitude that helps him improve after every single game he plays. As captain, he had to focus as much on the field placements and bowling changes as his own game. Few cricketers have been able to perform with such consistency with the additional burden of captaincy on their shoulders. It remains to be seen if Kohli can sustain his form over the coming years. Will Kohli be remembered as the greatest cricketer to have played the game? He certainly has the talent and motivation to achieve the same.

Virat Kohli's Batting Performances over the Years (till 15 September 2022)

	Matches	Innings	Not Outs	Runs	Highest Score	Average	100s	50s
Tests	102	173	10	8,074	254 (not out)	49.53	27	28
ODIs	262	253	39	12,344	183	57.68	43	64
T20Is	104	96	27	3,584	122 (not out)	51.94	1	32

4

Consistency Has No Age

Martina Navratilova

I have been at the twilight of my career longer than most people have had careers.[1]

MARTINA NAVRATILOVA

At the tender age of three, a Czech-born young girl was hitting tennis ball against a concrete wall. Since then, that girl has witnessed many events and changes in her life and each has brought new opportunities. This is the story of Martina Navratilova, who became one of the greatest tennis players of all time, holding the World No. 1 position for a total of 332 weeks in singles (second only to Steffi Graf) and a total of 237 weeks in doubles. She is the only player recorded holding the top of singles and doubles for more than 200 weeks. She is known for her extreme physical conditioning and for having brought big serve and volley back to the women's tennis game.[2] In her tennis career, she has won 18 Gram Slam singles titles, 31 women's doubles titles and 10 major mixed doubles titles. She has won nine women's single

---

[1] Navratilova, Martina, *Shape Your Self: My 6-Step Diet and Fitness Plan to Achieve the Best Shape of Your Life*, Rodale Books, US, 2006, p. 107.

[2] De Giulio, Bill, 'The Top 10 Greatest Women's Tennis Players of All Time', How They Play, 15 September 2022, https://bit.ly/2EDUTRv. Accessed on 26 September 2022.

titles in Wimbledon and has reached the finals 12 times, which include nine consecutive years from 1982 to 1990.

EARLY LIFE

Martina Navratilova was born on 18 October 1956 as Martina Šubertováin in Prague, Czechoslovakia (now Czech Republic). Her initial years were full of grave events. When she was only three years old, her parents got divorced. Her mother, who was a gymnast, tennis player and ski instructor, later married Miroslav Navrátil, who became Martina's first tennis coach. Martina later adopted her stepfather's last name, tweaking it to Navratilova. Her biological father, who was a ski instructor, died by suicide when Martina was just eight. Overcoming these setbacks, Navratilova won the Czechoslovakia National Tennis Championship at the young age of 15. A year later, she debuted with the United States Lawn Tennis Association.

TURNING PROFESSIONAL

In 1974, at the age of 18, Navratilova won her first professional title in Orlando, Florida. In 1975, she lost in the final of French Open to renowned American tennis player Chris Evert over three sets. She also lost the finals of the Australian Open to the Australian tennis player Evonne Goolagong. Due to the repressive communist government in Czechoslovakia, Navratilova applied for US citizenship, leaving her family and home country behind to continue pursuing her game. She knew how to shut the noise out and focus on the game.

In 1978, she won her first major singles in Wimbledon, where she defeated Evert and captured the World No.1 ranking for the first time. She defended her title the following year by defeating Evert again. This was just the beginning. In the years to follow, Navratilova won 167 top-level singles titles, which was more than any other player in the Open Era[3], and 177 doubles titles. In the 2006 US Open, she capped her career by winning the mixed doubles title with American doubles specialist, Bob Bryan, making her the oldest-ever major champion at 49 years and 10 months of age.[4] She embarked on the next destination of her life as a 'tennis coach'.

CORE PRINCIPLES

Navratilova's life is a clear indication that age is no barrier to consistency. She had a gloriously long career with the racquet. From the age of three to the age of 50 (in 2006), her racquet never stopped. How did she manage to work consistently towards her goal of being a successful tennis player? Let's look at the core principles she followed to be so successful at her game.

Learn from your competitors

Chris Evert was known as the 'Ice Maiden' of her time. She was the World No. 1 in the game of tennis when Navratilova had just entered the arena. The on-court rivalry between Navratilova and Evert refuted the public perception that 'women should play nice'. This was during the time when male tennis players like Jimmy Connors, Björn Borg and John McEnroe were

---

[3]Tennis, starting 1968, has been referred to as the Open Era because the Grand Slam tournaments agreed to allow professional players to compete alongside amateurs. Hence, the events were 'open' to all players.

[4]'Martina Navratilova', International Tennis Hall of Fame, https://bit.ly/3ppvD8r. Accessed on 18 August 2022.

attracting more public attention towards men's tennis. The quality of Evert and Navratilova's game brought women's tennis the same popularity as men's. Their on-court rivalry was much talked about in the 1980s. Each of them had a fair share of fans and detractors, and this rivalry positively increased the fan base of the game.

Their contrasting playing styles and on-court demeanour became the hottest topic in tennis circles for years to come. Navratilova was an expert in serve and volley game, whereas Evert was a powerful baseline player who had a two-handed backhand, which was one of the best in the game at that time. Navratilova, on the other hand, played left-handed tennis (one-handed backhand) despite being born right-hand dominant. Evert and Navratilova played each other 80 times during 1973–88, with 59 of those matches in the finals.

Evert had the advantage of good speed and footwork, which helped her gain a lead against Navratilova in their earlier matches, but the latter soon picked up speed, polished her serve and volley style, and started gaining momentum. Navratilova played better on grass and indoor courts, while Evert played best on clay and hard courts. Evert faced Navratilova in 14 Grand Slam finals, out of which she lost 10. During their face-offs, the World No. 1 ranking was held by either Navratilova or Evert. These two women were good friends outside the court but fierce competitors while on the court.

Navratilova's and Evert's personalities were also contrasting. The latter was known to be more focussed, consistent, patient and determined. On the other hand, Navratilova displayed more agitation and volatility in the earlier days of her playing. She often engaged in arguments with the chair umpire. However, the later years saw Navratilova rein in her excesses on the court and developed her mental strength. As a result, she holds the record of 43 wins versus 37 losses against Evert.[5]

Learning Tip: Analysing your competitor will help you identify your loopholes and build your USPs.

In 1981, Evert defeated Navratilova in the finals of the Amelia Island Championship, which was a Women's Tennis Association (WTA) event, with the score of 6-0 and 6-0 in two straight sets. This was Navratilova's only professional double bagel loss. Her initial losses motivated Navratilova to incorporate certain changes in her fitness regime. Known to have a broad and sturdy built, she hired a coach and got back in shape to defeat the American tennis star. At this point, Navratilova also started working with basketball player Nancy Lieberman and adopted her exercise plan to improve her fitness and toughen her mental approach towards the game. Her dedicated fitness routine and hard work resulted in her achieving major milestones. In the same year, Navratilova won her third major singles after defeating Evert in the finals of the Australian Open. The next year, she won both the Wimbledon and the French Open. She avenged her earlier Amelia Island defeat with the score of 6-2 and 6-0, at the same place, in 1984. Witnessing Navratilova revamp her approach towards tennis with various forms of cross-training, fitness and diet, her long-term rival, Evert once commented, 'She brought athleticism to a whole new level with her training techniques—particularly cross-training, the idea that you could go to the gym or play basketball to get in shape for tennis.'[6]

---

[5]'Chris Evert Recalls Ups and Downs of Long Rivalry with Martina Navratilova', *The Indian Express*, 30 July 2020, https://bit.ly/3fuwWkV. Accessed on 1 November 2022.
[6]Kettmann, Steve, 'Martina Navratilova', *Salon*, 18 April 2000, https://bit.ly/3QPie58. Accessed on 18 August 2022.

Another prominent rival in Navratilova's life was Steffi Graf. The 28-year-old Navratilova had a face-off with a 16-year-old Graf in the semifinals of the 1985 US Open, where she defeated the young rising star 6-2 and 6-3. On 6 June 1987, Graf defeated Navratilova at the Grand Slam final at Roland-Garros, with the score of 6-4, 4-6 and 8-6. This marked a change in the top ranks of the game. Two months later, she took over the World No.1 rank from Navratilova. In the same year, Navratilova made a comeback by winning the grass court match in Wimbledon finals against Graf. She also won the hard surface match in the US Open semifinals against Graf the same year. After winning the third tie-breaker with a score of 10-8, Navratilova tried to console Graf, but the latter stormed out of the court disappointed. The Graf–Navratilova rivalry was a shift in the era of tennis. The two players were among the topmost in their own generation. Six months later, Graf avenged the loss with a victory in the semifinals of the Lipton Championships in Key Biscayne, Florida. To this Navratilova said, 'Today she was the best player of the world. And she will be until I play her again.'[7]

Steffi Graf and Martina Navratilova too shared contrasting playing styles. The latter was a net rusher, who liked pressurizing the opponent and moving them out of position. Graf, on the other hand, was a steady baseliner, who liked striking forehands repeatedly from the back of the court. Navratilova studied Graf's weakness, her one-handed slice backhand and delivered her most lethal weapon—her lefty serve, which Graf had a tough time dealing with. In the 1987 French Open finals, Graf and Navratilova faced each other in three sets. It was a match between Navratilova's serve and

---

[7]Tignor, Steve, '30-Love: Thirty Years Ago, Steffi and Martina's Unsung Rivalry Crested', Tennis, 5 June 2017, https://bit.ly/3QzvRWf. Accessed on 18 August 2022.

approach style and Graf's backhand approach. Navratilova's punches were too strong for Graf to counter punch and it was evident that the latter would taste defeat that day, but Navratilova double faulted twice granting Graf victory. The interesting thing after this match was that Graf was actually apologetic for winning because Navratilova had given her such a tough competition during the match.

At times, failures make us question our capabilities. Especially when others start predicting the end of our career, we seriously start doubting ourselves. These self-created insecurities cloud our decision-making abilities. What could have been just a brief setback becomes a huge hurdle to our growth. It is imperative to take a step back, analyse the bigger picture and realize that one loss or some small losses have not yet tarnished your entire career and you can definitely make a comeback whenever you want.

There is much to learn from Navratilova and her 'rivalry' with both Evert and Graf. The first half of 1987 saw Graf celebrating victories after victories. At this point, Navratilova thought of analysing her losses and trying something new. She called her former coach Renee Richards back and tried a new racquet. She trained extensively under her coach and eventually defeated Graf at the finals of both US Open and Wimbledon in 1987.

In the initial years, Apple closely followed in the footsteps of its tech rivals LG and Samsung in the smart phone business. In September 2014, Apple launched its 4.7-inch iPhone 6 and 5.5-inch iPhone 6 plus. Tech commentators were surprised, as they thought Apple would not go beyond the 4-inch screen segment. Steve Jobs himself disregarded the importance of big phones and said no one would buy them.[8] *However, Apple's rivals Samsung and LG were selling bigger screen handsets and people were buying them. Apple took a leaf out of the rival companies' books and followed the trend of producing phones with bigger screens. It is never wrong or late to learn from rivals.*

Learning Tip: Follow your rival's actions closely and learn from their successes as well as their failures.

Develop your own style

When Navratilova turned nine, her stepfather took her to Czech champion George Parma for tennis lessons. He made her ditch her two-handed backhand, which she had been using until then, so that she could increase her reach and deliver better volleys. She developed the attitude of mental play under him. She worked on her strategy to master the routine shots. Today, Navratilova's fast serve and volley style are renowned all through the world. She served a wicked serve, rushed to the net and surprised the opponent with a ferocious volley. Her speed and footwork on a grass court were unmatched. Her playing style was predominantly aggressive and attacking. She had the unique ability to adapt to situations. She tweaked her playing strategy depending on the court she was playing on, grass or clay.

Her popular rival, Evert, played cautiously from baseline and resolutely returned shot after shot. She preferred to tire out the opponent with long rallies. The opponent would inevitably make an unforeseen error and lose the point. This

---

[8] Petrovan, Bogdan, 'Finally Vindicated, Samsung Recalls Steve Jobs' Opinion on Big Phones', Android Authority, 10 September 2014.

was a strategy followed by many players whom Navratilova faced. Navratilova, on the other hand, played the 'power game'. She would decisively charge towards the net and tear down the opponent by delivering a powerful volley. She avenged every defeat with a spectacular victory soon.

Navratilova's winning percentage was extremely high—87. In doubles, her winning statistics were 747 wins and 143 losses, capping her winning percentage at 84. These numbers are till date on the highest in terms of winning percentage. She has won a total of 305 grass matches and 47 consecutive encounters at the WTA from 1985 to 1987. She was tough to be defeated even in indoor matches. She won 48 consecutive matches on the carpet from 1986 to 1987 and has a total of 516 carpet wins in her kitty.

> **Learning Tip:** Your own unique style allows you to express who you are. It makes you memorable and helps you enhance your self-image and confidence.

Build your unique image

Navratilova had a unique image. She was a left-hander among all right-handed players. She was a proud lesbian in the so-called straight world[9]. She was a gallant volleyer in the crowd of baseline players. She was an immigrant among the Americans. She was old as compared to the new players. Initially, the public perceived Navratilova as physically imposing and cold. It took them a long time to accept her.

For Navratilova to come out as lesbian in 1981 was difficult. There was a constant fear of losing her endorsements

---

[9] Ennis, Dawn, 'Celebrating LGBTQ Sports History: The Complicated Champion Martina Navratilova', Outsports, 30 October 2020, https://bit.ly/3dDSgTX. Accessed on 18 August 2022.

and sponsorships. However, she decided to be open about her sexuality, as she believed she would not be able to embrace her true identity without being open about it. She proposed to her long-time girlfriend Julia Lemigova at the US Open in 2014 and the couple got married in New York in December 2014.

In 1992, Navratilova participated in a lawsuit against Amendment 2, which was designed to prevent sexual orientation from being a protected class. In 1993, she participated and spoke before a large political rally named 'March on Washington for Lesbian, Gay and Bi Equal Rights and Liberation'.[10] She received the 'National Equality Award' from Human Rights Campaign, US's largest gay and lesbian activist group.

Apart from this, she has authored many books and has been a keynote speaker on several platforms. Post-retirement, she became a tennis coach. She has frequently spoken up for WTA players and has advocated equal pay and better playing conditions for women. She has also made a number of appearances on-screen in movies and television shows such as *Will & Grace* (1998) and *The Adventurers* (2017) and in TV series *Married to a Celebrity: The Survival Guide* (2017).

Players like Navratilova look beyond their 'athletic identity' and strive to establish themselves as multitalented individuals. In 'Athletic Identity: Hercules' Muscles or Achilles Heel?' the authors define athletic identity as 'the degree to which an individual identifies with the athlete role and looks to others for acknowledgement of that role'.[11] Navratilova created her own unique image, which became her personal brand.

---

[10]Ibid.
[11]Brewer, B.W., et al., 'Athletic Identity: Hercules' Muscles or Achilles Heel?' *International Journal of Sport Psychology*, Vol. 24, 1993, pp. 237–54.

Consistency Has No Age

Learning Tip: Looking beyond one's popular identity helps create alternative opportunities for recognition. It is like creating a solid back-up plan in case anything goes wrong.

Individuals often identify themselves with the organization they work with. An individual will proudly say, 'I am the business leader at ABC organization'. However, if tomorrow the said organization undergoes a massive transition rendering you jobless, you will have to start again from scratch. Therefore, it is imperative for individuals to build their own personal brand. More than building a personal brand, it is imperative to have a voice as well.

Janine Allis, founder of Boost Juice and a board member of Retail Zoo, is a classic example of someone who has built an impressive array of personal brands. Over and above her business initiatives, she has also made an appearance as a 'shark' on the well-known television series Shark Tank, which shows her supporting small businesses. She has made a personal brand for herself for having a voice. She is also the author of the book, The Accidental Entrepreneur: The Juicy Bits. *Allis is a voice for working mothers and has been an advocate for the problems they face. She has also spoken about small businesses and given talks in support of mental health. She has a dedicated following on Twitter and usually uses it to voice her opinion.*

Learning Tip: Concentrate on having a voice. Your personal branding is dependent on how strong a voice you have.

Develop good analytical skills

Navratilova made diet, fitness and strength training a part of her mandatory daily routine. Veteran tennis player Leander Paes, who was Navratilova's long-time doubles partner, owes his ability to endure the rigours of the tennis tours to Navratilova, who transformed him to a fitness freak. Paes once said in an interview, 'Navratilova taught us on how physical fitness was a pre-requisite. Navratilova taught me the importance of physical fitness and that is the reason I had such a long career.'[12] Navratilova is the epitome of perseverance. She believes it is important for an athlete to reinvent oneself and make a winning routine. She surrounded herself with a support staff comprising nutritionists, trainers and others who helped her improve her game. It included championship bodybuilder Lynn Conkwright and tennis kinetics expert Rick Elstein.

Navratilova was smart enough to analyse her defeats, identify the missing element in her routine and make necessary changes in her support staff to boost the missing element. After her loss in the quarterfinals of the 1982 US Open, she analysed that though she was training hard, she lacked the right nutrition to support her game. She on-boarded Miami-based nutritionist, Dr Robert Hass, under whose close watch, Navratilova cut down on red meat, fats and sugars. Dr Hass conducted daily blood tests on the player for 39 variables and planned her diet accordingly. The result was spectacular, as was seen in 1983, when she won 86 of the 87 matches she played.

Navratilova looked at everything as science. Her nutritionist, Dr Hass used to sit by the courtside during the Navratilova–Evert matches and track their strokes and

---

[12]'Martina Navratilova Inspired My Longevity: Leander Paes', *The Indian Express*, 16 October 2019, https://bit.ly/3QED7R1. Accessed on 22 August 2022.

reactions on his laptop. Navratilova would check the analysis before every match and strategize accordingly. This programme was nicknamed 'Smartina'. This computer analysis made her bulldoze her opponents effectively. As a result, in 1984, she won 74 matches in a row starting from the US Indoor Championship in February.[13] This streak did not end until the Australian Open in December, where she lost to tennis star, Helena Suková.

Tennis involves higher-level decision-making skills. Everything, from playing a particular kind of shot to directing the ball to a particular part of the court, involves high analytical skills. Navratilova used analytical thinking in approaching every match. Her every strategy or move was backed with data and statistics. She thought through the entire match logically and did not rely on emotions to make a decision.

Learning Tip: Every decision you make should be based on logical thinking and not emotions.

A person with good analytical skills develops goal-oriented thinking and approaches the decision-making process logically. Such people are better equipped to understand the cause–effect relationship in every problem. To deliver a correct solution, one needs to understand the problem completely. A good analytical person is a capable conflict manager as well. They handle difficult situation tactfully and approach a problem with logic rather than emotions. Similarly, better critical skills and problem-solving abilities in turn enhance one's analytical skills. Critical thinking involves evaluating information and then coming out with solutions accurately. A company or corporation faces new challenges every day. It

---

[13]Allen, Scott, 'How Martina Navratilova Became the Smartest Player in the Game', Mental Floss, 26 August 2013, https://bit.ly/3T97a4C. Accessed on 22 August 2022.

is imperative for leaders to have good analytical skills, so as to ensure that their companies run smoothly with their foresight and planning. The logical assessment in several situations helps the company strategize its business in a proper direction. Today, we see almost every company including a root cause analysis in their problem-solving process.

Turn adversity into opportunity

When Navratilova was 18, she fled from her home country to the US. She said that the authorities in the communist Czechoslovakia were objecting to her decision to play in the US, where major tournaments were held.[14] Her decision angered the Czech regime and they stripped off her citizenship. Instead of being disheartened by this adversity, she chose to seek out the opportunity to be an American citizen for the sake of her career. Years later, when the situation in Czech Republic came under control, she reapplied for citizenship and currently holds dual citizenship of the US and Czech Republic.

She believed every adversity had a hidden opportunity. In 2010, she was diagnosed with breast cancer. Subsequently, she started promoting breast cancer awareness. When she was diagnosed, she said that it was her 'own personal 9/11'.[15] She was the health and fitness ambassador for the American non-profit organization, AARP. She used this as an opportunity to promote breast cancer awareness and the importance of periodic health screenings. She admitted that she had been so

---

[14]P., Pranjali, ' "I Cried When I Left, Not When I Got There"– When Martina Navratilova Spoke about Her First Trip to Communist Czechoslovakia after Becoming a US Citizen', Sportskeeda, 18 October 2022, https://bit.ly/3NY7yRt. Accessed on 9 November 2022.

[15]McVeigh, Karen,'Martina Navratilova Says Breast Cancer "My Personal 9/11"', *The Guardian*, 7 April 2010, https://bit.ly/3pxWeAf. Accessed on 22 August 2022.

involved in diet and exercises that the annual health check-ups had fallen behind on her to-do list—something that she deeply regretted. In an interview, she said, 'It's not all about eating right and exercising. Preventative steps can make just as much, or in some cases more, of a difference. Getting my mammogram literally saved my life.'[16] She reiterated the fact that early diagnosis is crucial in getting the right treatment at the right time, which can be life-saving at times.

Navratilova is an incredible woman, who has never been disheartened by adversities. She has fought on and made herself what she is today. What has made her successful has been the consistency with which she has moved ahead in life. Indeed, she has proven that consistency has no age. From the age of three till now, she is still going strong, despite several setbacks that she faced in her life. She is, indeed, the greatest gift to the world of tennis.

Some of Navratilova's Major Recognitions over the Years

- ATP Female Athlete of the years 1983 and 1984
- ITF World Champion 1979, 1982, 1983, 1984, 1985 and 1986
- WTA Player of the Year 1978, 1979, 1982, 1983, 1984, 1985 and 1986
- BBC Sports Personality of the Year Lifetime Achievement Award 2003
- Czech Sport Legend Award 2006

---

[16]Ibid.

5

Fighting Adversity

Mary Kom

Because I realize that the hardships I faced in my formative years are the foundation of my strength.[1]

MARY KOM

May 2011. A 28-year-old mother of two was in the boxing ring facing Asian champion Kim Myong Sim of North Korea. Hundreds watched the match at the 2011 Asian Cup in Haikou, China, with bated breath. Though physically present inside the ring, mentally she was with her three-year-old son, Nainai, whose health was frail at that time. Just a few days before the Asian Cup, her son had been admitted to the Postgraduate Institute of Medical Education and Research, Chandigarh, for a heart surgery. The mother's heart tore apart at the thought of her three-year-old going through such a major surgery. That was a very tough moment for this mother—to walk into the boxing ring, cast aside her deepest fears, focus on the game and return with a gold medal for her sons. The 5 feet 2 inches boxer fought with strength, technique and agility, defeating the North Korean boxer with a score of 4-3 in the

---

[1]Katariya, Meenu, '14 Powerful Quotes by Mary Kom That Will Inspire You to Follow Your Dreams & Never Give Up', *Scoopwhoop*, 14 April 2018, https://bit.ly/3dwwgdW. Accessed on 20 September 2022.

final. This is the story of Mangte Chungneijang Mary Kom, a boxer, eight-time world champion, winner of Olympic bronze medal in 2012, a loving mother and an inspiration to countless women of this country to do something extraordinary.

EARLY LIFE

Born as Chungneijang to Mangte Tonpa Kom and Mangte Akham Kom in a remote village of Kangathei in Manipur, Mary Kom was an extremely hard-working and obedient daughter. Being the eldest of three siblings, she not only helped her parents in their farm work but also looked after her younger siblings. Her father believed that a woman should be competent in everything—not only household chores but also other errands. Kom helped her father in ploughing the fields, which required immense physical strength, as the bullocks were not easy to control and manoeuvre.

The quality of being fearless was something Mary Kom developed right from her childhood. Due to the absence of any affordable transport medium or potable water in her village, she used to carry heavy rice sacks and water over long distances, all by herself. She would often go to the hills with her father to collect firewood too. Apart from this, she helped her mother with cooking, washing clothes, gardening and cleaning the house along with pursuing her studies. Her feet were fast but hands faster, coping with work from both school and home. By the time she used to set out for school, her friends would already be on their way. She would run like the wind and catch up with them. The only shoes she possessed were made of rubber, which would easily wear out due to the long trek to school. Her mother would repair the shoes by heating old iron tongs and pressing them together on the tear to join the broken pieces. By the time school term ended, her shoes would be tattered. Young Kom did not bother about her shoes or her dress; she was keener on learning what was being taught in school. She was a good student.

INSPIRATION

I was the David who took on Goliaths in the boxing ring and I won, most of the time.[2]

For Mary Kom, the Biblical story of David and Goliath has been a constant inspiration. This story presents a typical 'underdog situation', where there is a contest between a smaller and weaker opponent facing a stronger and bigger adversary.

According to this story, a great Philistine giant, Goliath, who was over 9 feet tall, mocked David, a small Israeli boy who had walked up to him with a sling and a stone. David put a stone in his sling, aimed for Goliath's forehead and released the stone. The stone hit Goliath's forehead and he fell down. Sensing the opportunity, David pulled out Goliath's sword and killed him. This story is a lesson of courage and faith and of overcoming what might seem impossible.

Learning Tip: Never let your shortcomings come in the way of your dreams.

However, not everyone is blessed with the right resources, opportunities and abilities to play the game of life. Those who know how to capitalize on their strengths and the way to work around their weaknesses meet with success. Mary Kom had a short stature and this often let people to think that she was incapable of fighting tougher and sturdier opponents

---

[2]Mary Kom, M.C., *Unbreakable: An Autobiography*, HarperCollins, New Delhi, 2013.

in the ring, but she has proved everyone wrong throughout the course of her journey. Yes, good height is definitely an advantage, but she has never let her height and slim build come in the way of boxing. Mary Kom's life is, thus, full of fights, just not in the ring but outside as well.

ENTERING THE ARENA OF SPORTS

Right from her childhood, Mary Kom excelled in every sporting event in which she participated. Seeing her fierce passion for sports, her father started looking for ways to indulge her such that it would not interrupt her studies. She started training for athletics under Nipamacha Kunam, a National Institute of Sports-trained coach in Moirang, Manipur. She had to cycle to and from her village to Moirang around four times on an everyday basis. Due to the absence of appropriate nutrition, this was taking a heavy toll on her health. She discontinued training in 20 days with the realization that athletics was not what her heart desired. She was in the process of searching for her true passion. She continued practising stretching, stamina-building exercises and speed training, which she learnt at the institute. She knew in her heart that one day, the right opportunity would show up. She was faced with several constraints: financial challenges, health issues and the responsibility of looking after her family, among others. Yet, she was determined to not give up without a fight. She did not worry about her tribulations and, instead, decided to work her way around them. Let us look deep into her life and understand how she battled these adversities. Let us learn the qualities that made her achieve success.

Identifying Where Your Heart Is

In 1999, Mary Kom enrolled in the Sports Authority of India (SAI), Takyel, Imphal, while pursuing her schooling. She trained under Coach K. Kosana Meitei. Every day, she would be up by 4.00 a.m., cycle to the academy, practise there, return by 8.00 a.m. and then set out for school. She spent the next two years of her life with this schedule, which was extremely demanding. After those two years, she rented an affordable house near the academy with some of her friends. Laishram Sarita Devi, an Indian boxer, was one of her flatmates.

During her stay at the SAI, she tried her hand at a number of sports: pole vault, javelin throw and many other track and field events, but none of them appealed to her. She wanted to take up a sport that involved a lot of action, like martial arts, but SAI dealt with track and field disciplines only. Hence, she decided to leave the institute. Her true inspiration to take up boxing came from Ngangom Dingko Singh's gold win in the 1998 Bangkok Asian Games. After the 1999 National Games, where the senior women boxers, Laishram Sarita Devi and Sandhyarani Devi, put up a good show, there were speculations of introducing boxing in the SAI. Kom would also watch a lot of Muhammad Ali matches and was impressed by his combatting skills. After a chance meeting with a boxer named Rebika Chiru, she decided to pursue boxing.

We often try to follow the career path chosen by our parents and advisors. We start living their dreams and fulfilling their wishes, believing them to be our own. In the process, we either ignore or suppress our hearts' true desires. In the long run, we soon develop dissatisfaction for the job and our performance deteriorates. Before this happens, it is imperative to check on our inner desires and work in the direction of pursuing them.

Learning Tip: Recognize your true passion before embarking on your career path.

Ignoring External Pressures

Initially, Mary Kom did not tell her parents that she had chosen boxing as her profession. It was only after she won the state boxing championship in 2000 that her father saw her photograph in the newspapers. Her parents were worried about her choosing boxing as a profession because of the injuries one faces while battling an opponent inside the boxing ring. They thought those injuries would eventually ruin her chances of marriage. Mary Kom was adamant and eventually convinced her father. 'I like boxing and will not stop,' she told her father.[3]

Learning Tip: Dreams are achieved only when you are passionate about something and decide to pursue it without worrying about what anyone else thinks.

We often hear people say, 'Nobody from my family has ever chosen such a profession'; 'This is new for me. I have no background for this'; 'I lack the degree and expertise for pursuing something like this'; 'Such a profession is not meant for people from our community'; 'Pursuing this involves a lot of money and the return on investment is not good enough'; 'It is a risky profession. Very few have succeeded in the past'; or 'What will people think if I chose this profession?' These thoughts would have crossed Kom's mind too, but it takes a lot of courage to brush aside these insecurities and move ahead. She was battling many travails in her life and she knew with firm conviction

---

[3]Bhushan, Aditya, 'Mary Kom—The Journey of India's Boxing Hero', Sportskeeda, 1 March 2017, https://bit.ly/3pARee2. Accessed on 23 August 2022.

that throwing her boxing punches towards the narrow-minded society was the solution to most of her problems.

One interesting thing to note from Mary Kom's life so far is that she took her own sweet time to figure out what she actually wanted. She must have subconsciously done a complete SWOT (strengths, weaknesses, opportunities and threats) analysis of herself at that point of time, before embarking on the journey of boxing.

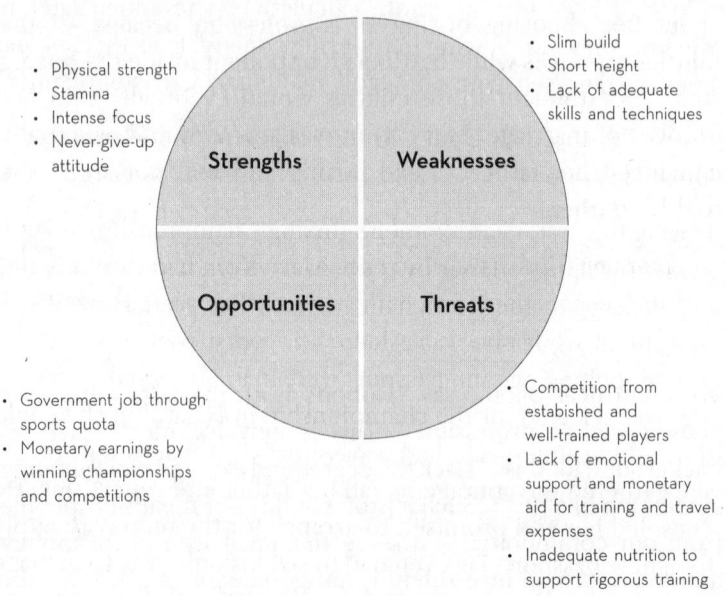

SWOT Analysis of Mary Kom

During the 2001 World Championship event in the US, Mary Kom won her first silver medal and returned home, having made a name for herself. 'In 2001, I was young and inexperienced; in fact, I would say I had no skill. I was only relying on strength and stamina to pull through. Just following my instincts at that time,' she had said during an interview.[4] Instead of celebrating, she took into account her weaknesses, studied her opponents and worked on a way to convert her weaknesses into strengths. Soon, the upcoming World Championships saw her winning gold after gold. 'But in 2018, I had the experience to ensure that I did not exert myself unnecessarily. I don't want to get hit anymore, I like to win bouts without getting struck and this is what I largely managed to do this time. No wasting of efforts. I have become more calculative,' she added later in the interview. Reviewing her journey, one realizes that she has converted herself from a 'no-skill' maiden to a 'master planner'.

Being Prepared to Deal with Situations When Planning Goes Haywire

During the first Asian Women's Boxing Championship in 2001, while travelling to Hisar by train, Mary Kom had carefully tied her luggage to the iron chain beneath her seat. However, it was stolen while she was asleep. The worst part was that her money, belongings and passport were in it. She was devastated. She was selected for the championship in Hisar, but she could do nothing unless she had a passport. In those tough times, she gathered the courage to call her father and report this. He consoled her and promised to arrange for the money to apply for a new passport. He even had to sell his only cow to manage this. Her mother overworked for days to gather the money. With help from the Kom community, he managed to raise the money and arrange for the documents required to issue a new passport. The next thing Kom remembers is holding her new passport in her hand. It was handed to her by a Manipuri boy called Onler Kom, who would eventually become her husband.

---

[4]'Mary Kom: From "No Skills" to Master Planner', *Sportstar*, 26 November 2018, https://bit.ly/3pIGfiA. Accessed on 23 August 2022.

So, the theft turned out to be a blessing in disguise.

Travelling abroad on her own expenses was difficult. The only 'wealth' Mary Kom had was her parent's support. She never let them down. From earning money, looking after her house and siblings, training for boxing, travelling for championships, embracing motherhood, winning medals to opening her own academy, she had to fight all along. She had a difficult choice to make: her passion or her family, but she managed to maintain a balance

Focussing on Performance Instead of Rewards

Money is just a by-product of success. One should aim for satisfaction. For Mary Kom, boxing gave her the ultimate sense of fulfilment. Her unwavering dedication to the sport gave her the title, 'Meethoileima', which can be loosely translated as 'great or exceptional lady'. She was named 'Magnificent Mary' as well.[5] Through her consistant hard work, she was able to pursue her passion as well as create a secure future for her family.

> **Learning Tip:** If you focus only on rewards, you will miss out the joy of giving your best fight in a sport. Enjoy the game; rewards and recognitions will eventually follow.

STRUGGLES: A MEANS TO SUCCEED, NOT A BURDEN TO BEAR

If I being a mother of two can win a medal, so can all. Take me as an example and don't give up.[6]

---

[5]Leivon, Jimmy, 'Manipur Government Confers Boxer MC Mary Kom with "Meethoileima" Title', *The Indian Express*, 12 December 2018, https://bit.ly/3pE9XWk. Accessed on 23 August 2022.

[6]Nair, Sharika S., 'Life Lessons from the Sporting Legend, Mary Kom, Who Saw and Conquered', YourStory, 1 March 2017, https://bit.ly/3pEtfL6. Accessed on 23 August 2022.

In 2007, Mary Kom gave birth to twin boys through cesarean delivery. The elders of her family advised her to retire and focus on motherhood. They thought it would be prudent to retire when she was at the peak of her career, so that she could happily move on to the next phase of her life. The doctor had advised her to rest for at least three years post surgery, but Mary Kom had other plans. Six months after her delivery, she started exercising and building her stamina again. By this time she had already secured a government job, garnered much recognition and made enough money to support her family. However, she still felt something was missing and she fought her way to make a spectacular comeback. Everyone was worried that her opponents would target her abdominal area and deliver blows over her stitches, but she brushed aside those fears with her conviction to return to boxing.

Having a cesarean section causes a lot of physical changes in a woman's body, but Mary Kom probably looked at it this way—if a woman's body can be so miraculous as have the ability to give birth, then it can do other wonders too.

It was, however, not easy. She was unwell and in much pain during her training. She developed mastitis, as she was unable to breastfeed while she was away training. Everyone thought her peak performance was behind her, as she was sick and nauseous half the time. With her determination, she proved everyone wrong, got herself selected for the fourth Asian World Championship and brought home another gold. A commendable feat indeed!

Learning Tip: The struggle you go through today toughens your mind, body and spirit for bigger challenges that you might face tomorrow.

Voicing Opinions Fearlessly

Mary Kom has a voice—a fearless one, and she has spoken up every time she has felt something was not right. Throughout her life, she has been vocal about the lack of proper amenities for emerging players in our country. Many a time, she has gotten into direct conflict with sports officials, which has affected her selection chances,[7] but she has answered all of them with her punches in the boxing ring. Whenever she has been questioned about her age and been advised to retire from her favourite sport, she has defeated younger opponents with the same agility as before and shut down her critics. Her age has improved her performance level rather than decreasing it.

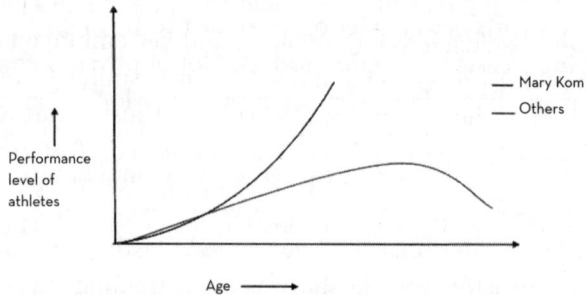

Mary Kom's Performance Level Versus Her Age

Learning Tip: You can achieve your dreams at any point of your life provided you have the desire and passion. Age will not deter your chances of following your inner calling if you have the endurance and determination to achieve your goals despite all difficulties

---

[7]Mary Kom, M.C., *Unbreakable: An Autobiography*, HarperCollins, New Delhi, 2013.

Visualizing Adversity as a Great Teacher

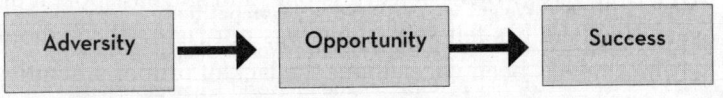

Hidden Opportunities in Every Adversity

Some people give up by trying to put the blame on adversities. Others challenge those adversities and move on. Mary Kom is in an entirely different category. She fights adversities and claims her victory. Imagine a girl from a remote village in Manipur, who had never seen the outside world before and had difficulties communicating in any language other than Manipuri. That girl challenged society by picking up a 'not-so-girly sport', struggled with finances and yet embraced every personal and professional setback with a smile. Instead of complaining, she adapted and learned not just about boxing but about adjusting to a life outside of her comfort zone. In short, she has become an inspiration for countless women in India who are fighting various battles at various stages of their life.

> **Learning Tip:** Adversity gives us an opportunity to develop resilience, which an easy life would not provide us. Adversity itself does not make you stronger. It is the reaction to the adversity that makes you stronger.

Mary Kom's Performance in Major Tournaments

Year	Place	Weight	Competition
2001	2nd	48	AIBA Women's World Championships
2002	1st	45	AIBA Women's World Championships
2002	1st	45	Witch Cup
2003	1st	46	Asian Women's Championships
2004	1st	41	Women's World Cup
2005	1st	46	Asian Women's Championships
2005	1st	46	AIBA Women's World Championships
2006	1st	46	AIBA Women's World Championships
2006	1st	46	Venus Women's Box Cup
2008	1st	46	AIBA Women's World Championships
2008	2nd	46	Asian Women's Championships
2009	1st	46	Asian Indoor Games
2010	1st	48	AIBA Women's World Championships
2010	1st	46	Asian Women's Championships
2010	1st	51	Asian Games
2011	1st	48	Asian Women's Cup
2012	1st	41	Asian Women's Championships
2012	1st	51	Summer Olympics
2014	1st	51	Asian Games
2017	1st	48	Asian Women's Championships
2018	1st	45–48	Commonwealth Games
2018	1st	45–48	AIBA Women's World Championships
2019	1st	51	2019 AIBA Women's World Boxing Championships

6

Giving Controversies a Big Punch

Muhammad Ali

Float like a butterfly and sting like a bee.
—MUHAMMAD ALI

25 February 1964, Miami Beach. A crowd of 8,300 spectators had assembled in the Convention Hall Arena to witness a tense situation. The 22-year-old Cassius Clay Junior was planning to dethrone the world heavyweight boxing champion Sonny Liston, who had demolished former world champion Floyd Patterson in 1962 and 1963 in the first knockout round itself. With massively muscled arms, Liston's jabs were like shockwaves. He also had ties with organized crime.[1] Cassius seemed unperturbed by Liston's reputation. Rather, he began hurling insults at the boxing champ, saying, 'Liston even smells like a bear [...]After I beat him, I am going to donate him to the zoo.'[2]

This infuriated Liston, who charged at Clay at the start of the match, expecting to knock him out quickly. Clay used his superior speed and agility to dodge and win round one by

---
[1]"This Day, That Year: When Muhammad Ali "Shook Up the World"", *The Free Press Journal*, 25 February 2020, https://bit.ly/3qWvIRA. Accessed on 21 September 2022.
[2]Ayegi, Steve, 'He Who Is Not Courageous Enough to Take Risks Will Accomplish Nothing in Life', Medium, 14 February 2016, https://bit.ly/3QYREXy. Accessed on 24 August 2022.

hitting continuous jabs at Liston. Round two was dominated by Liston. However, in round three, Clay used a combination of agile feet and hand movements that buckled his rival's knees and opened a cut beneath Liston's left eye. By the end of round four, Clay started experiencing blinding pain in his eyes. It was later understood that it was due to the ointment that was used on Liston's cuts, which may have been deliberately put on his gloves as well. Luckily, tears and sweat rinsed the irritation from his eyes and Clay dominated Liston in the sixth round by repeatedly hitting him. By the end of the seventh round, Clay was declared the winner. That day, the 22-year-old became the youngest boxer of that time to snatch away the title from a reigning champion.

EARLY LIFE

Muhammad Ali, born Cassius Marcellus Clay Junior, was an American professional boxer born and raised in Louisville, Kentucky. He was dyslexic and this condition led to difficulties in reading and writing all through his life. Some doctors felt his ability to dodge a punch was because of the fact that he was dyslexic. It was said that he could read the body language of the opponent better and knew from where a potential punch may come.[3]

At the age of 12, an unexpected turn of events introduced him to the world of boxing. One afternoon, he was riding his bicycle to the Columbia Auditorium. He parked his bike outside. When he went to get it, he found that it had been stolen. Someone told him that there was a policeman in the basement. He went to the basement and found that it was

---

[3]Davies, Dave, 'New Muhammad Ali Biography Reveals a Flawed Rebel Who Loved Attention', NPR, 4 October 2017, https://n.pr/3WiNFZd. Accessed on 1 November 2022.

police officer Joe Martin, who had his own boxing gym in the basement. Clay started hurling verbal threats against whoever had stolen his bike. After listening to Clay's determination of beating up the thief when he was found, Martin invited him to take boxing lessons. Martin said to the young Clay, 'Well, you better learn how to fight before you start challenging people that you're gonna whup.'[4] Within six weeks of training under Martin, Clay won his first match in 1954. Martin grew increasingly impressed by Clay's speed and strength. He had the mental agility to take a punch without panicking.

ENTERING THE PROFESSIONAL TURF

His high-school days saw Clay turn into an amateur boxer. In 1956, he won the Golden Gloves tournament for novices in the light heavyweight category. In 1959, he won the National Golden Gloves tournament of Champions as well as the Amateur Athletic Union's title in the light heavyweight category. He went on to win six Kentucky Golden Gloves championships and two national championships. Just after his graduation, he won the gold medal in the light heavyweight boxing championship in the 1960 Rome Olympics. By this time, he was considered America's hero due to his spectacular performance at the Olympics. His footwork and speed were well noticed. With this major victory, he decided to turn professional with the help of Louisville Sponsoring Group. This was the start of his remarkable career, interspersed with fights with opponents as well as several controversies. Let us study in depth the various controversies he faced during his life and how he combatted them.

---

[4]'Muhammad Ali: What They Said', BBC, 4 June 2016, https://bbc.in/3QWxJbA. Accessed on 24 August 2022.

FROM CASSIUS CLAY TO MUHAMMAD ALI

A day after he created news by defeating Liston, Clay shook the world by announcing that he will be joining the 'Nation of Islam', denouncing his slave name, 'Cassius Clay' and taking the name Cassius X.[5] However, he renamed himself Muhammad Ali a month later. In a letter to his second wife, Khalilah Camacho-Ali, he wrote that he was influenced by a cartoon in the Nation of Islam newspaper, *Muhammad Speaks*, which showed a white slave owner beating his Black slave and insisting the man pray to Jesus. Since Ali grew up in the midst of racial segregation, he felt drawn to the ideologies of the Nation of Islam and decided to embrace it. He took a political stance at a time when athletes preferred to remain neutral. His personality can be summed up perfectly in his own words, 'I don't have to be who you want me to be. I don't want to say what you want me to say. I don't want to do what you want me to do. I'm free to be who I want.'[6]

> **Learning Tip:** Be yourself. Don't accept the world's definition of you.

FIGHT WITH PATTERSON

Another big controversy in Ali's life was his fight with Patterson, who was a former heavyweight boxing champion. It was believed that Patterson had insulted Ali before the

---

[5] Nguyen, Stacey, 'One Night in Miami: The Major Reason Muhammad Ali Changed His Name', *Popsugar*, 15 January 2021, https://bit.ly/3TX5Ulp. Accessed on 1 November 2022.

[6] Davies, Dave, 'New Muhammad Ali Biography Reveals a Flawed Rebel Who Loved Attention', NPR, 4 October 2017, https://n.pr/3WiNFZd. Accessed on 1 November 2022.

Giving Controversies a Big Punch 77

1965 match owing to his background as a Black Muslim. He was quoted to have said, 'The image of a Black Muslim as the world heavyweight champion disgraces the sport and the nation. Cassius Clay must be beaten and the Black Muslims' scourge removed from boxing.'[7] This angered Ali, who had by far tried his best to create an identity for himself in the field of boxing.

On 22 November 1965, the fight between them went on for 12 rounds, where Ali used his tall stature to his advantage and dominated Patterson. The latter had already been injured at the training camp, but he did not cancel the match, as he desperately wanted to defeat Ali. During the match, when his injury became apparent, Ali refrained from knocking him out, thus ending the match to a 'technical knockout'. Patterson was perplexed upon seeing that Ali was not using his full power against him. On a later date, Patterson gave an interview stating that he had never been hit by punches as soft as Ali's. W.K. Stratton, Patterson's biographer, said in an interview, 'Ali knew that Floyd was hurt, and to his way of thinking, it would bring him no pride to injure a man who was already hurt. So, he essentially backed off, waiting for the fight to stop.'[8]

After the fight, Patterson kept addressing Ali as 'Cassius', but the latter never took it as an insult. Ali had great respect for Patterson despite all the mockery. He had even praised Patterson's bravery in a post-match interview.

Learning Tip: Be strong and not harsh. Then, you will be a true champion in all aspects of life.

---
[7]Gregory, Sean, 'Why Muhammad Ali Matters to Everyone', *Time*, 4 June 2016, https://bit.ly/3PFAGfy. Accessed on 24 August 2022.
[8]Blickenstaff, Brian, 'Throwback Thursday: Patterson vs. Ali, the Culture War That Wasn't', *Vice*, 24 November 2016, https://bit.ly/3AbXBKu. Accessed on 14 November 2022.

LOUISVILLE LIP

Ali was well-known for using humour and taunts against his opponents, earning him the nickname 'Louisville Lip'. Some believed it charged him up. Others thought that it was a psychological trick to rattle his opponents. It was his way of getting inside the opponent's head before displaying his athletic ability. Ali was also renowned for his ability to rhyme spontaneously while hurling these insults. He was a good marketing person. It was a way of promoting his fights to bring in more money for everyone.

> **Learning Tip:** Laugh and joke to diffuse tension, to bring some fun into the monotonous way of living and understand yourself and this world better.

In 2004, he said in an interview, 'Comedy is a funny way of being serious [...] My way of joking is to tell the truth. That's the funniest joke in the world.'[9]

REFUSING THE VIETNAM WAR: INCORPORATING A NON-COMPROMISING ATTITUDE

> *There are only two kinds of men: those who compromise and those who take a stand.*[10]

In 1964, Ali failed the qualifying test of the US Army due to his poor writing and spelling skills. The qualifying criteria were eased in 1966 and he got reclassified as 1A. When he was asked

---

[9] Fussman, Cal, 'Muhammad Ali: What I've Learned', *Esquire*, 17 January 2012, https://bit.ly/3UjASE5. Accessed on 1 November 2022.

[10] Wolfson, Andrew, 'Muhammad Ali Lost Everything in Opposing the Vietnam War. But in 1968, He Triumphed', *USA Today*, 19 February 2018, https://bit.ly/2WNZwiu. Accessed on 25 August 2022.

to serve in the Vietnam War, he refused to be drafted. Ali did not like the idea of killing hundreds of innocent people in war. He said, 'My conscience won't let me go shoot my brother, or some darker people, or some poor hungry people in the mud for big powerful America.'[11]

Learning Tip: Solve in-house problems first before looking out for trouble outside.

Ali was vocal about the treatment Black Americans received in his home country. He said, 'Why should they ask me to put on a uniform and go 10,000 miles from home and drop bombs and bullets on Brown people in Vietnam while [the] so-called Negro people in Louisville are treated like dogs and denied simple human rights?'[12]

As a penalty for disobeying orders to join the army, Ali was stripped of his championship titles. He was convicted of violating service laws and sentenced to five years in prison. He eventually arranged for bail, but his passport was snatched away. He could not fight in America.

Despite being stripped of his identity, Ali continued to fight back. He started capturing the attention of the audience when he drifted from the Nation of Islam orthodoxy. He was now a crowd puller, as the crowd could sense his antiwar stance in a proper manner.

Learning Tip: Listen to your inner voice. Let your value system do the decision-making part.

From March 1967 to October 1970, Ali could not fight. During

---

[11]Ibid.
[12]Barbash, Fred, '50 Years Ago Today, Muhammad Ali Was Told to "Step Forward." He Refused', *The Washington Post,* 28 April 2017, https://wapo.st/3CvBtwv. Accessed on 25 August 2022.

this time, he won public sympathy, as the American people started seeing the cruelties of war and began adopting an antiwar stance. Eventually, through subsequent appeals by lawyers, his conviction was overturned in 1971 and his boxing licence was reinstated.

Ali lost some prime years (between ages 25 and 29) away from the boxing ring owing to being suspended for non-participation in the Vietnam War, but he did not compromise on his core values.

RIVALRY WITH JOE FRAZIER: BEYOND THE BOXING RING

Ali limited his rivalry to the boxing ring. Most of his insults and taunts were meant only to attract more audience and increase his popularity. He never really intended to offend anyone. However, one such rival of his, Joe Frazier, really got offended and took his rivalry off the ring.

The Fight was a heavyweight championship boxing match between heavyweight champion Joe Frazier and former undisputed heavyweight champion Muhammad Ali, on Monday, 8 March 1971, at Madison Square Garden in New York City. Dubbed as the 'Fight of the Century', it exceeded all the promotional hype and went on for the full 15 round championship distance. Ali started off with dominating the first two rounds, using his powerful jabs against Frazier's shorter body. In the closing seconds of the third round, Frazier landed a left hook on Ali's right jaw. By round 15, Ali's jaw started swelling considerably, but he managed to get up within three seconds of being pinned down. Frazier won by a unanimous decision by the judges, thus retaining his heavyweight championship title in 1971 and Ali faced his first major professional loss.

SUPER FIGHT II

On 24 January 1974, the duo engaged in Super Fight II at Madison Square Garden in New York City. This time, Ali came up with a new technique: a half-hook half-upper cut coming from both sides. This technique enabled him to land more punches on Frazier than before, when he had missed most of the punches. Frazier was a slow starter. Ali took advantage of this and maintained a fast pace by punching in flurries followed by clinching, which led to his victory. He was never scared of tougher opponents and he knew he could easily overpower them first with confidence and second with technique. In an interview, he had said, 'A man who views the world the same at fifty as he did at twenty has wasted thirty years of his life'.[13] With age, his views and perspective became more matured.

RUMBLE IN THE JUNGLE:- SELF-BELIEF MAKES THE UNDERDOG A WINNER

At the age of 32, Ali challenged George Foreman, the world champion, aged 25, to reclaim the heavyweight championship title. Everyone associated with boxing, including Ali's long-time supporter, Howard Cosell, thought Ali had the faintest chance of winning. Ali knew he was an underdog, but he strongly believed he could win. He even declared himself the greatest![14]

Defying the conventional style, Ali started off the match with disorienting right-hand leads, which meant he used his right hand to continuously punch without setting up the left.

---

[13] Ezra, Michael, *Muhammad Ali: The Making of an Icon*, Temple University Press, USA, 2009, p. 190

[14] 'In His Own Words: Muhammad Ali's Most Famous Quotes', NBC Sports, 5 June 2016, https://bit.ly/3TusSzm. Accessed on 9 November 2022.

This enabled him to land several blows on Foreman's head but failed to injure him severely. Foreman was known for his 'cutting the ring and preventing escape' technique. Ali applied the rope-a-dope technique by leaning on to the ropes and covering himself up with gloves. Foreman started punching Ali vigorously but did not win any points, as the punches either did not hit Ali or were deflected in such a way that they did not hit Ali's head. This was a carefully planned technique to drain Foreman of his energy. When Foreman started tiring, Ali used his fast jabbing technique and started hitting hard and fast jabs. Ali landed a left hook to get Foreman's head in position and a hard right straight to the face resulting in Foreman falling down in the canvas. Ali unanimously won the match.

One of the winning qualities of Ali was his immense self-belief. The bout mentioned above highlights Ali's tactical genius on how he outwrestled a heavily muscular guy with intelligence. After the fight, he proudly announced to his critics, 'I told you all, all of my critics, that I was the greatest of all time. [...] Never again make me the underdog until I'm about 50 years old.'[15] Ali won back his title and once again proved his words true that he was the greatest.

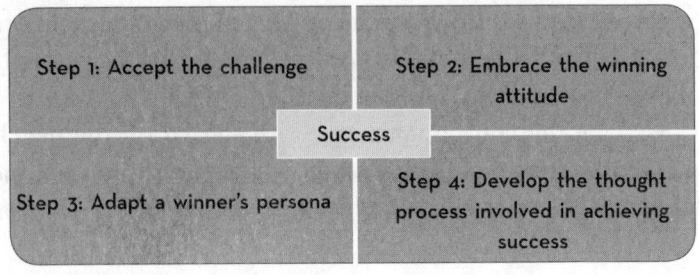

Four-Step Guide to 'Fake It Till You Make It'

---

[15]Ibid.

THRILLA IN MANILA 16: CONTROVERSY OF DELIBERATELY CREATING EXTENDED CLINCHES

On 1 October 1975, the final match between Ali and Frazier was held in the aluminium-roofed Philippine Coliseum, where the temperature was intensely hot at 125 degree Fahrenheit. For the first two rounds, Ali overpowered Frazier by landing several straight right-handed punches after his left jab.

In the later rounds, Frazier made the crucial mistake of listening to his adviser and standing upright to see where the incoming punches from Ali's side were coming. Ali saw this as his opportunity in round 12 and landed several punches on Frazier's face in quick succession with both hands. The punches landed so accurately that they did further damage to Frazier's limited eyesight. By round 13, Frazier was barely able to see. Ali dominated in both rounds 13 and 14 and, hence, Frazier had to quit. Little did somebody know, Ali himself was also not in a position to fight. He later acknowledged this to his biographer, 'Frazier quit just before I did. I didn't think I could fight anymore.'[17] Thus, Ali won this fight.

> **Learning Tip:** It is imperative to keep faith till the last moment. Luck favours those who have faith in themselves.

GETTING BOWLED BY PARKINSON'S DISEASE BUT CONTINUING TO SERVE

By the late 1970s, there were visible changes in Ali's speech and speed. In 1982, at the age of 42, three years after his retirement

---

[16] Mitchell, Kevin, 'Thrilla in Manila: 40 Years on from Sanctioned Manslaughter in Boxing', *The Guardian*, 1 October 2015, https://bit.ly/3fmiP0z. Accessed on 26 September 2022.

[17] Hauser, Thomas, *Muhammad Ali: His Life and Times*, Portico, 2012.

from boxing, he was diagnosed with Parkinson's disease. His wins started turning into a series of losses and he was on the receiving end of punches. His speed and agility went down. By the time he retired, he had already taken 200,000 hits.

Nevertheless, Ali was a symbol of hope for Parkinson's patients, showing that they do not have to limit themselves. In 1998, he worked with actor Michael J. Fox, who also has Parkinson's disease, to raise awareness and funds for research on this disease.

BEATING CONTROVERSIES

Ali's life was a fair mix of love, hatred, popularity and controversy. From changing his name, induction into the Nation of Islam, refusal to join the army, mocking and criticizing opponents to his marital life and affairs, he received a fair bit of negative publicity from the media.

Ali was a known philanthropist and humanitarian. He donated millions to charity. He is known to have fed 22 million people affected by hunger and starvation across the world. In 1990, he went to Iraq to meet the then president Saddam Hussein to negotiate the release of American hostages, which was a success. In 2002, he went to Afghanistan as the UN Messenger of Peace.

Looking at Ali, it can be said that while it is quite easy to punch an opponent in the ring, it is equally difficult to punch controversies in the face. Even though he passed away in 2016, his tale of triumph continues to inspire people.

Ali's Major Performances over the Years

Event	Year	Category	Position
Olympic Games	1960	Light Heavyweight	Gold
Intercity Golden Gloves	1959, 1960	Light Heavyweight	Gold
Chicago Golden Gloves	1959, 1960	Light Heavyweight	Gold
US National Championships	1959, 1960	Light Heavyweight	Gold

7

Reaching the Success Shore

Michael Phelps

I think goals should never be easy, they should force you to work, even if they are uncomfortable at the time.

MICHAEL PHELPS

Michael Phelps is arguably the greatest swimmer of all time. He is the most decorated Olympian ever, with 28 medals to his credit, of which as many as 23 are gold. This also includes his record of eight gold medals at the 2008 Beijing Olympics, the highest by an individual at any Olympic event.[1] He has set 39 world records (29 individual and 10 relays), which is more than any other swimmer in the world. He also holds 23 Guinness World Records, which is the highest number of accumulative Guinness World records held by any athlete. The manner and focus with which he has maintained his supremacy in the world of swimming over nearly two decades is a model to emulate.

---

[1] Venkat, Rahul, 'Michael Phelps: The Man Who Dominated the Olympic Pool Like No Other', Olympics.com, 23 March 2022, https://bit.ly/3AJHwwq. Accessed on 25 August 2022.

EARLY LIFE

Being the youngest of three siblings, Phelps began swimming at the age of seven, largely owing to the influence of his mother and sisters, who already swam at a local aquatic club. It was there that, after the initial resistance, Phelps discovered his love for water. Initially afraid to get his head underwater, he decided to swim on his back. This eventually led to him mastering the backstroke. In his book *Beneath the Surface: My Story*, he recollects feeling like a dolphin in water. In his own words: 'I could go fast in the pool, it turned out, in part because being in the pool slowed down my mind. In the water, I felt, for the first time, in control.'[2]

At the age of six, Phelps was diagnosed with attention-deficit/hyperactivity disorder (ADHD), which is marked by the inability to pay attention, listen and follow directions, as well as impulsiveness and hyperactivity. In his book, he recalls that he had trouble paying attention as early as his kindergarten days. In fact, his teacher had once told his parents that he would not be able to focus on anything. He loved being the centre of attention and often resorted to playing mischief. However, a major turning point came after his parents divorced, leading him to the realization that he needed to focus his attention on something.

While it was challenging for him to sit through an academic class, he loved being in the swimming pool for more than three hours after his classes. His mother, Debbie Phelps, played a huge role in fuelling her son's passion for swimming. She accompanied him to all major competitions and practice

---

[2]Phelps, Michael, and Brian Cazeneuve, *Beneath the Surface: My Story*, Sports Publishing, New York, 2017, p. 24.

sessions, as she felt that this was an apt way to get rid of the extra energy in his body.

While we tend to focus on the negative aspects of ADHD, it should be noted that it also provides an additional boost of energy levels for risk-taking individuals.[3] Sir Richard Branson of Virgin Atlantic is another celebrated personality diagnosed with ADHD, and just like Phelps, he, too, was able to turn it around in his favour. Though such individuals lack focus on minor aspects of life, they tend to hyperfocus and become the best in their chosen field. In the case of both Branson and Phelps, the statement holds true. They identified their primary weakness and made it their greatest strength. Similarly, we should turn our weaknesses into the fuel that drives our spirit.

Any individual can become the best in their chosen specialization by maintaining focus and discipline. This can be achieved by following a simple five-step strategy.

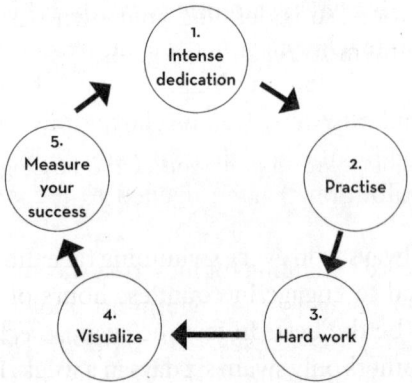

Five-Step Approach to Ensure Success

---

[3]Sherrell, Zia, '6 Strengths and Benefits of ADHD', Medical News Today, 20 July 2021, https://bit.ly/3L6mOdv. Accessed on 12 September 2022.

1. **Intense dedication:** One needs to focus on the goal with a single-minded approach and become obsessed with achieving the end objective.
2. **Practise:** According to author Malcom Gladwell, if an individual performs the same activity over a period of 10,000 hours, he can attain a level of perfection in his chosen field. In order to be successful, one needs to put in the effort towards achieving one's goals.
3. **Hard work:** There is no substitute for hard work. It is hard work coupled with direction that eventually leads to success. Once success is achieved, it is all about replicating the same in a consistent manner.
4. **Visualize:** It is important to visualize the journey and focus on reaching the destination.
5. **Measure your success:** Define parameters to measure your progress over time and keep track of it. Just like a project plan is essential to determine the progress in any implementation, so is defining your own parameters and monitoring them to reach your goals.

Learning Tip: Maintaining your focus and discipline towards attaining your goal is one of the key ingredients for success.

Phelps almost always won every swimming race that he entered. However, he had to engage in countless hours of preparation and practice to be the best. In fact, he swam *every day* for six years, whereas others only swam six days in a week. In the end, it made a lot of difference to his approach and preparation. He also uses visualization techniques to determine his goal and works hard towards it. In a similar manner, any young professional should also focus his energy towards attaining his goal. Define the goal, figure out an action plan and then pursue it.

On qualifying for the 2000 Sydney Olympics, Phelps became the youngest American to accomplish the feat in the last 68 years—which in itself was a huge achievement. Yet, he failed to have a single podium finish. He bounced back in the 2008 Beijing Olympics with eight gold medals and the rest, as they say, is history. In fact, before the Olympics in 2008, he had already announced he would win gold in his events.[4] If he had given up, he would never have become the greatest. We too should not call it quits and persevere till the very end. The best way to answer our critics is not through words but through our actions, as goes the age-old adage: actions speak louder than words.

One of the reasons why Phelps is so good at swimming is because of his body features that are ideal for it. His imposing height (6 feet 4 inches) and broad hands and feet are perfect for the sport. His physical features enable him to swim faster, since his hands and feet are good enough to work as paddles. He was quick to realize that he was exceptionally good at swimming and, hence, stuck to it and became an Olympic champion. It is important to enjoy the work we do and the team we work with. Companies such as Google dominate the field of technology, as they allow their employees to work on projects that they love. This, in turn, propels them to build products that are a class apart.

In a similar manner, as individuals, we need to identify our strengths and weakness. Performing a SWOT (strengths, weaknesses, opportunities and threats) analysis on oneself is a good way to start.

---

[4]Mohan, Vishnu, '"I Got to Throw That Race Out" – Michael Phelps on His Mental Preparation to Do the 8-Medal Run at the 2008 Olympics', Sportskeeda, 31 August 2022, https://bit.ly/3BzfQL0. Accessed on 12 September 2022.

> **Learning Tip:** Always love what you do. This will propel you to be successful in spite of all adversities.

Another reason for Phelps's success was his long-standing association with his coach Bob Bowman. It was Bowman's mentorship that helped Phelps steer his focus towards being the very best in his sport. It was at the age of 11 that Phelps met his coach for the first time, leading to an association that has lasted throughout his career. Bowman was quick to spot the talent in the young Phelps and used his authority to make Phelps practise gruelling drills. According to Phelps, Bowman was more like a drill sergeant to him. He had once said, 'Training with Bob is the smartest thing I've ever done [...] I'm not going to swim for anyone else.'[5]

Bowman too is vocal in praising his prodigy. In his words, Phelps is more of a solitary man with a rigid focus on the pool.[6] The keyword to look out for is focus. Post the 2004 Summer Olympics, Bowman was hired as the head coach at the University of Michigan, where Phelps joined him to train and attend classes. Phelps served as a volunteer assistant coach at Michigan. After the 2008 Summer Olympics, Bowman returned to Baltimore as the CEO of the North Baltimore Aquatic Club, where Phelps also joined him. Their association continued even in 2015, when Phelps moved to Arizona after Bowman was appointed the head coach for both the men's and women's swimming teams at Arizona State University. Each time Bowman made a switch, Phelps followed him. Bowman was also Phelps's coach during the

---

[5] Fernando, Shemal, 'Michael Phelps' Incredible 28 Medals that Crowned Him the Most Decorated Olympian', *Sunday Observer*, 1 August 2021, https://bit.ly/3qykeDU. Accessed on 12 September 2022.

[6] 'How Michael Phelps Became the Greatest Swimmer of All Time', MySwimPro, https://bit.ly/3DTHnGR. Accessed on 9 November 2022.

famed 2008 Beijing Olympics, where the latter broke all records by winning eight gold medals.

There is an important lesson to be learnt here. Good coaches and mentors are rare and when we find one, we should not let them go. In a similar manner, having a good mentor in your office can pave the way for success in your corporate career. A mentor can groom you to improve your skills while maintaining your focus at all times. They help in bringing out the best in you.

> Learning Tip: Finding the right mentor is extremely important for one's success. It provides you with an opportunity to discuss your problems and to be guided by their experience and wisdom.

Apart from ADHD, Phelps also suffers from depression and severe anxiety and had even contemplated suicide after the 2012 Olympic Games.[7] The intensity with which he competed and practised perhaps had a price of its own. Defeat is something that is not in his dictionary. His focus means everything. If there is an individual who has experienced setbacks during the prime of his career, it is definitely him. Soon after his first Olympic Games, he was arrested for driving under the influence of alcohol, which tarnished his image because he was just 21.[8] Phelps is a living example that we have to rise above our setbacks and win, no matter what.

Though he once said, 'Really, after every Olympics I think

---

[7]'Michael Phelps Reveals He Battled Depression, Contemplated Suicide After 2012 Olympics', *Scroll.in*, 20 January 2018, https://bit.ly/3cl6Pve. Accessed on 26 August 2022.

[8]*Reuters in Baltimore*, 'Michael Phelps Pleads Guilty to Drunken Driving Three Months After DUI Arrest', *The Guardian*, 19 December 2014, https://bit.ly/3FGVhPr. Accessed on 2 November 2022.

I fell into a major state of depression,'[9] Phelps was able to make a successful comeback and win five gold medals and one silver in the 2016 Rio De Janeiro Olympics. He battled his way through, even took drugs, retired in 2012, came back to the sport in 2014 and achieved the feat of making a successful return at Rio. It is believed that his comeback to professional swimming in 2014 was motivated by the US team's inability to win the butterfly relay in the 2008 Olympics. In 2016, Phelps was finally able to win the gold medal in the 4x100 metre butterfly relay and fulfil his goal.

In his personal life, too, Phelps has settled down with his girlfriend Nicole Johnson and is a proud father to three kids. He attributes his recovery to his ability to open up and share his problems.

One has to simply admire the resolute focus of Phelps in fighting his personal demons and still achieving greatness. His focus is not just on bettering himself but also on helping others. He presently volunteers as a coach for the Arizona State Sun Devils team. Phelps has also been working with his foundation (Michael Phelps Foundation), which promotes swimming and other sports.

> **Learning Tip:** Adverse conditions are a true test of our character. How we respond to such situations makes us who we are.

Phelps could have withered away like any other professional, yet he held on like a true champion. He teaches us that by focussing on our goals, we can achieve anything. We can apply the same principle to our career, relationships as well as any other aspect of our lives.

---

[9] Scutti, Susan, 'Michael Phelps: "I Am Extremely Thankful That I Did Not Take My Life"', CNN, 20 January 2018, https://Cnn.it/3OaGuOY. Accessed on 26 August 2022.

World Records that Phelps Holds

- Most world records set for swimming (male)
- Most gold medals in world championships for swimming
- Most individual swimming Olympic gold medals
- Most medals at the Fédération Internationale de Natation (FINA) Swimming World Championships
- Most Olympic gold medals in team swimming
- Most medals at the Olympics for swimming (male)
- Most 'Men's World Swimmer of the Year' awards
- Most Olympic golds at one game (male)
- Most searched for sportsman on the internet (2016)
- Most gold medals at the Olympics for an individual event (male)
- Most Olympic medals won (male)
- Most consecutive Olympic swimming gold medals in the same event (male)
- Fastest swim long-course 400-metre medley (male)
- Most gold medals won at the Olympics (male)
- Most individual Olympic medals (male)
- Most swimming Olympic medals won (male, single games)
- Most Olympic medals won (male, single games)
- Most gold medals won at a single FINA World Championship (individual)
- Most silver medals awarded in a single Olympic swimming race
- Fastest swim, short-course relay 4x100 metre freestyle (male)
- Fastest swim, long-course relay 4x200 metre freestyle (male)
- Fastest swim, long-course relay 4x100 metre medley (male)

8

Kicking Poverty to the Curb

Pelé

The more difficult the victory, the greater the happiness in winning.[1]

PELÉ

Born in abject poverty and unable to afford even a football, a little boy in Brazil played soccer by kicking newspapers stuffed inside a sock. He learnt the basics of the game from his father, who was also a soccer player and who struggled to make ends meet. This is the story of Pelé, who overcame all obstacles to become one of the greatest legends in the history of soccer. He was lovingly called 'Pérola Negra', or the 'Black Pearl', by the people of Brazil. In 1999, he was voted the 'World Player of the Century' by the International Federation of Football History and Statistics and jointly won the FIFA Player of the Century award.

EARLY LIFE

Pelé was born on 23 October 1940 as Edson Arantes do Nascimento. Though his family gave him the nickname Dico,

---

[1]Pelé and Brian Winter, *Why Soccer Matters: A Look at More Than Sixty Years of International Soccer*, Penguin, New York, 2014, p. 204.

he came to be called Pelé when he started schooling. There is an interesting story behind it. He was quite fond of Bilé, the goalkeeper of the Brazilian sports club, Club de Regatas Vasco da Gama. However, Dico would mispronounce his name as Pelé, so some of his friends mockingly started to call him Pelé.

Pelé impressed everyone with his soccer skills. With his friends, he formed a small team, which they called Shoeless, as none of them had shoes. They played soccer barefoot and were also known as Pélada, after Pelé, who would skip school to play these street matches. In these matches, he developed the unorthodox dribbling techniques that eventually made him famous. He was expelled from school after fourth grade, as his headmaster once caught him playing soccer during school hours. He became a cobbler's apprentice and worked on a meagre wage of $2 a day.

> **Learning Tip:** People with a strong willpower can make their own way.

TURNING PROFESSIONAL

Pelé was discovered by the former national-level soccer player Waldemar de Brito at the age of 11 and the latter started secretly training him. Eventually, de Brito convinced Pelé's family to let him leave home to participate in the selections of the Santos FC aka Santos Futebol Clube. Pelé impressed the Santos coach Luís Alonso Pérez, who was affectionately known as Lula, with his unique style of play. In June 1956, he signed the professional contract with Santos FC.

With the onset of the 1957 season, Pelé was granted the starting position in the team. By the age of 16, he became the top scorer of the league. Within 10 months, he became part of the Brazil national football team. In 1958, 1962 and 1970, he was part of the World Cup team, which won the Cup for Brazil. In 1961, the president of Brazil, Jânio Quadros, declared Pelé a 'national treasure'.[2]

Let's take a look at the life lessons we can learn from Pelé.

HAVE THE COURAGE TO TAKE THE FIRST STEP

If we wait until we are ready, we will be waiting for the rest of our lives.[3]

When Pelé started playing soccer, he was without shoes, a football or any real practice. He knew that if he waited for the shoes and football, he would lose the valuable chance to make a mark. In his book *Why Soccer Matters*, he says, 'Bauru was poor, like [the] rest of Brazil. It often seemed like a city with too many shoe shiners, and not enough shoes.'[4] Pelé knew he needed to work with the limited resources available to excel in his game. He started playing soccer with a rolled-up sock and picked up his dribbling skills using just that. He learnt to control the ball, and the delicate handling of it by playing with a mango. He mastered the art of juggling i.e. keeping the ball in the air by bouncing it upwards with his knees, chest and head after practising for years with a grapefruit.

Learning Tip: Wise men know how to grab an opportunity at the right time. Excuses are tools of procrastinators.

---

[2] Heffernan, Conor, 'How Brazil Turned Pelé into a National Treasure to Stop Him from Leaving the Country', *These Football Times*, 22 October 2017, https://bit.ly/3QWv0PG. Accessed on 29 August 2022.

[3] Quoted in Francia, Ben, 'If We Wait until Ready, We'll Be Waiting for a Long Time', Ben Francia, https://bit.ly/3CKKxOi. Accessed on 30 August 2022.

[4] Pelé and Brian Winter, *Why Soccer Matters: A Look at More Than Sixty Years of International Soccer*, Penguin, New York, 2014.

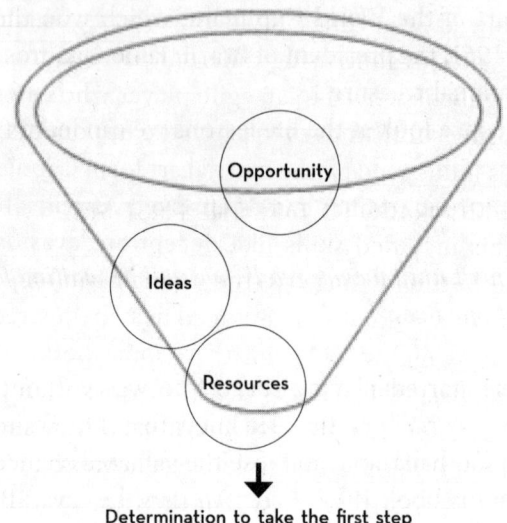

Determination to take the first step

Determination Supersedes Opportunities,
Ideas and Resources

Opportunities, ideas and resources may influence your first step, but in reality, they are only a subset of your determination to take the first step. Even if these three are absent and the person has a lot of determination, they can move ahead and create opportunities for themselves.

CREATE YOUR OWN SIGNATURE STYLE

Always be yourself! Don't try to imitate or be like someone else. Create your own individual style. Don't try to make yourself a "Pele" [sic]. It is much more important to be yourself than Pele [sic].[5]

---

[5]Pelé, 'Pelé – Learn to Play 360 Soccer', 360 Soccer, https://bit.ly/3U5EWIP. Accessed

Pelé followed the Ginga style of soccer, which involves dribbling and juggling using different parts of the foot. This style is highly beneficial to an agile player who can sway with the ball using subtle moves to catch the opponents off guard. Ginga was influenced by the martial art form Capoeira, which developed from combat games enslaved Africans brought to Brazil. This included skills like deception, evasion, kicking and head-butting. Ginga is the fundamental footwork of Capoeira. This style was encouraged heavily in street football and Pelé was highly adept in it. At some points in his life, he was told that the style would have worked in Santos FC matches but not at a global level. It was even suggested to him to adopt other players' style. Pelé, however, was a strong believer of his roots. He knew that the Ginga style was a part of his identity. He popularized his signature bicycle kick, which is world famous today. He first used it in the 1968 match between Belgium and Brazil. He received a cross from the left wing, but instead of facing the goalpost, he turned his back towards it. He tilted backwards and sprung in the air to shoot the ball with his right foot. The ball landed straight in the goalpost. Everyone was stunned and speechless by this manoeuvre. In his book, *Why Soccer Matters*, he says, 'The bicycle kick is not easy to do. I scored 1283 goals and only two or three were bicycle kicks.'[6]

Pelé was a prolific goal scorer. He played in a variety of attacking positions. Irrespective of his placement in the field, he had the ability to score a goal. His trademark moves *drible da vaca* and *paradinha* (little stop) are famous all over the world.

---

on 12 September 2022.
[6] Menon, Rohan, 'How Pele Made the Bicycle Kick Famous', Sportskeeda, 3 October 2015, https://bit.ly/3NRYU74. Accessed on 9 November 2022.

Learning Tip: You increase your personal brand value by associating your own unique signature with it.

People love and respect you for your uniqueness, so learn to embrace it. Be confident in your own skin. You gain an edge over the crowd by being different. Brands too employ unique strategies to gain an edge over others, thus refusing to follow the popular practice.

For example, consider Tesla, Inc. There is a widespread market habit of launching a minimum viable product at a minimum price point first and then proceeding to add higher-end luxury products in the kitty. Tesla, on the other hand, launched a luxury battery electric vehicle (BEV) sports car called Roadster at the first go. It targeted the affluent buyers first and then introduced products at a lower price point. Tesla's focus is more on electric cars rather than the traditional fuel-driven ones. It predicted that the market will need batteries for electric cars, so it went on to manufacture batteries as well. Even while adopting its sales strategy, Tesla decided to sell its cars online and via company-owned showrooms instead of conventional dealers, further allowing customers to customize their carrs. It thought of playing the long-term game and focussed on its uniqueness rather than blindly following the crowd.

LEARN FROM YOUR MISTAKES

Pelé's father, João Ramos do Nascimento (nicknamed Dodinho) was also a professional soccer player, but he had to discontinue playing due to a knee injury in 1953. He had to retire and take up the job of a hospital cleaner to support his family. Many close to the family believed that Dodinho suffered the injury due to his Ginga style of playing soccer. However, his father always reiterated that that had not been the cause of his injury but it had also been his self-doubt. During a game, when his father was unsure of his next move with the ball, he accidentally collided with an opponent on the field and injured himself. He advised his son not to repeat the same mistake. Self-doubt leads to hesitation and even one second of hesitation in shooting or passing the ball can give the opponent an ideal opportunity to score.

Pelé convinced his team to follow the Ginga style, which gave them an edge over the professional Swedish team in the 1958 soccer finals. He knew that the only way Brazil could have an edge over their opponents was by concentrating on their roots and own style of play.

LEARN THE 'WHY' OF THE TRADE BEFORE THE 'HOW'

The best way to learn is by asking questions. Pelé was always inquisitive. Before learning the various shots, he read up on the centre of gravity and the force of inertia. Even in his book, *Learning Soccer with Pelé*, he explains the basics of the game first by explaining the 'why' followed by the 'how'. Before learning to hit the ball in a certain way, it is imperative to know the reason behind making that particular move. Most people focus on the what and how instead of concentrating on the 'why' behind their actions. 'Why' needs to be the central question of all activities. The answer to the 'why' provides the vision statement, which is extremely important to grasp before beginning any work. 'Why' promotes curiosity, which leads to innovation.

BE ALERT

In the field, Pelé often surprised his opponents with his ability to gauge who was approaching from behind and then acting quickly. He had a great peripheral vision and was extremely agile in passing the ball, linking up with his teammates and providing powerful assists. He had his concentration on the ball while dribbling but was alert all the time. He knew who was coming towards him and accordingly made a swift move, much to the opponent's surprise. For any sportsperson, it is imperative to display a heightened sense of alertness to combat and prevent accidental injuries.

ALWAYS BE A TEAM PLAYER

Pelé was a firm believer in teamwork. Great teams may not always comprise all-rounders, but they make the most of each player's strengths. It is important to capitalize on those strengths and cover up for each other's weakness. Pelé said, '[...] Football is a team game. No one plays alone. Success depends on your whole team being a single unit. There are eleven players and also the reserves helping each other to fight for the same objective.'[7] He credited his teammates for every goal he scored and similarly assisted in numerous goals being scored from their side. To produce great results, we need teams that comprise individuals willing to brainstorm and work together. TEAM is about Together Everyone Achieving More. From the conception of an idea to its execution, it's all about teamwork. An individual may be a terrific contributor, but if they lack collaborative abilities, their talent is of no use.

---

[7]Miguel Díaz, Luis, 'Pele: An Inspiration for Teamwork in Negotiated Solutions', Mediate.com, 9 June 2008, https://bit.ly/3Q0LMvJ. Accessed on 30 August 2022.

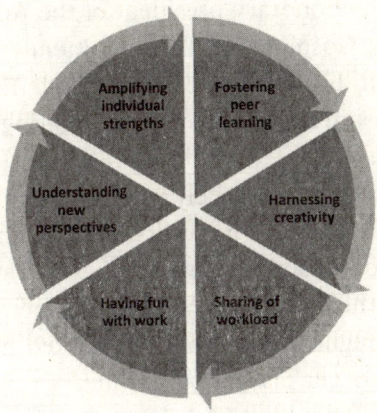

Advantages of Working as a Team

EXCELLING IN MULTIPLE DIMENSIONS

Pelé was an all-rounder who played as a centre forward, main striker, inside forward, second striker and also as an attacking midfielder. He was equally adept at shooting with both his feet. He had amazing ball control that allowed him to literally move the ball from any corner of the field straight to the goalpost. He was never intimidated by the strong defences of the opponent. He could swiftly cut past any player with the ball.

Apart from being a soccer player, Pelé authored several books like *Pelé, the Autobiography*, *Learning Soccer with Pelé* and *Why Soccer Matters,* among several others. He also starred in movies like *Escape to Victory* and *Mike Basset: England Manager* (cameo role), and documentary films like *Once in a Lifetime: The Extraordinary Story of the New York Cosmos* and composed musical pieces including the soundtrack of the film *Pelé*.

He was an active philanthropist. He was also appointed as the UNESCO goodwill ambassador in 1994. In 2010, he was introduced as the honorary president of the American soccer club, New York Cosmos. In 2012, he attended the Olympic Hunger Summit hosted by former British Prime Minister David Cameron and made an appearance during the Olympic's closing ceremony.

Pelé has taught us to actively believe in our dreams and to work on converting them to reality. There will be obstacles, misfortunes and constraints, but a true warrior is one who can overcome them. He was a true dreamer. With limited resources, he fought his way up. He worked hard to be one of the greatest soccer players of all time.

Pelé's Performance for the National Team

Tournaments	Matches	Goals Scored	Goals: Matches
World Cup 1958	4	6	1.5
World Cup 1962	2	1	0.5
World Cup 1966	2	1	0.5
World Cup 1970	6	4	0.67
Total in World Cups	14	12	0.86
Overall	92	77	0.836

9

Breaking Stereotypes

Lewis Hamilton

Nothing can really prepare you for when you get in the Formula One car. Knowing that you're driving a multimillion-dollar car, and if you crash it it's going to cost a lot of money, and they might not give you another chance, is scary.[1]

Lewis Hamilton

Lewis Hamilton is regarded as one of the best Formula One (F1) drivers of all time. Formula One is a fascinating sport if we look at the wide variety of racing tracks coupled with the need for both speed and accuracy. A miscalculation of adjusting to a turn by even a few seconds can be disastrous for both the rider and the automobile company. Yet, a young gentleman from England defied all odds and shattered stereotypes to emerge as the numero uno behind the steering wheel. He has been successful in winning seven world championship titles (equal to Michael Schumacher's) along with the most championship points, amassing a total of 4345.5 (as of October 2022). The achievement becomes even more fascinating if we

---

[1]Rose, Charlie, 'Lewis Hamilton', CBS News, 14 August 2016, Accessed on 9 November 2022.

consider that Hamilton is also the only F1 driver of Black descent.

EARLY LIFE

Hamilton was born on 7 January 1985 in Hertfordshire, England, to Carmen Larbalestier and Anthony Hamilton. His parents separated when he was two years old and he continued to live with his mother and half-sisters till he was 12, after which he moved in with his father and half-brother Nicolas Hamilton, who also happens to be a professional racing driver. It is interesting to note that despite surviving a broken home, Lewis was able to keep his mind focussed on his dreams. His humble beginnings is why he cherishes success so much and always refers to his childhood as one of the key drivers of his success. He also owes his success to the sacrifices his father made. He used to work three jobs to support Lewis's dream of becoming a racer. When Lewis was all of seven, his father got him a go-kart for Christmas and promised to support his racing career. Young Lewis did not let his father down. He won races and cadet class championships at the Rye House Kart Circuit.

Lewis himself acknowledged the pivotal role his father played in his career. During the go-karting championships, his father would always stand several metres closer to the corner where the other racers were braking. This resulted in Lewis taking a cue and trying to hit the brakes at those points. Initially, he would lose control and crash. However, it later paved the way for him to learn to hit the brakes late and manage the most difficult of tracks in his F1 career. In his own words, 'I really do aspire to be like him, as a strong, black man and as a father and as a human being for doing what he did in the difficult times with the little that he had.'[2]

> Learning Tip: The support we receive from our family and the sacrifices they make in shaping us should always be acknowledged and respected.

It is important to have someone you admire and respect as coach, since it helps build the foundation for a strong and long-standing relationship. In the case of Lewis, having his father as his coach was one of the key reasons for his successful career. In 2019, during the Hungarian Grand Prix, the Mercedes team agreed to a second pit stop tyre change for Lewis with just 20 laps remaining. Torger Christian 'Toto' Wolff, the team principal, used his father's words—'you can do it'—to keep motivating Lewis, as he was not sure about taking the second pit stop which would result in further delay. This in turn forced the Belgian-Dutch racing driver Max Verstappen, who was leading the race, to continue on his own disintegrating tyres. Lewis, on resuming the race after the tyre change, closed in on the gap and eventually won the race.

Similarly, having the right coach in our corporate career can pave the way for success. While organizations often focus on profit by encouraging a coaching culture, they end up indirectly helping employees to be more prepared during critical decision-making and always being focussed on self-improvement.

Even though his father's influence and support built his career, there was a moment when they fell apart and were not even on talking terms for several years. From the time he was a rookie till he became the youngest F1 champion, Lewis Hamilton had little say in making decisions about his

---

[2]Richards, Giles, 'How Lewis Hamilton's Family Ties Fuelled His Desire to Be a Champion', *The Guardian*, 20 October 2018, https://bit.ly/3Q58iDP. Accessed on 31 August 2022.

career. Eventually, in 2010, he decided to remove his father as his manager leading to a strained relationship between them. However, Lewis publicly acknowledged that he wanted to mend his relationship with his father and the two have since patched up. No matter how successful we are, we should never forget our roots. There is little doubt that without the guidance of his father, the world would definitely not have discovered this champion driver.

HUNGRY FOR SUCCESS

When Lewis was 10 years of age, he approached McLaren F1 head Ron Dennis for an autograph and told him that one day he would race his cars. The self-belief that Lewis had at such a young age is clearly astounding to say the least. In his autograph to the young and confident Lewis, Dennis asked him to call him back in nine years' time. In fact, by 12, his driving skills were already so advanced that the betting firm Ladbrokes took a bet that he would win an F1 Grand Prix by the time he was 23. In 1998, Lewis was signed for the McLaren Young Driver Programme by none other than Dennis himself. He also clinched an F1 seat making him the youngest driver to secure such a contract.

Self-belief and the desire to work hard eventually lead to success. There are several smaller steps that we can make use of to enhance our self-belief and improve our performance. These are:

- **Understanding one's support system**: Always remember that there are others who trust you and believe in your abilities. In case of Lewis, his father was his strongest pillar of mental support in his formative years.

- **Consistency and focus:** Just like Lewis, we too must be consistent in our performance if we seek to fulfil our dreams. One of the racing tracks that every F1 driver aspires to win on is the Monaco Grand Prix and Lewis was no different. Even though he did not succeed in his first season, he came back stronger, winning in 2008, 2016 and 2019.
- **Mental preparation:** It is important to mentally plan and prepare to succeed. One of the most useful techniques is mental visualization, whereby you can practise seeing the outcome before it actually happens. Lewis also uses mental visualization to understand his competitors in racing along with the various turns in the track to adjust his speed and strategy accordingly.

Any individual too can set targets and achieve them. The key in succeeding lies in breaking up the target into smaller manageable parts and then achieving them one at a time. One must remember that to achieve one's goals, they must be patient and willing to work hard in a sustained manner. Our path to our goals should be like a project plan with clearly defined timelines and tasks.

Learning Tip: Define your goals and create short-term targets that will help you achieve them. Monitor your progress at regular intervals and focus on improvement in each phase.

BATTLING RIVALS (AND TEAMMATES) ON THE TRACKS

Fernando Alonso

Two-time world champion Fernando Alonso was Lewis Hamilton's teammate in his debut season with McLaren, in 2007. Tensions soon surfaced between the two drivers after the Monaco Grand Prix (where Lewis finished second) over suggestions that McLaren was imposing team orders and favouring Alonso. This was followed by the incident at the Hungarian Grand Prix, where Lewis was delayed in the pits by Alonso during the final qualifying session. The relationship between the two drivers turned so sour that they reportedly stopped talking to each other for a few months. It was even believed that Lewis might race with Ferrari for the 2008 season, but it was Alonso who left the McLaren team at the end of the season paving the way for Lewis to continue racing for McLaren. Lewis completed his first season, finishing second in the rankings, and narrowly missed being the champion by one point. During the 2007 season, he finished with four wins and 12 podium finishes, quite an impressive start to his F1 career.

Clash of egos and competition between two top performers who are both trying to attain a shared goal is common in any discipline. In such a scenario, it is important to manage such clashes through mutual discussion and resolution of any misconception. Sadly, in this case, the McLaren team management was unable to play a significant role. Over time, the two champion athletes have resolved their differences and often expressed mutual admiration for each other. Alonso rated Lewis as one of the five greatest F1 racers of all time. During the cool-down lap after Alonso's last race in 2018, when he retired, Lewis, along with Sebastian Vettel, drove on each side of Alonso in a formation and paid tribute to the champion racer. Fierce competition improves one's performance, but such competition and rivalry should only be limited to the field, or here, track. Alonso and Lewis together would have made a formidable team, but that was not meant to be. There is, however, no doubt that by competing with the best, one inches closer to being the best.

> **Learning Tip:** Resolution of conflicts early on is important to prevent any misconceptions from arising in a team.

Nico Rosberg

Lewis's friendship and competition with Nico Rosberg, the German-Finnish racing driver, started when they were teammates for Mercedes-Benz McLaren in Formula A in 2000. Lewis finished the season as the European champion closely followed by Rosberg. The two became teammates again in 2013 when Lewis joined the Mercedes team. Despite the enormous success that the duo enjoyed over the period of four years when Mercedes dominated F1 racing, there were confrontations between the two both on and off the field. A look at the success record of the two drivers reflects the strength of the partnership the two had built from 2013 to 2016. Lewis had 32 wins with 55 podium finishes and two championship wins. Rosberg had 22 wins with 50 podium finishes and one championship win.

The two drivers have contrasting backgrounds. While Rosberg comes from a well-to-do family and his father was former F1 champion Keijo Erik 'Keke' Rosberg, Lewis hails from a middle-class background. In terms of performance, the latter is more focussed on speed, whereas the former is more analytical in nature. However, the success the two enjoyed as a team is noteworthy despite competing for the championship title.

It is quite common even in a workplace to find people with different backgrounds and varied strengths. In such an environment, all of them compete to become the best performer, however success will only be achieved when they start working on team goals by delivering their best performance. Rather than reacting to situations spontaneously, we should try, instead, to better our own performance and keep our focus on our goals.

RISING LIKE A PHOENIX

The domination of Mercedes in the world of F1 is quite evident in the era of turbo-charged engines post-2014. Some of the critics have often attributed Lewis Hamilton's success to having the best car, however for someone to win so many races, there is definitely more to it.

His success can also be attributed to his ability to manage levels of instability in racing cars, which other drivers find difficult. For F1 cars, even a small parameter change such as tyre pressure or rate of fuel propulsion can have disastrous results for the driver. Yet, Lewis is always willing to take the risk. Another reason for his success has been his ability to produce fast laps at crucial moments by carefully identifying the limits of the car along with a finesse for raw speed. In many ways, he has modelled himself along the lines of Ayrton Senna, the two-time world F1 champion, who was also known for the same style of driving. Lewis even rates him as the greatest driver ever. This goes to show how important it is to have a role model in one's career and then mould ourselves by adopting their best principles. This is something that each one of us can learn from Lewis.

Lewis is also known as the master of driving in bad weather conditions. He was unbeaten for a record period of five years from the 2014 Japanese Grand Prix to the 2019 German Grand Prix in races affected by bad weather. When the going gets tough, the tough gets going, and no one shows that better than Lewis. Champion athletes get an adrenaline rush when the situation becomes unpredictable, and it drives them to perform even better. This is an invaluable learning that all of us should learn. For someone who had seen the humble roots of his family and faced challenging economic conditions in childhood, giving up has never been an option. This is primarily one of the major reasons for his success.

> **Learning Tip:** One needs to raise his game to overcome tough situations. Life can sometimes be unfair but we must deal with it accordingly.

BREAKING THE GLASS CEILING

It is indeed ironic that in more than 70 years of F1 as a sport, Lewis is the only Black driver to have participated in it. During the course of the journey, he has often had to face racial abuse because of his skin colour. In 2008, he was abused by Spanish spectators during pre-season testing at the Circuit de Barcelona-Catalunya. They wore black face paint and wigs along with black t-shirts marking the word 'Hamilton's family'.[3] This could have also partly been fuelled because of his rivalry with Fernando Alonso, a Spaniard, in the previous season. This even led the Fédération Internationale de l'Automobile (FIA) to launch a 'Race against Racism' campaign. How do you silence such people and give them a fitting response? Is it through reciprocation of similar hate? The answer is a definite no. Lewis silenced his naysayers by winning the 2008 F1 championship, becoming the youngest driver to do so.

Stereotyping—either in terms of gender, region, caste or

---

[3]Taylor, Matthew, et al., 'Spanish Racists Vent Hate for Hamilton', *The Guardian*, 1 November 2008, https://bit.ly/3EhyhFr. Accessed on 9 November 2022.

religion—is quite common even in workplaces. The best way to deal with such discrimination is by striving to do better and better. We must collectively stand against such biases and any such harassment and ensure that the strictest actions are taken. Lewis was bullied as a kid and so he took to learning karate for self-defence. There too, he faced racial abuse on several occasions. This only made his resolve stronger and he pledged to speak up for others in similar situations. In fact, Lewis has been quite vocal about encouraging drivers from different backgrounds to participate in the sport so as to foster diversity and inclusivity.

> **Learning Tip:** We must look at biases as opportunities to become stronger mentally and perform our actions to perfection.

Lewis is also known to take a stand for his views and opinions. In 2020, he unveiled a special tribute helmet to F1 legend Ayrton Senna ahead of the Brazilian Grand Prix. He has also been a strident supporter of the Black Lives Matter movement and has participated in protest marches against racism. He has also been quite vocal of his choice of becoming vegetarian, citing pollution and animal cruelty. In January 2020, during the Australian Bushfire crisis, he donated $500,000 towards fire services and animal-welfare charities. His business interests include a clothing line called TommyxLewis, which he has created in collaboration with Tommy Hilfiger. He has also been the executive producer of the documentary movie *The Game Changers* (2018).

Lewis is presently the highest-paid F1 racer in the history of the game, with earnings worth over £40 million a year. Despite this, he has not forgotten his humble beginnings. His success has only made him more resolute to continue his winning spree. The diversity that he brings to the world of F1 will definitely encourage others to break stereotypes and make their own mark in their chosen fields.

Lewis's Performance in Formula One over the Years (as on 8 November 2022)

Season	Team	Races	Wins	Poles	Podiums	Points	Position
2007	Vodafone McLaren Mercedes	17	4	6	12	109	2nd
2008		18	5	7	10	98	1st
2009		17	2	4	5	49	5th
2010		19	3	1	9	240	4th
2011		19	3	1	6	227	5th
2012		20	4	7	7	190	4th
2013	Mercedes AMG Petronas F1 Team	19	1	5	5	189	4th
2014		19	11	7	16	384	1st
2015		19	10	11	17	381	1st
2016		21	10	12	17	380	2nd
2017	Mercedes AMG Petronas Motorsport	20	9	11	13	363	1st
2018		21	11	11	17	408	1st
2019		21	11	5	17	413	1st
2020	Mercedes-AMG Petronas F1 Team	16	11	1	2	347	1st
2021	Mercedes-AMG Petronas F1 Team	22	8	8	1	387.5	2nd
2022	Mercedes-AMG Petronas F1 Team	20	0	2	8	216	5th (still in progress)

10

Serving with Perfection

P.V. Sindhu

Pressure and responsibility are always high. It's just that I need to give my best rather than thinking about others. You should play well and win—and it's good for everyone.[1]

P.V. SINDHU

It was the 2016 Olympic finale. The badminton court was packed with an audience holding anticipated breaths. A 21-year-old Indian girl was about to compete with Spain's Carolina Marin, then World No. 1. Hyderabad's young lioness, Pusarla Venkata (P.V.) Sindhu, fought with utmost tenacity. Though she lost the match by a slim margin, she nevertheless created history, becoming the youngest Indian ever to win an Olympic medal. That day, India got its second badminton woman champion after Saina Nehwal and badminton got a new star.

When asked what makes her so focussed during championships, a smiling Sindhu said, 'Well, each match was important for me and every point too. Obviously, I did a lot

---

[1]Mohammad Ali, Qaiser, 'Exclusive/World Championship Title Will Particularly Motivate Me; Will Give a Lot of Confidence: PV Sindhu', *Outlook*, 4 September 2019, https://bit.ly/2jYqiXp. Accessed on 1 September 2022.

of preparations, like practising and changing a few things in my game.'[2] That has always been the driving force for Sindhu's success. From winning her Grand Prix titles, to making a place in the Badminton World Federation (BWF) rankings, to being the recipient of the Padma Shri, Padma Bhushan, Rajiv Gandhi Khel Ratna and Arjuna Award for badminton, the list is endless. 'The most striking feature in Sindhu's game is her attitude and the never-say-die spirit,' says Pullela Gopichand, her coach who transformed a passionate teenager playing badminton at her courtyard to a national sensation.[3]

Born to ace volleyball players, Sindhu chose badminton as her sport. She drew inspiration from the 2001 All England Open Badminton champion Gopichand, who was the second Indian, after Prakash Padukone, to achieve this victory. In the words of a media correspondent, 'The fact that she reports on time at the coaching camps daily, travelling a distance of 56 km from her residence, is perhaps a reflection of her willingness to complete her desire to be a good badminton player with the required hard work and commitment.'[4]

For Sindhu, practice is a daily essential, just like bathing, eating and sleeping. It is her prayer. It reflects her passion for the game. And what are the end results? It started with her winning the Fifth Servo All India Ranking Championship in the doubles category and the singles title at the Ambuja Cement All India Ranking in the under-10 category, and this was just the beginning. She went on to win the singles title at the sub-juniors in Puducherry, the doubles titles at the Smt Krishna

---

[2] Ibid.
[3] Kulkarni, Bhushan, '3 Performance Lessons from PV Sindhu's Final Match', *Entrepreneur India*, 20 August 2016, https://bit.ly/3B3oDVg. Accessed on 1 September 2022.
[4] Ibid.

Khaitan All India Junior Ranking Badminton Tournament, the IOC All India Ranking, the Sub-Junior Nationals and the All India Ranking in Pune, all in the under-13 category. She then proceeded to win the under-14 team gold medal at the 51st National State Games of India.

Sindhu, like any other sportsperson, has had her fair share of wins and losses, but the outcome of any game did not change her attitude, which was: there is always scope for improvement. She loves to keep running across the court and roars like a lion on hitting her masterstroke. She likes to give back the same way she receives shots. So, how did Sindhu stay at the pinnacle of her game? It was years and years of dedicated practice.

Life is similar to the game of badminton. Life may attack you with a clear shot, smash, drive, drop, net lift or net kill. It is up to you to analyse the shot and give it back with full force. It is the pursuit of perfection that makes an ordinary person extraordinary.

Such is a story of Zhang Ruimin, who converted a humble refrigerator-manufacturing company to what it is known as Haier today. Such was his obsession with perfection that quality meant more for him than profits on a balance sheet. He was asked to look after a debt-laden plant of Qingdao General Refrigerator General Factory. When he arrived, he found his company manufactured poorly designed refrigerators. However, the company did not look into this problem, as the public demand for the products was still high. Zhang believed that for the product to be viable in the market in the long term, it needs a good reputation. One fine day, he handed over his workers a sledgehammer and ordered them to break down 76 refrigerators. That was the start of a new era for Haier. He tried and did not give up till he got the desired quality of output. The famous 'sledgehammer' is preserved in the company's in-house museum.5 It signifies that each unsuccessful attempt is like 'net practice' for the final match.

Learning Tip: Success is a product of practice and dedication. Mastery is achieved by the repetitive execution of a specific task. Talent and skill may not always lead to perfection, but talent can be developed and moulded with the help of practise.

Practice comprises eight components—all of which are equally important to achieve success.

- Perseverence
- Resilience
- Acumen
- Cognizance
- Tenacity
- Intelligence
- Calmness
- Earnestness

P: PERSEVERANCE

After a major loss, Sindhu often modifies her attacking strategy. It is only through constant practise that one can attain the acumen to make split-second decisions and adapt accordingly. One such instance was when she lost against former

---

[5] Mahajan, Neelima, 'Haier CEO Zhang Ruimin: Challenge Yourself, Overcome Yourself', Founding Fuel, 18 October 2015, https://bit.ly/3ee85ks. Accessed on 2 September 2022.

World No. 1 and London Olympics silver medallist Wang Yihan at the Australian Open in 2015. She had a good lead in the first game, but Wang Yihan made a perfect comeback in the second. The third game was the decider where Wang Yihan held her nerve till the end and knocked Sindhu out of the competition. Gopichand was not agitated and, in fact, temporarily removed all dietary and exercise-related restrictions post this. Sindhu spent the next few days partying with her sister in Australia. These were supposed to be the last few days of her enjoyment before preparing for a long journey ahead.

After returning to India, Gopichand handed over a letter to her listing the dos and don'ts to be followed for the next eight months. One of the conditions listed in the letter was that Sindhu would have to hand over her phone to her coach. It was a big sacrifice, but soon this discipline became an integral part of her personality. Even today, her day starts at 3.30 a.m. and she starts training as early as 4.00 a.m. Her workout regime consumes almost six to eight hours of her day. A hundred push-ups and 200 sit-ups are a part of her daily warm-up routine. This adds up to 700 push-ups and 1,400 abdominal exercises in a week.

Several months prior to the Rio Olympics in 2016, Sindhu was asked to repeatedly practise one particular shot—the backhand cross court defensive block. It was her weakest shot and her coach believed that if she was somehow able to convert her weakness into her strength, she could present an element of surprise on the match day. It was during her Olympic stint in Rio that the shot came out perfectly balanced, poised and positioned. It caught her opponent, the Canadian Michelle Li, totally by surprise. The months of intense training and dedicated practice finally paid off. This is a tale of perseverance and success.

Learning Tip: You can achieve anything you set your mind to, but it takes persistence to overcome the odds and courage to face your fears and rejections.

R: RESILIENCE

Whenever anyone questioned Sindhu's form, she was quick to respond with a victory in her next match. She faced her first major defeat on 14 June 2012, when she lost to Germany's Juliane Schenk in the Indonesia Open with an extremely unimpressive score of 21-14 in both the sets. Disappointed, but not heartbroken, Sindhu started practising harder. In less than a month, on 7 July, she added a major victory to her kitty by winning the Asian Youth Under-19 Badminton Championship, beating Japan's Nozomi Okuhara in the finals by 18-21, 21-17 and 22-20.

Unfortunately, Sindhu injured her knee during the China Open which made her lose her match against the Air India shuttler, Sayali Gokhale in the 77th Senior National Badminton Championships at Srinagar, but this did not stop her from hitting the court again with a vengeance. The lioness won her Malaysian Open title in 2013, defeating Singaporean shuttler, Gu Juan, by a close call of 21-17, 17-21 and 21-19 and claiming her first Grand Prix Gold title.

Learning Tip: Resilience is important, as it helps us develop mechanisms to cope with stressful situations. It helps us maintain balance and rebuild ourselves after a major failure.

When we set out to achieve something new, there are bound to be challenges and hurdles. For many entrepreneurs, getting their first client may take years. There are highs and lows in the journey. It is imperative to focus on the activity and not the emotions. One must learn not to react to the ups and downs and keep the focus trained on the goal.

A: ACUMEN

At the 2018 BWF World Tour finals, Sindhu had to face Taiwan's Tai Tzu-ying. She had faced six successive losses in the 13 meetings with the Taiwanese badminton star till that time. Tai Tzu-ying was a tough opponent because of the deceptive strokes she played. After being defeated in the first set with the score of 14-21, Sindhu used her technical acumen to reciprocate the opponent's body smash with a body blow and then a lucky net chord helped her gain four match point advantage, which ultimately paved the way for victory.

> **Learning Tip:** Practise enhances the technical acumen of the trade.

Often, decisions are to be made in split seconds. There is no time for second-guessing. One needs to be completely sure of arriving at a conclusion before taking any action. It is only through dedicated practise that one can gain an edge over others in delivering results.

C: COGNIZANCE

One of the major highlights of Sindhu's career is her success at the BWF World Championship. The phrase 'third-time lucky' suits her, as she won this feat in her third consecutive attempt. She gave her mother, P. Vijaya, her best birthday gift when she became the first Indian shuttler to win a gold medal at the BWF World Championship. This win was extraordinary, as she defeated her opponent, World No. 3 Nozomi Okuhara with the impressive score set of 21-6 and 21-7 in just 38 minutes. She finished the match in just two sets.

During the Swiss Open, Sindhu studied Okuhara carefully before the match. The knowledge of her opponent's strengths helped her prepare better for the match. She started developing early pressure on her opponent and adopted an aggressive stance. Her earlier stance had been that of engaging in long rallies, which would eventually tire her opponents and force them to make mistakes. However, her past encounters with Okuhara had shown that this was an ineffective stance against her. She knew she had to guard herself, which she had not been doing earlier, resulting in her losses.

Learning Tip: Complete awareness of the opponent's strengths and weakness helps in analysing and forming better decisions.

One cannot lead a trade without the knowledge of the market and rivals. To launch a product in the market, one needs complete data on the target consumers, the available resources, the risks involved and the competition in hand.

T: TENACITY

More than being a quick learner, it is important to be a firm learner. Having a grip of the basics is important. A surgeon often goes back to his basic textbooks before performing a complicated surgery. New technologies and developments emerge every day, but we should not forget the basics.

Besides her coaches, Sindhu learnt a lot from her opponents, such as Carolina Marin, Nozomi Okuhara, Tai Tzu-ying, Akane Yamaguchi and Saina Nehwal. Every time she lost a match against them, she reflected on her deficiencies, went back to the court and reworked her basics. When Sindhu defeated Okuhara in the BWF Championship match, one thing left the audience amazed. Her smashes seemed more polished and firmer from what they had been two years ago. Her earlier rounds before the finals also saw her displaying varying skills, including the receding fraction smash. It was evident that she had worked extensively on her wrist, defence and variations.

> **Learning Tip:** The degree of tenacity is far more important than that of talent. Tenacity provides the perspective to look beyond an obstacle and treat it as an opportunity to improve.

Sindhu had the power to land a full-blooded power smash in the range of 350 kilometres per hour. After losing twice in the finals of the BWF Championships, she decided to rework on her fundamentals and try out variations of her shots. The third attempt saw her incorporating all these variations. She started using the half smash conveniently as a set-up shot. She leveraged her tall stature and improved her on-court agility. After hitting half smashes conveniently, she would rush towards the net for follow-up. She handled the incoming assaults of smashes as if facing a barrage of missiles. She started using her wrist more effectively in returning with an inside-out backhand flick from midcourt to the opponent's forehand corner. Picking up on the areas where she had lost earlier, she persevered to come back a stronger opponent and a better player.

I: INTELLIGENCE

One should possess the ability to develop one's skill set. We learn the basics from our school education, but during the due course of our lives, we acquire new skills depending on the requirement of the market. The ability to adapt reflects a person's practical intelligence. Life is a game in constant motion. One should study the dynamics and react accordingly.

In the 2017 India Super Series, Sindhu managed to defeat World No. 1 and Olympic champion Carolina Marin with her intelligence. The former used a combination of drape shots and smashes to lead right from the beginning. But soon, Marin caught up and changed the dynamics of the game. Sindhu realized that Marin's strong shots were making her play defensive most of the time. Sindhu then started pursuing long rallies. When the moment was right, she used her forte—smash and attack—won the first set.

In the remaining two sets, Marin tried to outwit Sindhu by playing shots close to the net. The latter started applying delaying tactics, such as using her left hand to make Marin wait between her serves and tying her shoe laces very often. She knew that Marin uses minimum time between points. This was a psychological move. Sindhu capitalized on this pattern of her opponent and ended up winning the tournament. She also played deceptive shots like a late flick from the backhand midcourt while giving the impression of a drop shot.

Practical intelligence helps you analyse situations quickly to get your work done. Those with practical intelligence tend to learn by doing and experimenting rather than reading and watching. After suffering a few blows from Marin, Sindhu analysed her game and quickly came up with deceptive moves to win the match.

C: CALMNESS

We all know that things don't always go as planned. Combatting a new opponent on the field or meeting a new client who turns out to be the exact opposite of what one has prepared for can make one anxious. This anxiety can ruin the whole game. The ability to stay calm comes with practise. A calm mind thinks better. As Sindhu once shared, 'I was positive, even when I was losing some points.'[6] When asked about her winning mantra in an interview, Sindhu had said that she meditates to keep herself calm and focussed. There are times when the match dynamics are in favour of the opponent, but being positive helps one stay calm and plan the next moves meticulously. Just as playing diligently and making smart moves require practise, keeping the mind still and centred also requires immense practice. That needs to be inculcated from the day one of taking up a sport.

E: EARNESTNESS

Everyone wants to win, but only the ones with a strong heart bring home a medal. More than convincing anyone else, it is important to convince yourself why you need this victory so badly. The moment you get the answer to the 'why', the other answers automatically follow.

A combination of perseverance, resilience, acumen, cognizance, tenacity, intelligence, calmness and earnestness is required to convert any game to a success. In every walk of life, there is no alternative to practise.

---

[6]'I Meditate to Stay Calm: PV Sindhu to NDTV', *ap7am.com*, 28 August 2019, https://bit.ly/3q1DHws. Accessed on 1 September 2022.

Sindhu's Performance at Major Events
(till 5 September 2022)

Record	Year	Position/Result
Olympic Games	2016	Runner-Up
	2021	2nd Runner-Up
BWF World Championships	2013	Bronze
	2014	Bronze
	2017	Silver
	2018	Silver
	2019	Gold
Asian Games	2018	Silver
Asian Championships	2014	Bronze
	2022	Bronze
Commonwealth Games	2014	Bronze
	2018	Silver
	2022	Gold

11

Quest for Perfection

Sachin Tendulkar

People sometimes throw stones and you converted (sic) *them into milestones.[1]*

SACHIN TENDULKAR

It was 16 November 2013. There was a huge crowd at the Wankhede. A cricketer was trying to hold back his tears as fans cried and chanted 'Sachin, Sachin'. The cricketer was saying goodbye to cricket. It was an emotional moment for the entire nation to witness the retirement of someone who had shut the mouths of critics, frightened bowlers and won people's hearts all over the world with his cover drives, straight drives, on drives and pull shots and someone who had dedicated his entire life to the 22 yards of a cricket ground retiring.

Cricket in India is more than just a game, it is a religion in itself and Sachin Tendulkar is revered as the God of Cricket. It was this Master Blaster who inspired many youngsters to take up cricket as a profession. One of the most respected sports personalities, Tendulkar came a long way from a 16-year-old with a squeaky voice and a mop of bushy, curly hair to being

---

[1] 'I Converted Stones Thrown at Me to Milestones: Tendulkar', *The Times of India*, 17 October 2008, https://bit.ly/3QZz5CJ. Accessed on 29 August 2022.

almost synonymous with the sport of cricket. He had the eye, strength and flexibility to play any kind of shot. He was never intimidated by seasoned players and faced each ball bravely. For his riveting performance in cricket, he received the Arjuna Award in 1994, Rajiv Gandhi Khel Ratna Award in 1997, Padma Shri in 1999 and Padma Vibhushan in 2008. In 2010, *Time* magazine included him in its yearly Time 100 list of 'Most Influential People in the World'. In 2019, he earned a place in the International Cricket Council (ICC) Cricket Hall of Fame.

EARLY LIFE

Sachin Ramesh Tendulkar was born on 24 April 1973 to Marathi parents in Mumbai. His father, Ramesh Tendulkar, was an acclaimed Marathi novelist and poet, and his mother, Rajni Tendulkar, worked with the Life Insurance Corporation of India. Sachin was extremely mischievous from his childhood. He was considered a bully and would knowingly pick up fights with the local children.[2] To curb his mischievous behaviour, his elder brother, Ajit, introduced Sachin to the world of cricket. He was gifted his first cricket bat, a willow bat from Kashmir, by his sister Savita. The family hoped that cricket would keep him out of trouble. However, little did they know that this young boy would one day make millions of cricket fanatics stay glued to their televisions.

Tendulkar was stubborn as a child. Once, he wanted a bicycle, as all his friends had one. He was so obstinate that he refused to go out and play for an entire week until his father conceded to his demand. On one occasion, he stuck his head

---

[2] Pandey, Aditya, 'Sachin Tendulkar Being a "Bully" Who Almost Got Beat Up by a Gang of Students Is Hard to Imagine', *MensXp*, 24 April 2020, https://bit.ly/3Cyr8QG. Accessed on 29 August 2022.

out of the balcony grille of their fourth-floor apartment. After several attempts, his mother was able to safely pull him out. This incident compelled his father to arrange for finances and get him a new bicycle. Nobody could have imagined that this stubbornness would one day take this Master Blaster on the quest for perfection.[3]

Soon after being introduced to cricket, Tendulkar started playing in the neighbourhood with his friends. Ajit would often watch his little brother play on the streets and soon recognized his unique talent with the bat. To further hone his talent, Ajit introduced his brother to Ramakant Achrekar, a well-known cricket coach at Shivaji Park, Dadar, Mumbai. Achrekar was quite impressed by the young boy's batting skills. Following his coach's advice, Tendulkar was shifted to Sharadashram Vidya Mandir (English) High School, which had a dominant cricket team and had the reputation of producing several notable cricketers. Tendulkar would come to play in the academy in the mornings and evenings and attended school in between. Due to his hectic schedule, he shifted to his uncle's house, which was nearer to the academy. For a bigger purpose in life, Tendulkar bid adieu to his house, school, friends and his old life to set forth on a new journey.

> **Learning Tip:** You need to come out of your comfort zone to fulfil your dreams.

To boost this young child's confidence, Achrekar would place a coin on the stumps and declare it to be a gift for the bowler who would successfully dismiss Tendulkar. If he stayed not out throughout the practice session, the coin would be given to him. The young boy won 13 such coins and has preserved them as

---

[3]Tendulkar, Sachin, 'A Star Is Born: Sachin Tendulkar on What Inspired Him', *Reader's Digest*, 18 February 2020, https://bit.ly/3fy6HKv. Accessed on 3 November 2022.

his most prized possession till date.[4] The seeds of perfection were, thus, sowed in him by his coach at a very young age.

TURNING PROFESSIONAL

On 14 November 1987, a 14-year-old Tendulkar was selected to represent Mumbai in the Ranji Trophy as a substitute player. About a year later, on 11 December 1988, he made his debut against Gujarat becoming the youngest player to score a century. He ended the season as the highest run-scorer. A star was thus born. Tendulkar was an eager learner. During his free time, after his batting practice was over, he would pick up the ball and bowl over to whichever batter was available. He learnt all forms of deliveries: medium pace, off spin and leg spin. He would make use of his alone time by practising in the nets. So, what was it that made Tendulkar aspire for the journey towards perfection? Perfection is a living experience that we can intensify if we dare to stretch our wings a bit more and fly a little higher.

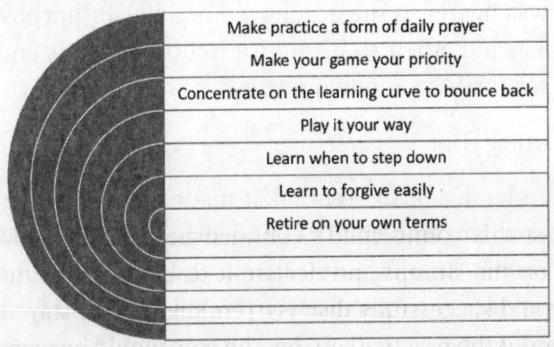

Steps to Follow to Achieve Perfection

---

[4] '40 Interesting Facts about Sachin Tendulkar', *India Today*, 11 October 2013, https://bit.ly/3qTYh2i. Accessed on 20 September 2022.

MAKE PRACTICE A FORM OF DAILY PRAYER

Even if it is for an exhibition match, Tendulkar practises in the nets rigorously before it as if it is his first. He plays every match with the same dedication as his first one. He treats every player—young or experienced, struggling or renowned—as an opponent with equivalent skill sets and strategizes accordingly.

This is the story of every start-up. Every idea, before it starts reaping billions of dollars, goes through several hours, days, months and years of slogging. In the enthralling psychology book, *Outliers: The Story of Success,* Malcolm Gladwell has popularized the 10,000-hour rule, stating that we need to put in 10,000 hours of work to achieve the level of mastery associated with being a world-class expert in any field of your choosing.

> **Learning Tip:** There is no substitute for hard work. Whether or not you are naturally gifted, the only road to perfection is through relentless effort.

MAKE YOUR GAME YOUR PRIORITY

At the tender age of 16, Tendulkar made his Test debut against Pakistan in November 1989, where he was bowled out by Waqar Younis, scoring just 15 runs. The way he handled the numerous blows to his body from the fast bowler and yet continued to bat is still etched in people's memory. In his fourth and final Test in Sialkot, a bouncer from Younis injured his nose, but he refused medical assistance and continued to bat. Such was his passion for the game!

Over the years, while playing professional cricket as well, Tendulkar endured much pain and many injuries. He had a toe injury while playing against Zimbabwe in 2001. This nasty injury flared up on several occasions, but he never let his physical discomfort affect his game. Another such incident came to the fore during the 2003 World Cup match against Pakistan, where Tendulkar emerged as a top scorer. However, it was only later that he revealed the severity of his left-finger injury.

Tendulkar faced a major setback in the form of a tennis elbow (lateral epicondylitis) at the beginning of 2004. He had already been suffering from a chronic back problem. The pain was so severe that he was unable to hold a bat. Some of the other major setbacks he faced came in 2006, when he had to undergo shoulder surgery for an injury, in 2007, when he had an ankle injury and then in 2008, when he missed the initial matches of the Indian Premier League (IPL) due to a groin injury.

CONCENTRATE ON THE LEARNING CURVE TO BOUNCE BACK

After the poor performance of Team India at the 2007 World Cup, many believed it would be best for Tendulkar to announce his retirement, with former Australian captain Ian Chappell urging the champion to hang up his boots. However, Tendulkar is the epitome of consistency. He never gives up. He returned to his form soon in the subsequent Test series against Bangladesh, where he emerged as the 'Man of the Series' shutting the mouths of all his critics. He continued this streak by scoring 99 and 93 in the first two matches of the 2007 Future Cup against South Africa. His bat answered everyone who questioned him

when he became the first to score 15,000 ODI runs.
You do not fail when you fall down, you fail when you give up trying.

You must have read Henry Ford's story. He used to say, 'Failure is simply the opportunity to begin again, this time more intelligently.' He had to go through multiple unsuccessful attempts at manufacturing the perfect car before Ford cars came into the picture. He used up all the money procured from his first group of investors without successfully bringing out a workable model. Eventually, he was able to come up with a model and raised further money, but soon his company went bankrupt. The third time, his hesitation to upgrade his car's model led to a decline in its sales. Rather than seeing each of his failures as inadequacies, he saw them as opportunities for improvement. He bounced back with a refined strategy, thus reducing assembly time of his Model T cars from 14 hours to 90 minutes.

Learning Tip: Form is temporary, class is permanent.

PLAY IT YOUR WAY

The cricket bat that Tendulkar used weighed almost a kilo and a half, one of the heaviest at that time. He was repeatedly advised to switch to a lighter bat, but he was adamant, which is unsurprising, given his stubbornness as a child. As he once said in his autobiography, *Playing It My Way*, 'I used a pretty heavy bat and I was sometimes encouraged to move to a lighter one. Again, I did try but I never felt comfortable, as my whole bat swing depended on that weight. When I was hitting a drive, I needed the weight to generate the power. It was all to do with the timing.'[5] That's not all. He was even advised to change his grip, but he did not change, as he was confident of this technique of holding the bat, which he had been practising over the years.

> Learning Tip: Be comfortable in your own skin. What works for others need not work for you. Last-minute changes can often be disastrous.

LEARN WHEN TO STEP DOWN

Tendulkar had two brief stints as captain of the Indian team. When he took over the captaincy for the first time in 1996, after Mohammad Azharuddin stepped down, Team India was more of a mix of young players, such as Rahul Dravid, Sourav Ganguly and V.V.S. Laxman, whereas he was one of the few experienced players on the team. The team heavily depended on Tendulkar for scoring bulk runs. Having one of the finest cricketing brains, it did not take Tendulkar long to realize that the team relied on him as a player more than as a captain. He voluntarily walked out of captaincy in 2000, handing over the reins to Ganguly. His third stint could have been when Dravid resigned from captaincy. He thought M.S. Dhoni was more suited for the role and suggested him for the captaincy. Both these decisions proved to be game changers for the team. Tendulkar never let any form of arrogance and ego come before his duties as a team player.

It's imperative to note that in real-life scenarios, stepping aside for someone else to fill in is often considered mature.

---

[5]Tendulkar, Sachin, *Playing It My Way: My Autobiography*, Hodder & Stoughton, London, 2014.

Google co-founders Larry Page and Sergey Brin stepped down from the top roles of their parent company Alphabet for Sundar Pichai to fill in the shoes of the CEO in 2019. They were ready to take up the role of parents, providing love and support.

> **Learning Tip:** Title does not always matter but contribution to the work does.

LEARN TO FORGIVE EASILY

History has proven that no one has ever succeeded by holding grudges. Ganguly and Tendulkar were often victims of harsh criticism, despite being cricketing legends of their time. But they remained calm and let their bats do the talking.

RETIRE ON YOUR OWN TERMS

When it came to announcing his retirement, Tendulkar decided to do it his way and on his own terms. On 16 November 2013, his cricketing journey came to an end at the Wankhede Stadium. After winding up his emotional and heartfelt farewell speech, he went on to pay his final visit to the 22 yards that had nurtured him for almost three decades. The legend concluded his batting journey with 74 runs against West Indies, thus falling short of 79 runs to complete 16,000 runs in Test cricket. He retired after creating a legacy.

> **Learning Tip:** Retire on your own terms. Your retirement should be such that everyone remembers your legacy.

The goal of every entrepreneur is to start an enterprise and turn it into a brand to reckon with. Narayana Murthy, who is also known as the father of the Indian IT industry, is one such example. Born to a family of limited means, he is a self-made man who founded Infosys, an IT giant that currently employs thousands of people. Murthy started his company in his house with a meagre capital of ₹10,000, from his wife Sudha Murty's savings. There was a phase when the company got into a joint venture that collapsed. At that point, his partners decided to move out. Murthy was firm in his belief that the company would survive the storm. He told his partners that under no circumstances was he going to shut shop, even if it meant buying his partners' stocks, in case they decided to call it quits. His self-belief and confidence drove everyone to reconsider their decision. Hence, Murthy proved himself yet again by reviving the company to its former glory during this difficult time. He was the CEO of Infosys from 1981 to 2002 and chairman from 2002 to 2011.

Tendulkar's Batting Performance over the Years

	Matches	Innings	Not Outs	Runs	Average	100	50
Tests	200	329	33	15,921	53.78	51	68
ODIs	463	452	41	18,426	44.83	49	96
T20Is	1	1	0	10	10.00	0	0
First class	310	490	51	25,396	57.84	81	116
List A	551	538	55	21,999	45.54	60	114
T20s	96	96	11	2,797	32.90	1	16

12

Defying Critics

Cristiano Ronaldo

I am not a perfectionist, but I like to feel that things are done well. More important than that, I feel an endless need to learn, to improve, to evolve, not only to please the coach and the fans, but also to feel satisfied with myself. It is my conviction that here (sic) *are no limits to learning, and that it can never stop, no matter what our age.*

CRISTIANO RONALDO

Cristiano Ronaldo is arguably one of the greatest football players of all time. He holds the record of being the only European player with four European Golden shoes, having won 34 trophies. He is also one of the few players to have made more than 1,100 professional appearances and scored more than 800 goals. He is nothing short of a legend. In a career spanning over two decades, Ronaldo has defied his critics with his goal-scoring prowess and fitness levels, which are next to none. Let us try to decode the reasons behind his success.

EARLY LIFE

Ronaldo was born on 5 February 1985 in São Pedro to Maria, a cook by profession, and José Aveiro, a municipal gardener and a part-time kit man in the club where Ronaldo played amateur football. He was named after former US president and actor Ronald Reagan as his father was a huge fan of his acting. Ronaldo is the youngest among his siblings and they had to share a room in their impoverished home. However, this did not deter him from chasing his dreams. It is worth recalling that our background and humble beginnings should pivot us towards achieving greater success. One should look at such circumstances as obstacles that can be easily overcome through dedication and hard work. Did you know that former Indian president A.P.J. Abdul Kalam used to deliver newspapers as a kid to help out his family? Did he let his financial condition come in the way of his pursuing his dreams? Well, no.

> **Learning Tip:** It is our response to situations that determines our path in life. If we are determined enough and willing to work hard, we can overcome any obstacle in life.

It was quite early on in his career that Ronaldo started showing potential. As a 12-year-old, he was signed by Sporting Clube de Portugal, or Sporting CP, for a fee of £1,500. Within four years, he was promoted from Sporting Clube de Portugal's youth team by first-team manager László Bölöni. He went on to become the first player to play for the club's under-16, under-17 and under-18 teams, along with the B team and first team, all in the span of a single season. His maturity and skills as a player catapulted him to the senior team in the first season itself. It is akin to an intern making it to senior management within the first year of service.

In 2002, Ronaldo made his debut in Primeira Liga, the top level of the Portuguese football league system and scored two goals in their 3-0 win. In 2008, he won his first Ballon d'Or and 'FIFA World Player of the Year' awards. He won the Ballon d'Or award again in 2013, 2014, 2016 and 2017, making it the most by a European player. In 2015, he scored his 500th senior career goal for club and country. He began his senior club career playing for Sporting CP before signing with Manchester United at the age of 18 in 2003. He had the most expensive association football transfer, worth €94 million ($132 million), when he moved from Manchester United to Real Madrid in 2009. After playing for nine seasons for Real Madrid, he made a shift to play for Juventus for the 2018–19 season in a blockbuster €112-million deal. In 189 appearances for the Portugal national team, he has scored 117 goals.

While there is no doubt that Ronaldo is enormously talented, what really drives him is his insatiable desire for success which, in turn, drives his work ethics. In fact, Ronaldo himself admits that talent is not a sufficient ingredient to be successful; it is important but definitely not enough. Virat Kohli sums it up beautifully in these words: 'I love his (Ronaldo) work ethic, drive, passion and ability to deflect all the noise from the outside, He moves ahead and just gets it done.'[1]

In the battle between talent and hard work, the latter always wins. In any organization, what separates the top performers from the rest is their hard work and discipline, and not talent. Real magic happens when talent and hard work come together—as is the case with Ronaldo. Now that is what we call a lethal combo.

> **Learning Tip:** No matter how talented you are, you still need to put in the hours to excel in your field. Talent without hard work does not yield results.

---

[1] '"Work Ethic, Drive, Passion"—Virat Kohli Reveals Why He Prefers Cristiano Ronaldo over Lionel Messi', *Hindustan Times*, 4 April 2020, https://bit.ly/3KQ4be1. Accessed on 1 September 2022.

It is seen that successful players have a great personal rapport with their coaches. In Ronaldo's case, however, things are a bit different. He has had a love–hate relationship with his coaches throughout his career. Ronaldo once had an obvious disagreement with Coach Carlos Queiroz with regards to changing tactics and his own position after Portugal's loss against Spain in the 2010 World Cup match (round of 16). Ronaldo was so upset that he refused to take questions from the press and only said, 'Ask Queiroz (Ask the coach)'.[2] Things were not much different after Portugal lost in the 2014 World Cup. The team's national coach Paulo Bento was sacked within months of the debacle. It is believed that Ronaldo had a role to play in this sacking. In fact, the rift between the two was also visible during Euro 2012, when Bento reportedly said in an interview that Ronaldo can't win the 'group of death' on his own.[3] Such a statement does not auger well and also points to a 'superstar versus rest' culture in the team.

Every organization has their fair share of star performers or super achievers, but the real test of the manager is in ensuring that they manage everyone equally, forging a cohesive unit. As a sport, soccer is very similar to an organization, as they both focus on teamwork and respect unique skill sets.

Ronaldo's relationship with Real Madrid coach José Mourinho was also bittersweet. Despite playing together for three years, between 2010 and 2013, the duo never quite got along and repeatedly had ego clashes over strategy and team selection, among others. In this regard, it is important to

---

[2]Wilson, Jack, 'Why Are Cristiano Ronaldo and Carlos Queiroz at War? Full Story behind Bitter Relationship', *Express*, 25 June 2018, https://bit.ly/3RuVkQZ. Accessed on 1 September 2022.
[3]"Paulo Bento: "Cristiano Ronaldo Can't Win Group of Death on His Own"', *The Guardian*, 4 June 2012. https://bit.ly/3dtYWEs. Accessed on 20 September 2022.

highlight Mourinho's remarks on Spanish television regarding Ronaldo, 'I had only one problem with him, very simple, very basic, which was when a coach criticises a player from a tactical viewpoint trying to improve what, in my view, could have been improved. At that moment, he didn't take it very well because maybe he thinks he knows everything and the coach cannot help him develop further.'[4]

Such ego tussles are common between employees and their reporting managers. Often, such clashes are triggered by small incidents of mistrust owing to the lack of transparency. Ronaldo and Mourinho's relationship deteriorated further after it was announced that the latter was leaving Real Madrid for Chelsea in 2013. However, over time, the duo resolved their differences and have expressed mutual admiration for each other.

Regardless of the constant barrage of criticism hurled at Ronaldo, during his nine years of association with Real Madrid, he emerged as the single-highest goal scorer for the club. He actually scored 105 goals for Real Madrid in the Champions League, 312 goals overall in La Liga and the most goals by a Real Madrid player in a single season (61). He also set the record for the most goals in a Champions League season (17) and led the league in goal scoring in six of the club's seasons during his tenure. Such achievement, despite facing criticism from his coaches, speaks volumes of his mental strength and ability to focus on his performance.

Criticism is a part and parcel of life, but it should only push us to do better each time. Ronaldo's life mantra can be emulated by remembering a few key lessons:

---

[4]Rice, Simon, 'Jose Mourinho: "The Problem with Cristiano Ronaldo Is He Thinks He Knows Everything"', *Independent*, 5 June 2013, https://bit.ly/3Twy0nF. Accessed on 1 September 2022.

- **Be the best:** Always exceed expectations and strive harder each time.
- **Accept new challenges:** Look out for new avenues to succeed and do not limit yourself due to constraints.
- **Have self-belief:** During difficult times, it is self-belief that helps you sail through.
- **Accept criticism:** Remember, those critical of you are only helping you become a better version of yourself. For instance, many of Ronaldo's fans criticized his decision of moving back to Manchester United in 2021, but for him, it was more of a homecoming, as he himself said, 'I have a fantastic history with this amazing club. I was there at 18 years old and of course I'm so happy to be back home after 12 years.'[5] Ronaldo gets much flak for wearing diamond-encrusted boots, but it is his performance that silences his critics. We should let our work speak for itself.

Learning Tip: We should always believe in ourselves and perform a task to the best of our abilities, regardless of criticism.

Five-Step Approach to Handle Criticism

1. **Focus:** Instead of focussing on what others think of you, focus on the activity at hand and give it your best. If Ronaldo would have been affected by the tussles and arguments with his coaches, would he be where he is today?
2. **Understand:** Try to perform a root cause analysis to arrive at a pattern of the criticism you receive.

---

[5]Froggatt, Mark, 'Five Killer Quotes from Ronaldo's Signing Interview', Manchester United, 2 September 2021, https://bit.ly/3cCrriM. Accessed on 1 September 2022.

3. **Impress:** Maintain proper body language and conceal your inner thoughts by maintaining a calm and composed demeanour.
4. **Improve:** Start working harder and learn new skill sets that can help you further your objectives.
5. **Network:** Try to analyse how others are managing such situations. If required, connect with individuals who have faced similar situations in the past.

It is important to remember that Ronaldo shared a great rapport with Zinedine Zidane, the coach of Real Madrid. During this period, Ronaldo led the team to three consecutive Champions League titles and credited Zidane with making him feel very special. In Ronaldo's own words, 'The confidence that a player needs doesn't only come from himself but also from the players around him and the coach.'[6] The way we treat others is how others treat us. This golden rule defines almost all human relationships. As a coach, Zidane was appreciative of Ronaldo's talent and gave him the freedom to play his natural game, and so the results followed. In a similar manner, managers should keep a keen eye on talented resources and mentor them to achieve their full potential.

> **Learning Tip:** By following a consultative approach, any leader can build a great team that shares a common vision and goal.

---

[6]Pisani, Sacha, 'Ronaldo: Zidane Made Me Feel Special', *Sportstar*, 13 August 2019, https://bit.ly/3Q5NQTe. Accessed on 1 September 2022.

BUILDING BRAND EQUITY

Ronaldo invests a lot of his money into his own businesses. His investments include his own brand CR7, with which he has diversified into mobile apps, clothing, fragrance, apparel and footwear. He owns a restaurant chain in Brazil called Dona Dolores, named after his mother, which specializes in Portuguese cuisine. He also has a majority stake in a digital agency. He is the only footballer to have a lifetime contract with Nike, which is reported to be worth $1 billion and is the second-most highest paid athlete as per the 2019 Forbes ranking.

Ronaldo's Performance over the Years with Various Clubs (till 5 September 2022)

Club	Season	Total	
		Appearances	Goals
Sporting CP	2002–03	31	5
Manchester United	2003–04	40	6
	2004–05	50	9
	2005–06	47	12
	2006–07	53	23
	2007–08	49	42
	2008–09	53	26
Real Madrid	2009–10	35	33
	2010–11	54	53
	2011–12	55	60
	2012–13	54	53
	2013–14	48	51
	2014–15	54	61
	2015–16	48	51
	2016–17	46	42
	2017–18	44	44
Juventus	2018–19	43	28
	2019–20	46	37
	2020–21	44	36
	2021–22	1	0
Manchester United	2021–22	38	24
	2022–23	8	1
Total		**941**	**699**

13

Shattering the Glass Ceiling

Serena Williams

I really think a champion is defined not by their wins but by how they recover when they fall.[1]

—SERENA WILLIAMS

The youngest of five daughters, Serena Jameka Williams, born 26 September 1981, has generated a new era of power and athleticism in the world of tennis. She has won 23 Grand Slam singles titles—the most by any player in the Open Era. Serena also held the World No. 1 ranking for 186 consecutive weeks. She has five Olympic wins in her kitty. It is interesting to note that until 1999, Serena was living in the shadows of her elder sister, Venus Ebony Starr Williams, who reached the finals of the 1997 US Open, at the age of 17. In March 1999, Serena defeated German tennis player Steffi Graf in the Evert Cup finals in California, thus winning her first Tier 1 title.

It was at the 1999 Lipton International Players Championship that two sisters competed against each other in the history of Women's Tennis Association (WTA). This

---

[1]Rizvi, Ahmed, 'The Fall and Rise of Maturing Serena Williams', *The National*, 10 September 2012, https://bit.ly/3wMlsi3. Accessed on 2 September 2022.

tough nail-biting game was described as a 'bullfight' by their father, Richard Williams.[2] By then, Serena had made her name in the Top 10 by securing the rank World No. 9. However, she was still in the shadows of Venus. Serena won her first professional match against Venus that same year, in the finals, winning her first Grand Slam title in the US Open. Venus was then the only top player Serena had not defeated. The crowd had hoped for Venus to win, but Serena took everyone by surprise. They teamed up to win the Wimbledon doubles titles and Olympic gold medal in 2000.

In 2002, Serena won the French Open, US Open and Wimbledon after defeating her sister in each of the tournaments. The next year, she completed her Career Grand Slam by winning the Australian Open. She won again in the Wimbledon in 2003. That same year, both her Grand Slam victories had come after defeating her sister Venus. In 2005, Serena won her second Australian Open. In 2008, the two sisters teamed up again to win the second tennis gold medal in the doubles at the Beijing Olympics. Serena won her third US Open title the same year. In 2009, she won her 10th Glam Slam title by winning the Australian Open. She won her third Wimbledon singles title that same year, defeating Venus once again. Then, the world saw a new form of Serena, who had come out of the shadows and surpassed her sister in winning several matches. In 2010, she was successful in defending her Australian Open and Wimbledon titles.

During a time when every female tennis player dreamt of reaching somewhere close to the glass ceiling, Serena dreamt of breaking it. She did not want to set a limit to her potential. She did not have a life filled with just rose petals; she had

---

[2]Roberts, Selena, 'TENNIS; Serena Williams Wins as the Boos Pour Down', *The New York Times*, 18 March 2001, https://nyti.ms/3Qg1kvW. Accessed on 5 September 2022.

to step on thorns as well. So, what was it that made her so successful in life? How did she shatter the glass ceiling? Here are a few principles she followed in her life.

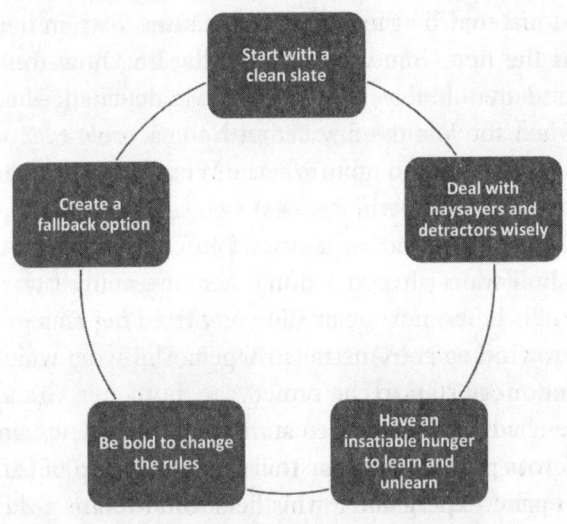

Steps to Break the Glass Ceiling

START WITH A CLEAN SLATE

Serena got into the world of tennis at a time when nothing much was expected from Black women. No one expected her to be the face of tennis. There were times when she was booed by her home crowd, but she took everyone by surprise by delivering powerful strokes.

In 2001, Venus pulled out of the semifinals of the Indian Wells Tennis Masters Series that she was supposed to play against her sister because of a right-knee injury, though many suspected it to be a case of match fixing by their father. So,

Serena had to face 17-year-old Kim Clijsters in the finals. The crowd started showering a crescendo of boos at her. She was deeply hurt. 'How many people do you know go out there and jeer a 19-year-old? I'm just a kid,' she said in an interview.[3] She was affected by the way people cheered when her shots touched the nets. She was perturbed seeing how the crowd celebrated her double faults. Her winning chances seemed bleak when she lost the first set with the score 4-6. However, she channelled her thoughts in one direction and brought back her concentration to win the next two sets with the score 6-4 and 6-2, respectively. She later said in an interview, 'At first, obviously, I wasn't happy. I don't think mentally I was ready for that. To be honest, what I literally did on a changeover, I prayed to God to help me be strong, not even to win, but to be strong, not listen to the crowd.'[4]

When we venture out to start something new, we often come across phrases such as 'This is not your cup of tea'; 'You have no prior experience in this field' or 'You are not cut out for this'. We are often booed by the very people who matter the most to us. But, in order to move ahead, we have to put all this noise and negativity behind.

> **Learning Tip:** Every game is a new game with a new beginning. What happened yesterday need not define what will happen today or tomorrow.

---

[3] "Serena Williams on Booing: 'I'm Just a Kid'", ESPN Tennis, 18 March 2001, https://es.pn/3cHJjch. Accessed on 5 September 2022.

[4] Roberts, Selena, 'TENNIS; Serena Williams Wins as the Boos Pour Down', *The New York Times*, 18 March 2001, https://nyti.ms/3Qg1kvW. Accessed on 5 September 2022.

DEAL WITH NAYSAYERS AND DETRACTORS WISELY

Though ignoring critics is often not possible, it is imperative to come up with a witty reply, which will be like 'fighting fire with sugar'. Instead of taking an aggressive and defensive stance, which does no good to anyone, it is wiser to resort to wit as an effective tool to disarm detractors.

Serena has always been targeted for her muscular build and aggressive playing stance. Her fashion statements too have more often than not come under the scanner. In the 2018 French Open, the president of the French Federation criticized the cat suit she wore by saying, '[It] would no longer be accepted...you have to accept the game and place.'[5] Instead of getting angry, Serena responded by showering praises on her detractor, saying, 'The president of the French Federation, he's been really amazing. He's been so easy to talk to. My whole team is basically French, so we have a wonderful relationship. I'm sure we would come to an understanding and everything will be OK. Yeah, so it wouldn't be a big deal. He's a really great guy.'[6]

When Virgin Group founder Sir Richard Branson started out as an entrepreneur, his ideas were often ridiculed. Even when Branson wanted to help the unsigned singer Mike Oldfield get a record deal, none of the established companies entertained them. Branson had little knowledge and experience in the field of music, but he was passionate about getting Oldfield's music to the world. Branson decided to take the risk of starting his own music label with no clue

---

[5] Beaton, Eleanor, 'How to Handle Personal Criticism Just Like Serena Williams Did', *Inc.*, 29 August 2018, https://bit.ly/3CVYTeX. Accessed on 5 September 2022.
[6] Ibid.

> *how to run a record company. This is how Virgin Records was born in 1971.*

Most families discourage entrepreneurship because of the risks and uncertainties involved. When entrepreneurs approach investors and banks for seed capital, they often have to face rejection. Their ideas are questioned and pooh-poohed. But one needs to have faith, not give up and keep pushing through.

> **Learning Tip:** Accept feedback from all, even if it is from naysayers, but take it with a pinch of salt. Use their criticism to bolster your improvement. Stay away from unnecessary cynicism.

HAVE AN INSATIABLE HUNGER TO LEARN AND UNLEARN

Serena was at the zenith of her career in the beginning of 2010. She was ranked World No. 1. Unfortunately, she had an accident in Munich, where she stepped on a broken glass and consequently received 18 stitches on her foot. She could not play for the rest of the season and her rank stipped to fourth. She had to skip a number of tournaments the next year as well so her ranking dipped further to 12th. In 2012, she lost to Russia's Ekaterina Makarova in the fourth round of the Australian Open. At the French Open, she lost to 111th-ranked Virginie Razzano in the first round of the Grand Slam. According to *The New York Times*, this defeat served as 'an upset that ranked as one of the most stunning and unexpected in the recent history of French Open'.[7] This was the first time she had been knocked off in the opening round of a Grand Slam.

---

[7]Bishop, Greg, 'Serena Williams Loses in First Round', *The New York Times*, 29 May 2012, https://nyti.ms/3QgZlYb. Accessed on 5 September 2022.

People started speculating that her career was almost over. The average age of Grand Slam players is 24 and Serena was already 31 at that time. To make matters worse, she had not won a single Grand Slam in the previous two years. However, these setbacks did not deter her in the least. She realized that what had worked for her for years was no longer working in her favour. She needed to try something different. With this resolution, she started on a journey of rediscovering herself. She went to Junior Academy in Paris, where she met one of the owners, Patrick Mouratoglou, who also served as a coach there. Mouratoglou, however, had no classical coaching background and had not trained any world-class players. He watched Serena play for 45 minutes and gave his analysis: 'Every time you hit, you are off-balance, which makes you miss a lot—also, you lose power as you are not using your body weight and your game is slow as you are not moving up enough.' To this, she bravely said, 'Let's work on this.'[8]

Serena announced that Mouratoglou would be her new coach, replacing her father after the 2012 French Open. This was a risky move, as Richard had proved to be a remarkable coach for both Serena and Venus until then. Her new coach's methods were somewhat unconventional, so Serena had to unlearn and relearn everything. Mouratoglou followed a holistic approach, concentrating both on her game as well as her mentality and mindset. Because of his coaching, Serena won eight Grand Slam titles in the next two-and-a-half years, bringing her overall tally to an impressive 21. The year 2016 was tough for her, but the next year, she won the Australian Open without dropping a set. She achieved this feat despite the fact that she was pregnant.

---

[8]Thornley, Ross, "'How Serena Williams' Comeback Can Teach Us the Principle of "Un-Learning"', Medium, 22 September 2019, https://bit.ly/3qdk7gK. Accessed on 5 September 2022.

When she won her 23rd Grand Slam title, she was eight weeks into her pregnancy and 35 years of age.[9]

Had she followed the 'one-size-fits-all' approach, she would not have succeeded. Serena's willingness to unlearn and embrace new learning after being at the pinnacle proved to be her greatest strength.

Sometimes, the tried-and-tested methods no longer produce the desired results. Change is the only constant in the world. There are new rules, norms and competition arising every single day. One who does not want to learn and upgrade gets left behind. It is important to identify the change and make adjustments accordingly. The key is to stay relevant in a fast-changing world.

Learning Tip: Work on your AQ (adaptability quotient) to remain successful.

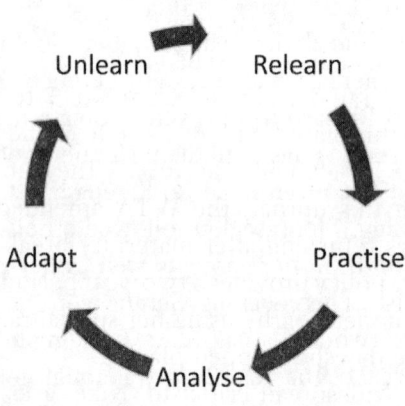

The Components of Adaptability

---

[9]Roxby, Philippa, 'Serena Wiulliams: How Did She Compete while Pregnant', BBC, 20 April 2017.

> *Charles Darwin said, 'It is not the strongest of the species that survives, nor the most intelligent that survives. It is the one that is most adaptable to change.' This was a lesson well learnt by the Lenovo-owned Motorola, once a leading brand among mobile handsets, which had been seeing declining sales since the introduction of newer brands like Xiaomi and Realme. Motorola failed to refresh its portfolio, whereas its Chinese counterparts started offering competitive models at a better price. Motorola missed the movement to 3G at that time, which was crucial, as that was what customers wanted. It was their reluctance to adapt that caused their business to slide down.*[10]

BE BOLD TO CHANGE THE RULES

In September 2017, Serena gave birth to her daughter Alexis Olympia Ohanian Jr and had to go on a maternity leave. As a result, her ranking dipped from No. 1 to No. 453. She fought against this biased ranking system, as she felt penalized for taking time off after her delivery.[11] The public supported her. Following this uproar, the WTA amended the seeding rule for players returning after maternity break. The current maternity leave policy provides a two-year period for an athlete to return to competition by using her special ranking, i.e. her ranking on the day she stopped playing.

Following widespread criticism, Nike, a leading sponsor

---

[10]'How Motorola Lost its Grip in India', *Communications Today*, https://bit.ly/3qhNQoA. Accessed on 5 September 2022.

[11]Bellshaw, George, 'Serena Williams Believes "Biased Ranking System" Played Role in French Open Injury', *Metro*, 8 March 2019, https://bit.ly/3SdNueM. Accessed on 20 September 2022.

for tennis stars, had to change its policy of slashing women players' pay during and post-pregnancy. Serena welcomed this change and spoke in favour of Nike stating that, 'It's about learning from mistakes and doing better.'[12]

Serena has always been vocal about gender equality. She has spoken up against the gender pay gap and sexist remarks. Her sister Venus too has been vocal about the gender pay gap. The night before her Wimbledon win in 2005, Venus made a failed plea about this issue to the governing body. In 2007, after her fourth Wimbledon victory, she was awarded the same money as the men's tennis champion, Roger Federer.

In the world of business too, unfortunately, many still consider women to be too soft for leadership roles. Often, they are not paid at par with their male counterparts.

Learning Tip: It is imperative for organizations to promote a culture of meritocracy and introduce a gender-neutral recruitment process.

CREATE A FALLBACK OPTION

Sustaining a career as a sportsperson throughout one's life is impossible. Serena realizes this pretty well. That is why, apart from creating a strong position in tennis, she decided to diversify. She has started her own line of clothing and accessories, invested in several companies, undertaken philanthropic projects and produced an HBO series, *Being Serena*. She has made several television appearances and provided her voice to animated shows. She has several product endorsements under her belt too. She is the board member of the consumer survey

---

[12] 'Serena Backs Nike after Maternity Pay Controversy', *Sportstar*, 28 May 2019, https://bit.ly/3Bf8yfj. Accessed on 5 September 2022.

start-up, Surveymonkey. She has secured her future by ensuring she has enough passive income-generating opportunities the day she decides to retire from tennis.

In business as well, diversification is considered a viable option to meet long-term financial gains and to minimize risks. 'Don't put all your eggs in one basket' is a saying we have been hearing since childhood.

Learning Tip: Have a contingency plan to bail out of difficult situations. Have a fallback plan too.

Serena's Performance in Finals of Major Tournaments (till 12 September 2022)

Career Finals					
Discipline	Type	Won	Lost	Total	Win Ratio (Won: Total)
Singles	Grand Slam	23	10	33	0.70
	Summer Olympics	1	-	1	1.00
	WTA Tour Championships	5	2	7	0.71
	Grand Slam Cup	1	-	1	1.00
	WTA Premier Mandatory	23	10	33	0.69
	WTA Tour	20	3	23	0.87
	Total	73	25	98	0.74

Career Finals						
Discipline	Type	Won	Lost	Total	Win Ratio (Won: Total)
Doubles	Grand Slam	14	-	14	1.00
	Summer Olympics	3	-	3	1.00
	WTA Tour Championships	-	-	-	-
	WTA Premier Mandatory	2	-	2	1.00
	WTA Tour	4	2	6	0.67
	Total	23	2	25	0.92
Mixed doubles	Grand Slam	2	2	4	0.50
	Total	2	2	4	0.50
Total		98	29	127	0.77

14

Combatting the Enemy Within

Tiger Woods

Winning is not always the barometer of getting better.
TIGER WOODS

Life is not always perfect and flawless. Along with success comes a platter of failures, mistakes and setbacks. Victory lies in combatting these adversities in a way exemplified by Eldrick Tont 'Tiger' Woods, the American professional golfer who is tied for rank one in PGA (Professional Golfers' Association) Tour wins and ranks second in men's major championships. Woods is the youngest player (at the age of 21) and first African-American to win the US Masters in 1997. He has won about 15 major professional golf championships and 18 world golf championships. He was named the 'PGA Player of the Year' an astounding 11 times and also elected to the World Golf Hall of Fame. Woods was World No.1 for 264 weeks (from August 1999 to September 2004) and then again for 281 weeks (from June 2005 to October 2010). In 2019, he became the 33rd sports figure and fourth golfer to receive the Presidential Medal of Freedom.

EARLY LIFE

Tiger Woods was born in 1975 to Earl Dennison Woods, a US Army infantry officer and Kultida Punsawad Woods, who used to work as a secretary in Bangkok in a US Army office and later in a bank in Brooklyn, New York, during the early years of moving there. Woods was nicknamed Tiger after the nickname of his father's friend, Col. Vuong Dang Phong. Earl was an amateur golfer and introduced his son to the game at the age of two. Owing to his military background, the former had access to the Navy golf course, where he took Tiger for his lessons. Tiger was a quick learner and soon started mastering the game. At the age of five, he appeared in the monthly golf magazine *Golf Digest* and on ABC's reality show *That's Incredible!* At the age of eight, he became so proficient in his game that he featured in the television show *Good Morning America*, where he showed off his skills. He also won the Junior World Golf Championships, participating in the youngest age group of 9-10 in 1984. Additionally, he broke 80 in the same year. For most golfers, breaking 80 is the achievement of a lifetime. Woods defeated his father at the age of 11, with his father trying really hard to win. At just 12 years of age, he broke 70.

A SHOT AT FAME

In 1994, Woods enrolled in Stanford University under the golf scholarship. He turned professional in 1996 at the age of 20, but by that time, he had already collected a number of amateur golf titles. He created history by winning the US Masters at Augusta in 1997, setting a record score of 270 at the tender age of 21. With this feat, he secured his position as the youngest player and also the first African American to win this title.

Woods signed lucrative advertising contracts with Nike, Inc. and Titleist in 1996. The same year, the American sports magazine *Sports Illustrated* named him the 'Sportsman of the Year' and 'PGA Tour Rookie of the Year'. The following year, Woods won the 1997 Masters Tournament, making him the youngest to do so. He had the fastest ascent to World No. 1 in the Official World Golf Rankings just two months later. He maintained this streak for 264 weeks.

In 2000, *Sports Illustrated* called his US Open performance the 'the greatest performance in golf history'.[1] He became the youngest golfer to achieve the Career Grand Slam at the age of 24. *Sports Illustrated* again named him the 'Sportsman of the Year' in 2000. He was ranked the 'twelfth best golfer of all time' by *Golf Digest* in 2000. In 2009, Woods became the first-ever athlete to make it to the 'billion-dollar club' after winning the $10 million FedEx Cup title.

Woods's life has been a sort of roller-coaster ride. There were times when the media wrote him off, but he had the tenacity to prove everyone wrong. In an interview, he said, 'I have to overcome all my inner demons to perform, 'cause no one's gonna bail me out'.[2] By his inner demons, he meant all the controversies that surrounded him due to his misbehaviour, affairs, alcoholism, etc. These hampered his image. He soon realized he needed to fight an inner battle first before he could become a truly exceptional and remarkable athlete.

It takes immense courage to battle the enemy within. We all have our inner demons to fight. They could be our habits,

---

[1]Burnes, Jerry, 'Greatest Sports Accomplishment: Tiger Woods Wins U.S. Open by 15 Strokes', Bleacher Report, 17 June 2008, https://bit.ly/3SAbbyJ. Accessed on 28 September 2022.

[2]Juneau, Jen, and Lindsay Kimble, 'Tiger Woods Talks About Overcoming "Inner Demons to Perform" in Upcoming ESPN "G.O.A.T.s"', *People*, 2 March 2021.

relationships or weaknesses. We are all human and it is only natural to be imperfect and flawed. We have to understand the underlying psychology behind our negative thoughts and actions.

NEVER QUIT

When Woods was battling injuries and surgeries that affected his performance, the media declared that it was the end of his reign. Surprisingly, he rose like a phoenix and is on the race to reclaim his lost position. Had he thought of quitting when his ranks were dropping, we would not have been reading about him now.

Overcoming stuttering problem

As a child, Woods had a speech disorder. To overcome the problem of stuttering, he practised for hours to get his speech correct. 'The words got lost, you know, somewhere between the brain and the mouth. And it was very difficult, but I fought through it.'[3] On a later date, he wrote a letter to a young boy with the same problem. In his letter, he motivated the boy to keep fighting and achieve something great in life. 'I know what it's like to be different and to sometimes not fit in. I also stuttered as a child and I would talk to my dog and he would sit there and listen until he fell asleep. I also took a class for two years to help me, and I finally learnt to stop,' he wrote.[4] He further added that the stuttering did not stop him from achieving his dreams but only inspired him to fight harder.

---

[3]"Tiger Wins at Golf and Stuttering', The Stuttering Foundation, https://bit.ly/3KQvpkx. Accessed on 7 September 2022.

[4]"Tiger Woods Writes Letter to High School Boy with Stuttering Problem', ESPN, 13 May 2015, https://bit.ly/3Qnk6kQ. Accessed on 17 November 2022.

Difficulties with myopia

Woods had severe myopia with 11 dioptre and used to wear contact lenses, which caused a problem during rainy and windy conditions. He underwent laser eye surgery in 1999 to rectify the issues with his vision and got a 20/15 vision without contacts. His vision started deteriorating in 2007 and he had to undergo a second laser eye surgery.

Dealing with injuries

In 1994, while studying at Stanford, Woods underwent a surgery for the removal of a benign tumour from his left knee. Yet, he dominated the USGA (United States Golf Association) championships. When he won the 1994 US Amateur Championship at the age of 18, he created history as the youngest player to win the title.

In 2008, he underwent an arthroscopic surgery to repair the cartilage damage in his left knee. He immediately returned to win the 2008 US Open. Woods had been playing with a torn anterior cruciate ligament (ACL) in his left knee since the 2007 British Open. He underwent reconstructive surgery to repair his torn ACL 12 days after winning the 2008 US Open.

Just a few weeks after the WGC-Cadillac Championship (where he finished 25th), in 2014, Woods underwent his first back surgery, which was a microdiscectomy (a minimally invasive surgical procedure) to treat a pinched nerve in the back. Despite the surgery, he played the Quicken Loans National in 2014. The next year, he finished tenth at the Wyndham Championship. In 2015, he had another back injury and surgery because of which he missed the Masters Tournament. He underwent two more back surgeries in 2016 and 2017. However, he still made a spectacular comeback to competitive golf in the Hero World Challenge in Bahamas.

His world ranking improved from 1199 to 668, which was the biggest jump in his rankings.

Woods did consider the option of quitting at the age of 39 due to his injuries, but after staying away from the game for some time, he rethought his decision, regained the lost motivation and reinvented himself.

Sometimes, when the going gets tough, we need to accept our fate and take things in our stride. If we don't lose hope and keep persevering, sooner or later, things do fall in place.

Learning Tip: Learn to accept finite disappointment, but do not lose infinite hope.

FOCUS ON WINNING THE WAR, NOT JUST THE BATTLES

Every game requires physical as well as mental toughness. You need to keep fighting. Woods not only fought to maintain his standing as a sportsperson but also had to fight his inner demons. After the 2018 annual Tour Championship, the year Woods staged his comeback, he was reported to have said, 'I loved every bit of it. The fight and the grind and the tough conditions, and just had to suck it up and hit shots, and I loved every bit of it.'[5]

Losing the World No. 1 position

In September 2004, a Fijian professional golfer, Vijay Singh, overtook Woods as the World No.1 after the latter had held the ranking for 264 weeks. Woods reclaimed the spot next year after winning six PGA Tour events.

---

[5]Harig, Bob, 'Tiger Woods Caps Comeback by Winning Tour Championship', ESPN, 24 September 2018.

Learning Tip: Struggles and adversity present you with better skills to face the future. Be patient enough to endure the entire process rather than rushing through it. When things do not go as planned, take a brief pause to rebuild and repair yourself before preparing your comeback.

Answering the 'Tiger who?' question

In 2000, Woods won three out of four majors. The only major he lost was the one clinched by Vijay Singh, a close friend of Paul Tesori. In the 2000 Presidents Cup, when Tesori was directly facing Woods, the former wore a hat with 'Tiger Who?' inscribed on it. Woods gave a befitting reply by winning the match. Tesori meant the act to be funny and later apologized to Woods. He said in an interview, 'It probably just pumped Tiger up to play better.'[6]

Father's death

Woods suffered a personal setback when he lost his father in 2006. It was at that time that Tiger took his first major break from the sport. He went for 24 days without touching the club. After all, it was his first mentor and coach that he had lost, not to mention a loving and supportive father. However, he soon bounced back and that year saw him win the British Open. Being deeply attached to his father, Tiger felt a deep emotional loss after his demise. He soon realized that his father would have wanted him to continue playing and it was this thought that gave him the courage to go back to the golf course and win the PGA Championship that year.

---

[6]Welnman, Sam, 'The All-Time Biggest Tiger Woods Snubs', Golf Digest, 5 April 2011, https://bit.ly/3QqTPT1. Accessed on 8 September 2022.

Tiger-proofing

Since Tiger Woods played golf effortlessly, there were some changes made to the golf course to make it more challenging. These changes were called 'Tiger-proofing'. This was done to neutralize Woods's length of the tee. The golf courses were made longer, the holes were lengthened and fairways were made narrower. He had to use more golf clubs and deploy wider shots to master the new changes. However, he gave a befitting reply when he mastered these as well and started playing the new shots effortlessly.

> **Learning Tip:** A person with a winning attitude is not disturbed by changes in the course syllabus. He can easily adapt and emerge victorious.

Rejecting social stigma and seeking help

Our success graph is not always a straight line, everyone's career graph is a mix of highs and lows. Some of these lows could have been the result of our own bad decisions, mistakes and inner demons. It is imperative to not pay heed to what society's perception is of us and focus on our own reality. Woods recovered from the lows in his life, professional and personal, because he sought help especially while facing allegations for adultery.

Infidelity issues

In October 2004, Woods married model Elin Nordegren. They were blessed with a daughter in 2007 and a son in 2009. In 2009, there was trouble in paradise as rumours of Woods having an affair with New York City nightclub manager Rachel Uchitel started doing the rounds, though the latter denied the claim. In November 2009, allegedly a voice clip of Woods was released by the media. It was said that the voicemail was left by Woods for a woman who was suspected to be his mistress. This time, he owned up to his mistake and apologized publicly. Over the next few days, several women came forward claiming to have been in an affair with him.[7]

After Woods admitted to his multiple infidelities, several companies, including Accenture, AT&T, Gatorade, Nike, General Motors, Gillette and TAG Heuer, among others, cancelled their contracts with him.[8]

Woods recognized his inner demons and underwent rehabilitation therapy for sex addiction. In 2011, he landed an exclusive endorsement deal with a sports nutrition firm, Fuse Science, Inc. In 2012, he made a comeback by winning the Arnold Palmer Invitational, which was his first PGA Tour victory since 2009. The same year, he topped the field at AT&T National.

Thus, following his admission to having had numerous adulterous affairs, Woods sought help and underwent therapy, having to fight social stigma at the same time. When we admit our shortcomings and seek help or feedback, the battle is half won.

Arrest for driving under influence

On 29 May 2017, Woods was arrested for driving under influence near Jupiter Island, Florida. The toxicology reports showed that he was on painkillers and sleeping medication. He got himself in a diversion programme and did 50 hours of community service as redemption.

Woods has experienced fall-from-grace moments several

---

[7]Liston, Barbara 'UPDATE 4-Tiger Woods Admits "Transgressions," Apologizes', *Reuters*, 2 December 2009, https://reut.rs/3TTCkNM. Accessed on 8 September 2022.
[8]'When Scandal Engulfs a Celebrity Endorser', *Harvard Business Review*, May–June 2019, https://bit.ly/3sW5mjV, Accessed on 4 November 2022.

times in his life. First you struggle with all your might to get to the top, and then you keep sliding down with every mistake, every mishap. It is imperative to recognize your weaknesses and vulnerabilities and seek help to overcome them.

> **Learning Tip:** You can be a hero one day and a villain the next. People will love to associate with you when you are successful and desperately try to break all ties when you are in trouble or are falling.

BE DOWN TO EARTH

When Woods was at the peak of his career in the mid-2000s, he took his life for granted. Newfound fame and wealth can be overwhelming at times and difficult to handle. There is a possibility of getting distracted by the attention one receives, thus making one lose sight of the big picture. It is important to keep reminding yourself that you are where you are because of your game and performance. So, it is imperative to remain humble and down to the earth, always. One of the markers of humility is gratitude. When you reach a certain level in your life, it is because of the sacrifices, hard work, guidance and support of several people in your life. It is not just about you. Therefore, express gratitude to them.

After making a comeback, Woods developed the attitude of gratitude'. He said, 'I appreciate it a little bit more than I did because I don't take it for granted that I'm going to have another decade, two decades in my future of playing golf at this level.'[9]

---

[9]Omnisport, 'I Couldn't Sit or Stand – Tiger Woods Reflects nn Back Woes after Ending Drought', Sportskeeda, 24 September 2018, https://bit.ly/3Qos25l. Accessed on 8 September 2022.

Woods's life is a perfect example of how despite several setbacks both professional and personal, one can rise.

Woods's Performance over the Years (till 2022)

Tournaments	Number of Wins by Tour
PGA Tour	82 (1st all time)
European Tour	41 (3rd all time)
Japan Golf Tour	3
Asian Tour	2
PGA Tour of Australasia	3
Other	17
Best results in major championships (wins: 15)	
Masters Tournament	Won: 1997, 2001, 2002, 2005, 2019
PGA Championship	Won: 1999, 2000, 2006, 2007
US Open	Won: 2000, 2002, 2008
The Open Championship	Won: 2000, 2005, 2006

15

Racing Ahead with Passion

Michael Schumacher

Once something is passion, the motivation is there.
MICHAEL SCHUMACHER

Michael Schumacher is regarded as the greatest Formula One (F1) driver of all time. He has won the World Drivers' Championship title a record seven times and his passion for the sport even led him to come out of retirement at the age of 41. In terms of statistics, Schumacher has won more races than anyone else in the history of the sport and is the only racer to have won five consecutive World Championships. In 2002, he was appointed the 'UNESCO Champion for Sport'. He is the two-time winner of the Laureus World Sportsman of the Year Award. His prowess on the racing track has helped popularize the sport among the young generation and he has often served as a role model for them. So, what was it that really drove his insatiable desire for racing? Let us decode this further to understand more.

EARLY LIFE

Schumacher was born on 3 January 1969 in an ordinary household in North Rhine-Westphalia, Germany, to Rolf

Schumacher, a bricklayer by profession, and Elisabeth Starking, who ran a canteen at the local kart track. His father was the one to identify his son's interest in driving. When Michael was four years old, his father modified his pedal kart with a small motorcycle engine, but Michael crashed into a lamppost. This did not discourage him or his parents. On the contrary, soon, Michael became the youngest member of the karting club in Kerpen-Horrem after his parents decided to take him to the karting club. His father built him his first racing kart from discarded parts, with which he won his first club championship at the age of six. His parents were supportive of his interest in racing despite their limited means. This led to his father taking up a second job repairing karts. It was on the foundation of this strong parental support that Michael followed his passion for racing.

Each one of us has unlimited potential. However, there are several factors that determine whether we are able to achieve our true potential. One of the critical factors is the support received from one's parents. It is believed that a parent's role in a child's life has far-reaching impact. Parental involvement is extremely important for a child to do well in school and later too. When young Schumacher crashed the pedal kart into the lamppost, his parents could have put an end to his interest in racing. Yet, they decided to support his passion, which resulted in the making of a world champion.

> **Learning Tip:** Each child is unique in their own way. We must always support our children so that they can pursue their dreams and we must encourage their talent and passion.

EARLY CAREER

To obtain his kart licence in Germany, Schumacher had to be at least 14 years of age. His skills at that time already superseded that of his peer racers. Hence, he decided to circumvent this rule by obtaining the licence from Luxembourg, which did not have this age limit. It was with this licence that he won his first German Junior Kart Championship. He later worked as a mechanic and joined EuroKart dealer Adolf Neubert, which eventually led to him becoming both the German and EuroKart champion driving for them. He even quit school to pursue his passion for racing. He could have waited for the right age but decided, instead, to take a bold step forward. Furthermore, his stint as a mechanic helped him understand the components of the kart better, paving his way to becoming a better racing driver.

Just as Schumacher did not wait for the right time to seize an opportunity, we should also believe in creating opportunities for ourselves. In fact, there is never a better time to start your journey than today. A case in point is the Covid-19 crisis, where Indian apparel manufacturers started making personal protective equipment (PPE) kits instead of regular apparels. This catapulted the country to become the second-largest manufacturer of PPE kits in the world by May 2020.

> **Learning Tip:** Adverse situations always present us with an opportunity to grow. It is important for us to be receptive to such opportunities.

In 1989, Schumacher signed up with Wilhelm 'Willi' Friedrich Weber's WTS Formula Three (F3) team, following which he won the championship in 1990. It was this association with

Weber that proved extremely critical not just for Schumacher but also for his brother Ralf's career. Weber served as manager for Michael till 2012 and was known for his sharp negotiation skills and eye for talent. The story of the association of the two is nothing short of what we believe to be destiny. It was during a Formula Ford race in Austria that Weber first spotted Michael, whom he invited to test his F3 car. During the testing, Weber was convinced that he had found the right man for the job, so to say. Furthermore, a close connection of Weber later provided the financial guarantees needed for Michael's F1 debut with the Jordan Grand Prix F1 team. Was it just destiny that Weber spotted Michael? Or was it Michael's passion that propelled him to become one of the best drivers on the track? One thing is for certain: none of it would have been possible without Michael's hard work and drive.

As individuals, we must always respect those with talent and provide them with the right opportunity, though within our limits. Great partnerships at workplaces survive on the basis of understanding and such foundations are built on trust and mutual respect. Since we spend a major chunk of our time at work, cultivating such strong relationships not only furthers our career goals but also helps build a personal connect with those around us.

> **Learning Tip:** It is important to identify talent and support it. This helps in creating leaders and champions of tomorrow.

FORMULA ONE CAREER

Throughout his career, Michael Schumacher was known for his ability to produce fast laps at crucial moments in a race. He made his debut with the Jordan-Ford team at the 1991

Belgian Grand Prix and finished seventh in the qualifying stage. This was quite impressive given that he had only seen the track as a spectator and learned the track by cycling along it. Unfortunately, he had to retire in the first lap of the race owing to clutch problems. For the rest of the season, he drove for Benetton Formula, as no final contract had been signed with Jordan-Ford. Schumacher finished his debut season with four points out of six races. His first podium finish came in his second season in 1992, when he finished third in the Mexican Grand Prix and his first victory came in the Belgian Grand Prix. He finished the season at third place. In his third season, in 1993, he finished fourth in the F1 World Drivers' Championship with nine podium finishes. The consistency that he showed in his earlier years was remarkable and gave a glimpse of the future to come.

If we consider the trajectory of Schumacher's career, it was initially dotted with controversies. In 1994, he won his first Drivers' Championship. The season, however, was marred by the fatal accident of the former world champion Ayrton Senna when his car crashed into a concrete barrier while he was leading the 1994 San Marino Grand Prix in Italy. Schumacher, who was directly behind Senna in the second position, was an eyewitness to the tragic accident, which had a deep impact on him.

The season was also dotted with controversies, as the Benetton, Ferrari and McLaren teams were investigated for breaking the Fédération Internationale de l'Automobile (FIA)-imposed ban on electronic driving aids to ensure the emphasis of the race was on the driver's skills, not on the systems.

At the British Grand Prix, Schumacher was penalized for overtaking on the formation lap. He then ignored the penalty and subsequently received the black flag[1]. This resulted in him facing a two-race ban. The final race in Australia was marked with a bigger controversy. Schumacher was leading Damon Hill by just one point at the start of the race. However, in lap 36, both the drivers collided with each other, resulting in them retiring from the race, though Schumacher managed to clinch his first Drivers' Championship. At the press conference after the race, Schumacher dedicated his title to Senna. In the following season, he successfully defended his title with Benetton and became the youngest two-time world champion in F1 history.

Controversies only propelled him to work harder and improve his skills. From winning just one race in the 1992 season to becoming the youngest two-time world champion speaks much about his mental strength. He was always viewed as a 'win-at-all-costs' driver, which drew much criticism. But that did not deter him from achieving his goals. In 1996, he joined Ferrari. Its V12 engine was no longer competitive against the more fuel-efficient V10s of its competitors. However, Schumacher was convinced that the team was good enough to win the championship. It was this belief that led to the transformation of the struggling team into the most successful team in F1 history. In the 1996 Drivers' Championship, he came third, which, in turn, aided Ferrari in securing second place in the World Constructors' Championship, ahead of his old team Benetton.

His efforts helped Ferrari win the Constructors' title in the 1999 season. He lost his chance to win the Drivers' Championship because during the British Grand Prix, his rear brake failed, which sent him off the track resulting in a broken

---

[1] The black flag implies that the driver must immediately return to the pits.

leg. After missing six races and a 98-day absence, he made his return at the inaugural Malaysian Grand Prix qualifying in the pole position by almost a second. It is not easy for any sportsperson to make a comeback and assume the pole position, yet Schumacher was able to achieve the same.

The years 2000 to 2004 saw his dominance when he won five consecutive world championships, a feat that has not been accomplished by any other driver. His dominance in the 2001 season was so significant that with nine wins, he had already clinched the Drivers' World Championship although four races were remaining in the season. During the same season, he also finished second to his brother Ralf in the Canadian Grand Prix, resulting in the first 1-2 finish by two brothers in the history of F1. In 2002, he won the championship with six races remaining in the season, won a record 11 races and finished every race in the podium. He finished with 144 points, leading his teammate Rubens Barrichello by a record 67 points in the second position. The following season, in 2003, was a closely contested one with Kimi-Matias Räikkönen, who only won the championship in the final race of the season (Japanese Grand Prix). The year 2004 saw Schumacher dominating once again, winning 12 of the first 13 races of the season, earning him his seventh world championship title (a feat equalled by Lewis Hamilton in 2020).

If we consider the consistency with which Schumacher won, it indicates not just perseverance but also respect and passion for the game. When one attains glory at the highest level, a sense of complacency tends to creep in. This has happened even with large corporates such as Nokia. During its period of domination over the mobile handset industry, Google had proposed to Nokia for Android OS to be installed in

> *its devices instead of Symbian OS, but the discussion fell through and Nokia continued with Symbian OS. The rest, as they say, is history, as Nokia lost its market share and Microsoft eventually purchased its handset business within the next decade.*

Despite his wins, Schumacher continued with his record-breaking spree in world of F1. He wanted to win every race he competed in. It is this attitude that all of us should cultivate. Every day is a new day with new possibilities. So, the moment we grow complacent is the day we stop growing.

In 2005, however, a rule change in racing required the tyres of a car to last an entire race. This tipped the advantage in favour of teams using Michelin tyres and was specifically done to reduce the dominance of Ferrari over the last five years. The latter used Bridgestone tyres, which required their drivers to take pit stops for tyre change during the race. Despite the rule change, he finished the season in third position. The 2006 season was the last in his Ferrari career, during which he broke Senna's record of maximum pole positions. His skill level was on complete display in the Brazilian Grand Prix, when, owing to a tyre puncture, he slipped to the 19th position and yet managed to finish in the fourth position.

It was during the Italian Grand Prix in 2006 that Schumacher announced his retirement from racing though he continued to stay associated with Ferrari as part of their development team. He focussed on testing the electronics and test driving for the brand. In 2008, he even competed in motorcycle racing in the IDM-series and described riding a Ducati as the most exhilarating experience of his life. He even came back from retirement in 2010 at the age of 41 but could not recreate his magic with the Mercedes team. He raced for Mercedes for three seasons, from 2010 to 2012, before formally retiring from the sport for a second time.

In fact, it is very similar to business leader Ratan Tata who, despite his age, still continues to oversee the operations of the Tata Group. If you are passionate about anything, you will want to continue regardless of the situation. Just like an entrepreneur is passionate about his venture, we too should try to be passionate in our work and roles.

Schumacher was regarded very highly for his strict fitness regime and his ability to make any race 'him versus the rest'. It is extremely difficult to race in wet conditions, yet he won 17 of the 30 races he participated in such conditions. As some of his best performances came in rainy weather, he was often referred by the nicknames 'Regenkönig' (rain king) and 'Regenmeister'(rain master). He also helped popularize the sport in Germany. He played an important role in developing the first lightweight carbon helmet for F1 drivers in association with the German manufacturer Schuberth.

Business leaders should focus on nurturing talent and inculcating the same passion in the workplace. This can be done by ensuring the right environment using the following steps:

- Focus on hiring the right people rather than the best ones.
- Have a culture of open communication so that people can freely express their views and concerns.
- Focus on creating a strong sense of purpose.
- Allow individuals to work on their own ideas for a small part of the day.

Schumacher believe that it is his duty to give back to the sport and continue to be associated with racing. In honour of his racing career and efforts towards improving safety, he was given the FIA Gold Medal for Motor Sport in 2006. He has served as a special ambassador to UNESCO and made donations towards several social causes, including the construction of schools for the economically backward in the West African country Senegal. There is little doubt that his passion for the sport has provided the necessary impetus and thrust for achieving excellence.

LIFE BEYOND RACING

In August 1995, Schumacher married Corinna Betsch and together they have two children. He has always been a very private person, avoiding the spotlight when with family. In 2013, Schumacher, while skiing on the slopes of the French Alps, slipped and hit his head on a rock, sustaining a serious head injury, despite wearing a helmet, and slipped into coma. He is still in the process of recovering completely from the same.

Tragedies can happen to any one of us in our lives. It is important to always keep fighting and never give up. There is little doubt that the champion F1 racer, who overcame coma, will also recover in this journey ahead.

Schumacher's Performance in Formula One over the Years (as of September 2022)

Season	Team	Races	Wins	Poles	Podiums	Points	Position
1991	Team 7UP Jordan	1	0	0	0	0	14th
1991	Camel Benetton Ford	5	0	0	0	4	
1992	Camel Benetton Ford	16	1	0	8	53	3rd
1993	Camel Benetton Ford	16	1	0	9	52	4th
1994	Mild Seven Benetton Ford	14	8	6	10	92	1st
1995	Mild Seven Benetton Renault	17	9	4	11	102	1st
1996	Scuderia Ferrari S.p.A.	16	3	4	8	59	3rd
1997	Scuderia Ferrari Marlboro	17	5	3	8	78	Disqualified
1998	Scuderia Ferrari Marlboro	16	6	3	11	86	2nd
1999	Scuderia Ferrari Marlboro	10	2	3	6	44	5th
2000	Scuderia Ferrari Marlboro	17	9	9	12	108	1st
2001	Scuderia Ferrari Marlboro	17	9	11	14	123	1st
2002	Scuderia Ferrari Marlboro	17	11	7	17	144	1st
2003	Scuderia Ferrari Marlboro	16	6	5	8	93	1st
2004	Scuderia Ferrari Marlboro	18	13	8	15	148	1st
2005	Scuderia Ferrari Marlboro	19	1	1	5	62	3rd
2006	Scuderia Ferrari Marlboro	18	7	4	12	121	2nd
2010	Mercedes GP Petronas F1 Team	19	0	0	0	72	9th
2011	Mercedes GP Petronas F1 Team	19	0	0	0	76	8th
2012	Mercedes AMG Petronas F1 Team	20	0	0	1	49	13th

16

Charging Ahead

Usain Bolt

There are better starters than me, but I am a strong finisher.

USAIN BOLT

24 August 2004. An 18-year-old Jamaican boy raced the 200-metre sprint, finishing fifth and being disqualified from entering the semifinals by just 0.03 seconds. Though it was owing to a hamstring injury, this young boy—Usain St Leo Bolt—made it a point that this was his first and only defeat in his Olympic career. Today, he is the only sprinter to hold the record of winning a gold in 100-metre and 200-metre races in three consecutive Olympic Games (2008, 2012 and 2016).

As strange as this might sound, running was never his first love, it was cricket. He wanted to be a professional cricketer. It all started with a bet to win a free lunch. A local priest, Reverend Nugent, overheard two 12-year-boys arguing over who was a better runner between them. The two boys were Bolt and his close friend Ricardo Gedes. The priest suggested they contest in a race with the promise of providing free lunch to the winner. Bolt won. That day, the priest told him, 'If you can beat Ricardo, you can beat anyone.'[1] These words of encouragement propelled Bolt to take an interest in sports. He won the race in the annual national primary schools' meeting for his parish, where his sprinting potential was discovered.

EARLY LIFE

Born to hard-working parents who ran a grocery store in a rural locality of Jamaica, Bolt and his brother played cricket and football on the streets as kids. During his schooling days, Bolt stood out as a cricketer, but it was his performance as an athlete that caught his coach's eye and the latter urged him to train for track and field events.

TURNING PROFESSIONAL

Bolt's extensive training led him to win his first annual high school championship medal in 2001, where he won a silver in the 200-metre sprint with the timing of 22.04 seconds. He later participated in his first Caribbean region event, where he won a silver in the 400-metre and 200-metre race of the 2001 Caribbean Free Trade Association (CARIFTA) games, at 48.28 seconds and 21.81 seconds, respectively.

Bolt's talent was noticed in the 2002 Junior World Championships, where he won a gold medal in the 200-metre race, becoming the youngest-ever male world junior champion in any event. The medal was given by the former Jamaican Prime Minister P.J. Patterson, who arranged for Bolt to train with the Jamaica Amateur Athletic Association at the

---

[1] Thomas, Claire, '10 Facts You Didn't Know about Usain Bolt, the World's Fastest Man', *The Telegraph*, 3 August 2017, https://bit.ly/2oLoAYN. Accessed on 13 September 2022.

University of Technology, Jamaica. There, he rigorously trained under Pablo S. McNeil, who was a Jamaican track and field sprinter and sprinting coach.

Unfortunately, the 15-year-old boy didn't take athletics seriously at that time and had a mischievous streak. He hid behind the back of a van skipping the trials for the 2002 CARIFTA 200-metre finals. This led him to be temporarily detained by the police, resulting in a lot of public outcry against the coach and controversy at the same time.[2] His coach was blamed for not being able to control him. Bolt eventually silenced his critics with a set of impressive timings at the CARIFTA games with 21.12 and 47.33 seconds at the 200-metre and 400-metre races, respectively.

How did this mischievous lad become one of the fastest people in the world? Let us look deeper into his life and understand this.

KEEPING THE MIND CALM

The 2002 World Junior Championship was hosted in Kingston, Jamaica. The location should have ideally proved to be an advantage for Bolt, but it proved otherwise. He was so nervous facing his home crowd that he absentmindedly slipped his shoes in the wrong feet. Fortunately for him, he realized his mistake just in time. The incident was an eye-opener for him. He solemnly vowed to not let pre-match jitters affect his focus then on. Till this day, he has kept his word and displayed extraordinary calmness on the tracks prior to any match. And the rest as they say is history.

---

[2]Luton, Daraine, 'Pablo McNeil:The Man Who Put the Charge in Bolt', *Jamaica Gleaner*, 18 August 2008, https://bit.ly/3BBmlwP. Accessed on 13 September 2022.

Learning Tip: The biggest secret to playing your best is learning how to tame your mind to be calm and composed before the actual game.

Often, fear makes us nervous and uneasy. It puts unnecessary negative thoughts in our head. We start second-guessing ourselves. Bravery is not the absence of fear, but the act of overcoming it. Warren Buffett, American business magnate, investor and philanthropist, too suffered from stage fright and was afraid of talking to people. When he was 21, Buffett became a stock broker. At that time, he had two options: either to develop a way to overcome his fear or let go of his dreams. After much soul-searching, he decided to go with the first. He enrolled himself in a public-speaking course. That's how he carved out a future for himself.

IGNORING THE NEGATIVES AND FOCUSSING ON PREPARATION INSTEAD

Bolt was born with an abnormal curvature of the spine, a condition called scoliosis, which could easily have turned out to be a huge disadvantage for him as a sprinter. During his younger days, this condition delayed him in realizing his full potential. However, when he was assigned to Coach Glen Mills, Bolt was able to strengthen his core and back, becoming a consistent performer. The athlete worked for years to get his centre of gravity correct, as his head wouldn't point in the right direction, which affected his stance while running. He focussed on the factors that were under his control, such as working on biomechanics and strengthening his core.

There are two things in life that determine every outcome of a situation.

- **Factors that you can control:** These may include your preparation, studying the opponent in advance and strategizing, improvising techniques and acquiring new skills. You have complete control over the outcome that is a direct product of the amount of hard work and time invested in the preparatory phase.
- **Factors that you cannot control:** There are factors that may not be under your control, no matter how hard you work. These can be an illness, a personal tragedy, harsh weather conditions and superior competition. These can result in a different outcome from the one you anticipated. Leave them in the hands of the natural flow of things and have fun.

BEING A GREAT FINISHER IS MORE IMPORTANT THAN BEING A GOOD STARTER

Bolt usually has a sluggish start at the beginning of the race, whereas many other athletes have a great reaction time and start well. In an interview, he said, 'The more I run, the worse my reaction time gets. My coach knows that when it comes to the end of the season, I am not the perfect athlete.'[3] Irrespective of his poor reaction time, he manages to recover during the match and finish with style.

In real life, there are two kinds of people. First are those who have 'to-date-thinking'. They are good starters and like to evaluate their lives from the point where they have started

---

[3]'Usain Bolt Has a "Slow" Problem', Yahoo Sports, 31 August 2013, https://yhoo.it/3RX7Lp8. Accessed on 19 September 2022.

and where they are now. Second are those who have 'to-get-thinking'. They are good finishers. They like to visualize life from where there are now and where they want to reach.

PLAYING A FAIR GAME

Of the 30 fastest men's 100-metre sprint times, only nine have been run by an athlete not banned for drugs, all by Bolt. Almost every other athlete who ever ran more than 9.79 seconds has been under some doping charges. Bolt, however, has an untarnished anti-doping image. He has always played a fair game.

Incorporating the sense of fair play shows that you are an amazing person, with tolerance and respect for others as well as confidence in yourself. Former CEO of the Adidas Group, Herbert Hainer, had said, 'Any company can have a code of conduct and talk about a great game, but only companies that understand and value integrity can grow sustainably.'[4] In business too, short-term successes can be achieved by tweaking and bending rules, but only trustworthy brands survive, and this sense of trust develops from playing fair. In your workplace, it is imperative to set a positive and credible image and this can be done by maintaining your integrity and not falling prey to shortcuts.

SHOWING OFF YOUR SKILLS ONLY WHEN NECESSARY

Bolt never unnecessarily flaunts his speed. In the Rio Olympic semifinals, the rule was that the top two athletes would qualify for the finals. So, when Bolt was the first to near the finish line, he slowed down, whereas the Canadian athlete Andre

---

[4]'Fair Play: The Adidas Group Code of Conduct', Adidas Group, https://bit.ly/3UkOLmc. Accessed on 19 September 2022.

de Grasse sped up clinching the first position. Bolt jokingly wagged a finger at De Grasse implying that it was just the semifinals. Later, De Grasse accepted that he pushed so hard for no reason.

We are often tempted to show off our strengths to our peers and fellow competitors. Instead of impressing others, you are actually showcasing your insecurities. Play your cards at the right time.

DELIVERING WHAT IS PROMISED

Just before the 2016 Rio Olympics, Bolt declared that he would emerge as the greatest athlete. Upon this, many critics questioned his age and fitness level, but he made history again with gold medals in the 100- and 200-metre races and 4x100-metre relay.

We often end up bragging or overpromising results. This is the result of our nearsightedness. When a task is assigned, we often get overexcited and bite more than we can chew. If we don't deliver on our promise, we end up losing face. It is always better to underpromise and overdeliver than overpromise and underdeliver.

> **Learning Tip:** If we keep our word, we develop a reputation of being reliable, trustworthy and credible. We gain loyal followers, supporters and accomplices.

Even big brands sometimes fail to deliver what they promise. Sometimes, they do things that contradict the message they have previously articulated to the public. In 2017, videos of a passenger being manhandled in a United Airlines flight went viral. Immediately, the airline saw its share prices go

> *down. They defaulted on their core principles, which were ensuring customer safety, treating customers respectfully and delivering the service they have been paid for—'fly the friendly skies' (their tag line). In the weeks to follow, their CEO Oscar Munoz wrote in a letter, 'Each flight you take with us represents an important promise we make to you, our customer. It's not simply that we make sure you reach your destination safely and on time, but also that you will be treated with the highest level of service and the deepest sense of dignity and respect.'*[5]

LIFE BEYOND THE TRACK

Not just content being the 'fastest man on the planet', Bolt has ventured into business and authored several books too, including his autobiography, *Faster than Lightning: My Autobiography*. In 2016, an animated movie called *The Boy Who Learned to Fly* was made on him. He also starred in a documentary titled *I Am Bolt*. He has tried his hand at professional football and played at Soccer Aid, a British annual (formerly biennial) charity event. In 2013, he participated in the NBA All-Star Weekend Celebrity Game, where he scored two points from a slam dunk. In 2018, he co-founded a transformational personal transportation company called Bolt Mobility. The next year, he debuted as a dance-hall music producer by releasing *Olympe Rosé Riddim*, which featured five songs by Jamaican musicians. The same year, he released another compilation named *Immortal Riddim*.

---

[5]Carolyn Crafts, 'Broken Promises: When Brands Don't Deliver What They Promise', Full Surge, 1 April 2019, https://bit.ly/3U6Fb5L. Accessed on 5 November 2022.

The Guinness World Records Held by Usain Bolt

- Fastest run 150 metres (male)
- Most medals won at the IAAF World Athletics Championships (male)
- Most gold medals won at the IAAF World Athletics Championships (male)
- Fastest relay 4x100 metres (male)
- Most World Athletics Championships Men's 200-metre wins
- Most consecutive Olympic gold medals won in 100 metres (male)
- Most consecutive Olympic gold medals won in 200 metres (male)
- Most Olympic men's 200-metre gold medals
- Fastest run 200 metres (male)
- Most Men's IAAF World Athlete of Year Trophies
- First Olympic track sprint triple-double
- Highest annual earnings for a track athlete
- Most wins of the 100-metre sprint at the Olympic Games
- First athlete to win the 100-metre and 200-metre sprints at successive Olympic Games
- Fastest run 100 metres (male)
- First man to win the 200-metre sprint at successive Olympic Games
- Most World Athletics Championships Men's 100-metre wins
- Most tickets sold at an IAAF World Athletics Championships
- Most competitive 100-metre sprint races completed in less then 10 seconds

17

Nurturing Mental Toughness

Roger Federer

What I think I've been able to do well over the years is play with pain, play with problems, play in all sorts of conditions.

ROGER FEDERER

Roger Federer can undoubtedly be regarded as one of the all-time greats in the world of tennis. He holds the record of being World No.1 for a period of 310 weeks, which is the highest by any player to have played the game. He has won a record eight Wimbledon titles, six Australian Open titles, five US Open titles and one French Open title. He is also only one of the eight male tennis players to have achieved a Career Grand Slam. His achievements make him a truly indispensable player in the modern era. Yet, the question arises: what makes Roger Federer the success story that he is? Clearly, there must be an X factor propelling him to reach such heights in his career. That X factor can be attributed to his mental toughness which enables him to accept and conquer any situation.

We all know Federer as a tennis world champion, but did you know that he lost the the opening rounds of his first two Wimbledon tournaments in 1999 and 2000? Many players before him have also faced similar situations, but unlike them, he refused to give up. It is this ability to bounce back that has made all the difference in his career. It is said that battles are both won and lost in the mind.

Imagine a scenario where you are faced with a crisis and the decision you take can not only make or break your career but also impact the company you work for. In such a situation, you can succeed only if you are mentally strong. Our life is similar to the stock market and the investor. There are moments when an investor is propelled to buy or sell looking at the stock movements, but the one who analyses with a sound mind is able to make the right decisions. Mental toughness is not just about making logical decisions but also about overcoming adversities in life.

Each of us goes through phases when we feel anxious about the given circumstance. There is therefore a need to define a clear-cut strategy to segregate the inner game from the outer game. The latter refers to our external actions, whereas the former is representative of our conflicting thoughts and how we attain mastery over them. It is for the same reason that despite the same level of skills, on certain days a team emerges victorious, whereas on others, it is on the losing side. The true potential of an individual's capabilities can only be realized at the intersection of these two skill sets.

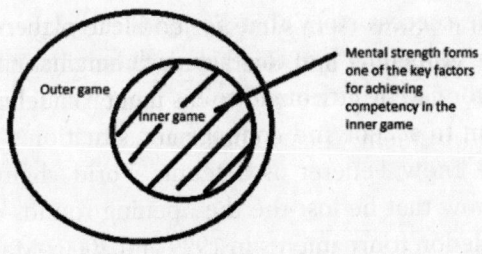

Mental Strength: Inner versus Outer Game

There is no doubt that being a master of the inner game has propelled Federer to achieve victories in the most testing conditions. Evidence in this regard can also be drawn with respect to the Australian Open final in 2018 when Federer defeated his opponent Marin Čilić over a five-setter (6-2, 6-7, 6-3, 3-6 and 6-1). The win was very significant, as it was the 20th Grand Slam for Federer, thereby making him the second-oldest player to win a Grand Slam at the age of 36 years and 173 days (Ken Rosewell being the oldest at 37 years, two months and one day). Owing to temperature conditions, the match was played under a closed roof.

On winning the match, Federer pretty much summed up his mental toughness when he said, 'I was surprised to hear they had the heat rule in place for a night match. I never heard that before. For me, it doesn't change anything.'[1]

It is important to lay emphasis on the part where he says that for him, it does not 'change anything'. It is impertinent to understand how differently Federer perceives things in comparison to others. External factors, like heat, did not seem to affect his performance. On the other hand, his rival Čilić had this to say about the match, 'Throughout the tournament I played all my matches outdoors, also preparing a hot day. Then first match for the final to play with the roof closed, it's difficult.'[2]

The conditions were same for both the players, yet it was how they perceived and dealt with them that made all the difference. Similarly, we too must make ourselves mentally strong and resilient to face challenges.

---

[1] 'Federer Wins Record 20th Grand Slam Title with Five-Set Win Over Cilic', Tennis, 28 January 2018, https://bit.ly/3BBMcET. Accessed on 13 September 2022.
[2] Ibid.

> *A corporate turnaround in this case can be aptly cited. Richard Teerlink, the former CEO of Harley-Davidson, took charge of the company when it had a market share of 15 per cent in the US and a reported loss of $15 million. Yet, through his focus on customer engagement, building world-class products and improving service, he was able to increase the company's share to 50 per cent of the US market, with a profitability of $1.7 billion, within eight years.*

Learning Tip: How we perceive a problem is key to finding its solution.

Federer returned to tennis with the 2017 Australian Open after a long break owing to an injury. Yet, he managed to push through to the finals.

In the finals, he was to face his arch-rival Rafael Nadal, who had won all six matches in the previous major tournaments between them. Yet, that day, Federer was able to get the better of Nadal in a five-set thriller. Neither the break nor the past history of losing to Nadal mattered to him. Federer defeated four top-10 players, including Nadal, to win the title. As against 2016, when he had to skip quite a few tournaments owing to an injury, 2017 saw him winning 54 matches, including seven major titles.

Because of a back problem, Federer was unable to enlist in the Swiss military, but he worked on his fitness so that he could perform on the court. There is much to learn from his resilience and mental toughness.

Business leaders too can build a culture of mental toughness in an organization. Just like any other skill, this too can be cultivated. When Federer started his career, he would often vent by throwing his racket. In an encounter with his rival Nadal in 2005 in Miami, Federer threw his racket on the floor in a huff and later justified it by stating that it helped him improve his game. This is in sharp contrast to the calm Federer that we see today. It is this calmness that helps him win sets that go into tie-breakers. Instead of emotionally reacting to a situation, we should have a mature response. This in turn helps in building a positive stream of thoughts and remove negativity. Building an attitude of 'Know, Can, Do' is of utmost importance.

It is equally important to make use of techniques such as visualization to control our mind and overcome self-doubt. Visualization is simply a mental rehearsal. When you create a mental image of what you want, your subconscious acts upon it.

There was a time when Federer had to undergo counselling to deal with his anger issues. In his own words, 'At 17, my family decided that I had to go to a psychologist, because I was so angry on the court. From that moment on, my growth has been constant.'[3] Today, he is one of the most calm, composed and benevolent players. This is reflected in the way he conducts himself on the court and also how he treats his fans, competitors and younger players. Regarding Federer's conduct, his arch-rival Nadal said: 'He's a good person, a fantastic player, and a great man on the court.'[4]

Learning Tip: It is important to have control over one's emotions to succeed in life.

It is equally important to understand and accept that obstacles

---

[3] Otway, Jack, 'Roger Federer: My Family Had to Stop Me Being So Angry After I Was Chased Off Court', *Express*, 21 November 2017, https://bit.ly/3eHNEwt. Accessed on 14 September 2022.

[4] Corpuz, Rachelle, 'Rafael Nadal on Roger Federer: "He's A Good Person, a Fantastic Player and a Great Man, On Court"', *International Business Times*, 24 October 2014.

are a part of life. In such scenarios, it is important to accept the situation and move ahead. Every time Federer is faced with a daunting task, he remembers his past experiences and the effort that he has put in so far. This thought provides him the much-needed comfort and mental strength to strive harder to achieve his goals.

Another important lesson to be learnt is that mental toughness allows an individual to bounce back from adversity. At 34, when Federer was ruled out for a period of six months owing to a knee injury, it was widely believed to be the end of his career. Yet, he bounced back to win the Australian Open for two consecutive years. If we are passionate about what we do, it propels us to work harder, which creates self-belief and, ultimately, mental toughness.

To emulate the same principles as Federer we need to follow a four-step strategy:

- Overcome pressure with a defined plan. This ensres the execution is as required.
- Create realistic expectations. This helps reduce unnecessary cause for worry.
- Build a strong team in doubles.
- Lead from the front.

Following these four simple steps helps an individual achieve his goals and remain focussed in any circumstances. This in turn helps build stronger organizations that are resolute enough to brave any storm.

On 16 September 2022, after 15,000 matches, 20 Grand Slams and a career spanning 24 years, Federer announced his retirement. Even while announcing his decision, his humility was there for all to see. In his own words, 'Tennis has treated me more generously than I ever would have dreamt, and now I must recognize when it is time to end my competitive career.'[5]

Roger Federer is undoubtedly one of the greatest tennis players of all time. He is a true inspiration. Let's hope he reconsiders his decision to retire and we can continue to cheer him on for many more years to come.

Roger Federer's Career Highlights over the Years

Tournament	Record accomplished
Grand Slams	20 men's Grand Slam singles titles
	31 men's Grand Slam finals
	All four Grand Slam finals in one season reached three times (2006-07, 2009)
	2+ men's Grand Slam titles per year six times (2004-07, 2009, 2017)
	3 men's Grand Slam titles per year three times (2004, 2006-07)
	2 consecutive years winning 3 titles (2006-07)
	4 consecutive years winning 2+ titles (2004-07)
	46 men's Grand Slam semifinals
	57 men's Grand Slam quarterfinals
	10 consecutive men's Grand Slam finals (2005-07)
	23 consecutive men's Grand Slam semifinals
	36 consecutive men's Grand Slam quarterfinals
	25 consecutive victories in quarterfinals
	79 men's Grand Slam tournament appearances
	7+ finals at three tournaments
	4+ consecutive finals at three tournaments

---

[5]Hamilton, Tom, 'Roger Federer Is Retiring from Tennis—But His Mark on the Sport Is Indelible', ESPN, 23 September 2022, https://bit.ly/3BT2Lw6. Accessed on 20 September 2022.

	6+ consecutive finals at two tournaments
	5 consecutive titles at two tournaments
	5+ titles at three tournaments
	6+ titles at two tournaments
	10 titles defended overall
	70+ match wins at all four tournaments
	85+ match wins at three tournaments
	100+ match wins at two tournaments
	40 consecutive match wins at two tournaments
	191 hard court match wins
	8+ titles on two different surfaces (hard and grass)
	12+ finals on two different surfaces (hard and grass)
	362 match wins
	421 matches played
ATP World Tour	24 consecutive tournament finals won
	24 consecutive match wins against top 10 opponents
	71 hard court titles
	56 consecutive hard court match victories
	24 ATP 500 series titles
	6+ titles at seven different tournaments
ATP Rankings	310 weeks as World No. 1
	237 consecutive weeks as World No. 1
	3 consecutive calendar years as wire-to-wire No. 1 (2005–07)
	Oldest player to be ranked No. 1
	15 years he held ranking in top 3
Wimbledon	8 men's singles titles

18

Understanding the Mind of a Strategist

Viswanathan Anand

In chess, knowledge is a very transient thing. It changes so fast that even a single mouse-slip sometimes changes the evaluation.

VISWANATHAN ANAND

In the 1995 Professional Chess Association's final match, Viswanathan Anand was due to play against Garry Kasparov, the defending champion and the best player of his generation. Chess enthusiasts across the country sat glued to the Doordarshan channel, where the game was being telecast for the first time. Anand moved the chess pieces on the observation deck of the 107th floor of the World Trade Center in New York City and hundreds of chess lovers moved their pieces on their chess boards, copying his moves, to analyse the game. The match started with eight straight draws. People watched with bated breath. None of the two grand masters were prepared to shift their focus from the chess pieces. It was in the ninth game in which Anand said 'checkmate'. People were overjoyed. The tension was palpable. In the next game, Kasparov bounced back with a magnificent move with the white pieces. Anand was back to square one. The most crucial point was in game 11, where Anand had a good advantage with his white pieces, but he overlooked a simple combination, giving Kasparov an easy win. Kasparov defeated Anand after 18 games, with four wins, one loss and 13 draws. 'Everyone has their nemesis. For me, it was clearly Kasparov. I don't think I want to make excuses for that,' Anand said in an interview after the match.[1]

Due to its national coverage across India, this game was analysed in depth by all. Anand was a promising player, but unfortunately at that time, he lacked the preparation needed for first-class chess. Today, years down the line, he is feared by his opponents for his top-class opening style. Anand is, in fact, synonymous with chess in India.

EARLY LIFE

Born in 1969 in the town of Mayiladuthurai, Tamil Nadu, to Krishnamurthy Viswanathan, a retired general manager of the Southern Railways and Sushila, a homemaker, Anand started learning chess at the age of six. The credit for that goes to his mother, who hailed from a family of lawyers where everyone played chess. She started playing chess with young Anand, who was a keen and fast learner. He learned the intricacies of the game in Philippines when his family moved there. There, a television show on puzzles used to be aired during school hours. His mother would note down the puzzles and when Anand got back from school, they would solve them together and send the solutions to the channel. Anand received many prizes from the show. Seeing his eagerness, his mother enrolled him in a chess club in Manila, where he used to win most of the competitions.

---

[1] 'Kasparov Crushes Anand with Insane Sicilian Najdorf', iChess, 12 October 2012, https://bit.ly/3LeUZjb. Accessed on 14 September 2022.

TURNING PROFESSIONAL

Given Anand's talent for the game, he soon achieved a meteoric rise and tasted national success at the young age of 14. In 1983, he won the National Sub-Junior Championship after scoring 9/9 points. The next year, he won his first norm for International Master after winning the Asian Junior Championship in Coimbatore. The same year, he made his debut in the national chess team and also his second norm for International Master in the 26th Chess Olympiad in Thessaloniki, Greece. The following year, he won the Asian Junior Championship again, but this time in Hong Kong, thus, becoming the youngest Indian to secure the title of International Master. He became the national chess champion at 16. He defended the title for two more years. He is a master of blitz chess (more commonly known as speed chess), and the first Indian to win the World Junior Chess Championship in 1987. The next year, he won the Shakti Finance International Chess Tournament in Coimbatore and became India's first grandmaster. At the young age of 18, Anand became the recipient of the fourth-highest civilian award in India, the Padma Shri.

In 1991, he won the Reggio Emilia chess tournament, finishing ahead of the then world champion Kasparov and former world champion Anatoly Karpov, thus breaking the chain of Russians being among the top chess players. In 2000, Anand won his first World Chess Championship title. In 2003, he won the World Rapid Chess Championship. Three years later, he became the fourth player in history to cross the 2,800 mark in Elo Ratings. In 2007, Anand won the World Chess Championships held in Mexico City (double-round robin format) against renowned players such as Vladimir Kramnik. He won the world championship titles again in 2008, 2010 and

2012. So, what was it that made him a 'mind master'? Let us analyse his life in depth and understand the reasons for his phenomenal success.

Anand seems to be extremely calm while making his moves on the chess board, but of course, like every warrior, there must be a turmoil brewing within. During his career, Anand has played the game first in his mind, strategically, before making the next move. He has earned the title of a grandmaster not just because of his speed and intelligence. His ability to analyse numerous possibilities and counter-possibilities and predict his opponent's next move is what makes him a winner.

> **Learning Tip:** When you are calm, you are more in control of your emotions. Your thinking process is unhindered and you are able to visualize numerous possibilities ahead.

Chalking out a clear and focussed strategy is imperative. Even battles are not fought without drawing a blueprint of the battleground and planning an attack or retreat strategy. A surgeon does not go into an operating room without mentally visualizing the procedure and preparing for the expected as well as the unexpected outcomes of the surgery.

The greatest weapon in the game of chess, as in life, is the brain and its thinking process. Our thoughts have the ability to push us towards the winning as well as the losing side. Just like chess, life is a game filled with obstacles and challenges. To successfully navigate through life, one must be open to embrace these challenges and turn them into advantages. Analysing Anand's playing style can give us some clarity in this perspective. He had a strategy of his own. For a successful strategist, the following qualities are important.

KEEPING THE MIND ALERT

In chess as well as in life, events are dynamic and fast. One has to be smart and prompt enough to catch the changes and react accordingly. Mental alertness is one of the most important qualities of a player. Engage in activities that require you to think, analyse and reason. This keeps the grey cells working. Just like muscles, the brain, too, needs to be stimulated to function well.

Most of the times, there are certain predictable moves and preplanned strategies in chess. Being in those situations again and again and having to practise the same moves over and over again can lead to monotony and boredom and the the brain loses focus. During such times, a single drifting thought may cause defeat. Anand tries different combinations to open or respond to similar situations on the chess board. This helps him exercise his brain cells to come up with new solutions and strategies. Similarly, one should not get stuck in a formula. A little bit of lateral thinking can bring out creativity in every step.

> **Learning Tip:** The brain changes throughout a person's life, modifying and adapting according to what one learns through experiences. Keeping the mind alert and active improves your decision-making and reaction time, which can further boost your mental capabilities.

In real life as well, companies now spend a fortune on innovation. Customers do not want the same solutions to a problem. When the demand is dynamic, one should keep one's mind alert at all times to look for opportunities and bring out-of-the-box solutions. An alert mind thinks faster and functions better at troubleshooting and innovating new solutions. An alert mind is devoid of intense emotions, irritating thoughts and distractions. When one has mental clarity, awareness increases. One gets a better sense of what is going on in life, the causes of problems, probable solutions and its possible outcomes.

BEING CONFIDENT

Confidence brings out a sense of greater self-worth, which means the more one has faith in their capabilities, the more valuable they feel. It eliminates self-doubt too. When we are confident, we are not afraid to step out of our comfort zone, learn new things and go beyond our current level of expertise and capability. Confidence provides freedom from fear and anxiety. It also removes all the mental toxins from the mind, thus making more energy available to concentrate on the game and plan ahead. Being confident provides more energy and motivation to pursue the things one loves. It eliminates overthinking and channelizes one's energy for better productivity.

> **Learning Tip:** When you are confident, you can achieve what you have already started out to.

Leaders who are confident in what they say and do are respected and followed by one and all. They are often open to new and different ideas and are not afraid to execute them. Anand describes the significance of confidence in his own words as: 'Confidence is very important, even pretending to be confident. If you make a mistake but do not let your opponent see what you are thinking then he may overlook the mistake.'

In the game of chess, being underconfident means playing more passive moves and shutting off the brain from trying new ones. Such moves are easy for an opponent to deal with. Tactics require confidence. Mental agility gives ideas, but execution requires confidence.

The game of chess helps one realize the consequences of one's ideas.

GAINING FROM THE OPPONENT'S ERRORS

In the game of chess as well as in life, where there is competition, one must be vigilant and learn from the mistakes others make. Often, an opponent's mistake can be your opportunity. When you see your opponent underperforming, be patient. Sooner or later, they will slip-up, rather create favourable conditions that will maximize their chance of making errors.

Napoleon Bonaparte said, 'Never interrupt your enemy when he is making a mistake.' It is a golden rule that if an opponent challenges you for a fight in a fit of rage, be it in an office, business, match or in any walk of life, learn to trade space for time. It may be best to refuse the fight. At times, it may infuriate the opponent more, causing them to make more mistakes. Lose battles, but concentrate on winning the war.

HAVING A FUTURISTIC VISION

A futuristic person is generative, he has the creative ability to solve today's problems and plan for the future. In any game, planning is the most crucial stage of developing a strategy. It is essential to plan the entire game with crucial moves and tricks beforehand. Studying the opponent, recognizing their behavioural pattern, weakness and strengths, and preparing some basic countermoves in advance give you an edge.

Well-known author Alan Lakein said, 'Planning is bringing the future into the present so that you can do something about it now.' To be ahead of your opponents, you need to see what they cannot see. You need to prepare before they have the slightest suspicion and you need to be completely prepared when they get the first hint of the problem. The Chinese philosopher Confucius said, 'A man who does not plan long ahead, will find trouble at his door.' Sun Tzu, Chinese general, military strategist, author and philosopher, said, 'Victorious warriors win first and then go to war, while defeated warriors go to war first and then seek to win.' Sun Tzu strongly advocated planning to the tee before going to battle.

Learning Tip: If you fail to prepare, you prepare to fail.

TAKING RISKS

Often, we see chess masters sacrifice the queen to gain a suitable position on their chess board, which allows them an easy victory. The queen, which is an important game piece, is to be kept safe till the very end. However, great chess players are willing to take the calculated risk of losing their important game pieces to turn the game in their favour towards the end.

Most chess players are trained using the same software, thus they are aware of the general winning moves and tricks. But those who are willing to try something different and somewhat risky create more complicated situations for their opponent to deal with and are more likely to win.

We all know Edward Jenner as the inventor of the small pox vaccine. But did you know that this experiment was a risk in itself? He observed that milkmaids did not suffer from the deadly disease of small pox, as most of them had already suffered from cowpox, which was a common cattle disease. He inoculated his gardener's son, James Phipps, with cowpox, which the boy suffered from and eventaully recovered. Jenner then inoculated Phipps with small pox germs. This was done without informed consent and would have posed a huge risk for Jenner and Phipps if something would have gone wrong. Fortunately for them, the experiment was a successs. Phipps did not suffer from small pox and the world got its small pox cure.

Taking risks does not mean indulging in recklesss activities, without any calculation or without taking into consideration the consequences. A risk is to be taken only after assessing its benefits as well as side effects. A calculated risk often helps one get ahead of their opponents, as it is a kind of innovation, which this fast-changing world welcomes.

> **Learning Tip:** Your appetite for risk shows how willing you are to put everything at stake in order to achieve your goal.

CONTROLLING ONE'S EMOTIONS

It is not very difficult to gauge when our oppotent is stressed. Stress is easily reflected on one's face and in one's body language. Most games are played in the mind before they actually start. Once the game is lost in the mind, it is lost in actuality as well. In any competition, stress is unavoidable. Sometimes, seeing a new crowd can make you nervous. At other times, reading about an opponent's previous performance or too much pressure from the coaches and the home crowd may cause one to be stressed.

Emotions of any kind need to be masked and kept under check. We cannot let our emotions get ahead of us. Exposing them means showing our opponents our vulnerabilities and giving them a psychological advantage. It is only when we have our emotions under control that we can play a stable and logical game. The same goes for life too. When we are emotional, we often make hasty decisions and say things that we end up regretting later. Anand has the ability to keep calm in tense moments even if a battle is going on inside.

> Learning Tip: When you react instead of responding, you let others take control over you and the situation. Remember, respond, never react.

In today's world, emotional quotient (EQ) is more valued than intelligence quotient (IQ). A person with a better ability to deal with emotions, keeping oneself calm and composed, can be a better decision-maker and hence a better leader. Such people do not let negativity cloud their judgement. Those who can keep their personal and professional lives separate and not allow the problems of one affect the other succeed in the long run. On the other hand, a person who is too emotional tends to be passive-aggressive, harbours a victim mentality—constantly blaming co-workers, co-players and the situation—is not open to feedback and leads a dissociated life.

Anand's Major Achievements over the Years

Years	Achievement
2000–02	FIDE World Chess Champion
2000–06	World Blitz Chess Champion
2003–09, 2017	World Rapid Chess Champion
2007–13	Classical World Chess Champion

19

Facing Challenges Head-On

Nadia Comăneci

I don't run away from a challenge because I am afraid. Instead, I run toward it because the only way to escape fear is to trample it beneath your foot.

NADIA COMĂNECI

The name Nadia Elena Comăneci immediately brings a picture of perfection to the mind. In 1976, she was the first gymnast to score a perfect 10 at the Olympic Games when she was all of 14. She won as many as nine Olympic medals and four World Artistic Gymnastics medals. Nadia is one of the world's best-known gymnasts, someone who redefined perfection and competitiveness. She was able to stretch the boundaries and create benchmarks in her own way. In simple terms, she was her own competitor. Gymnastics, as a sport, is extremely competitive and requires the athlete to possess great strength, agility, flexibility and rhythm. Nadia's domination in the field of gymnastics despite the political hurdles she faced is reflective of her mental strength. Being born in a communist regime, Nadia continued her pursuit of excellence regardless of the strict monitoring and restrictions she was subjected to as an athlete.

She brought much popularity to the sport. She was the first

gymnast to successfully perform an aerial walkover, an aerial cartwheel back handspring flight series and a double twist dismount. Her spirit of competitiveness can be gauged from the fact that she always aspired to give her best performance regardless of her health and other factors.

EARLY LIFE

Nadia Comăneci was born on 12 November 1961 in Onești, a small town in Romania, to Gheorghe and Stefania-Alexandrina Comăneci. Right from her childhood, she was very active and full of energy, hence her mother enrolled her for gymnastics. Her parents separated when she was very young. She began practising gymnastics when she was just three years old as part of a local team called Flacara. By the age of six, she knew she wanted to be a gymnast. At an age when most kids are not aware of what they want to achieve in life or what their goal is, Nadia's focus was solely on becoming a gymnast.

At the age of six, she was coincidentally spotted by Béla Károlyi, an established coach who was looking for young gymnasts with potential. The early years she spent training were like an investment for her career. The more she practised, the better she got. She was one of the first students to be enrolled in the gymnastics school established in Onești by Károlyi and his wife. In the next two years, she trained very hard and quickly became a name to reckon with in local competitions. Even at such a young age, she trained almost three hours a day. In the initial competitions she participated in, she was somewhat imbalanced and even fell off the apparatus a couple of times, but that only made her more resolute.

Learning Tip: A strong belief system and the willingness to work hard is a recipe for success.

In 1969, Nadia competed in her first official event as a seven-year-old at the Romanian National Junior Championship. She finished 13th in the event. Did she let the initial failure affect her? No. On the contrary, she trained harder, as the event made her more aware of the level of competition she would be facing going forward. The following year, she won the same event, becoming the youngest gymnast to achieve that milestone. Nadia's winning mantra was simple: never give up. She refused to accept defeat as the final outcome. This is an important learning for us: no failure is permanent and if one works hard enough, they can be successful.

In 1971, she debuted in an international competition, a dual junior meet between Romania and Yugoslavia, and won her first title while also contributing to a gold medal for the team. At 12 years of age, she was practising eight hours a day, six days a week with her coach. Her story is a perfect example of practice makes perfect. It is through practise that one can gain consistency and also experiment with developing techniques. Before participating in any competition, one needs to perfect the techniques. We often tend to overlook the efforts that go into making a champion and pass it off as an overnight success.

Nadia's first major international success came at the age of 13, when she nearly swept the 1975 European Women's Artistic Gymnastics Championships in Norway, where she won all the events except the floor event. Her success story continued at the Champions All competition and the Romanian National Championships the same year. The pre-Olympic event was held in Montreal, where she won the all-around and balance beam golds, while the Soviet gymnast Nellie Kim won the other events. This was the beginning of a major rivalry.

Another major event in Nadia's life was the 1976 American Cup, where she met American gymnast Bart Connor, who she later married, for the first time. They met again at the 1976 Olympic Games. The American Cup was significant as Nadia was able to make her mark by scoring a perfect 10 for her vault in the preliminary stage and the floor exercise route in the final of the all-around competition. A perfect 10 score signifies no deduction in gymnastics and the feat had not been achieved earlier in the American Cup. This was the precursor to Nadia's performance at the Olympic Games.

HISTORY CREATED

Nadia created history at the Montreal Olympic Games when she was awarded the first perfect 10 for her routine on uneven bars. The Olympic scoreboard manufacturer Omega SA had not factored in that someone can score a perfect 10 and the scoreboard only represented a score of upto 9.9. Hence, the score of perfect 10 appeared as 1.00 on the scoreboard. It was clearly an act of redefining human limits for the game.[1]

Her performance was more remarkable considering the burst of energy the event requires in a span of mere 23 seconds. In fact, she used her hands just like any other part of her body, with remarkable balance and grace. In the same games, she also repeated the feat of scoring perfect 10s six additional times, indicating her consistency at the highest level of competition. During the competition, she won gold in the events of the individual all-around, the balance beam and uneven bars. Her performance also fetched the team the all-around silver medal and bronze as part of the floor exercise.

Nadia's feat of scoring a perfect 10 was also repeated in

---

[1] Biswal, Sattwik, 'This Day That Year: Nadia Comaneci Makes History at 1976 Montreal Olympics', *India.com*, 18 July 2017, https://bit.ly/3daKReQ. Accessed on 14 September 2022.

the same games by Kim in the vault event. But the latter was 19 at that time, unlike Nadia, who was only 14 at the time of scoring a perfect 10. In the previous Olympic Games, Soviet gymnast Olga Korbut had won four gold medals, but Nadia's performance completely overshadowed everyone else's performance. The world ushered in a teenager as the queen of gymnastics. Owing to her performance, she was awarded the Sickle and Hammer Gold medal and became the youngest Romanian to be named a Hero of Socialist Labour. Her popularity can be gauged by the fact that when an instrumental song titled 'Cotton's Dream' got linked to Nadia's performance in the Olympic Games, the composers of the song renamed it 'Nadia's Theme' in her honour.

Nadia is the first Romanian and youngest gymnast to win the Olympic all-around title. Ironically, her record can never be broken. The present rules of Olympic Games state a minimum age requirement of 16 years for competing in the games. At the time when Nadia competed, the age criteria had been 14. Clearly, some remarkable feats are meant to stand the test of time, this is one such record. Her achievements in the 1976 Olympic Games are pictured in the entrance area of Madison Square Garden in Manhattan (New York), where she is shown presenting her perfect beam exercise. The Romanian government also issued postal stamps in her honour—a remarkable achievement for a young gymnast indeed. However, her passion for gymnastics mattered more to her than anything else as can be judged by the fact that after celebrating for a couple of days, she always got back to practice.

Had Nadia scored the perfect 10 just once, there might have been questions about her credibility. However, achieving the perfect score as many as seven times proves beyond doubt that she was the best gymnast in the world. One time can be passed off as a fluke but not every time. Similarly, a star performer in a corporate organization is one who can boast of consistent performance.

Learning Tip: Consistency is what separates the best from the rest.

In 1977, Nadia successfully defended her title of all-around champion at the European Championship. In addition to this, she also won a gold medal in uneven bars. She would have won in balance beam too had the Romanian team not walked out of the games immediately after Nadia's performance. The decision to walk out was taken by the Romanian Federation, as they found the scoring methodologies being adopted to be inadequate and unfair.[2] Following the games, the Romanian Gymnastics Federation sent Nadia to train at a sports complex in Bucharest after removing her coach.

One has to look at the political scenario prevalent in Romania at that time. The country was being governed by a totalitarian regime under the leadership of Nicolae Ceaușescu. There was wide-scale surveillance of citizens, and Nadia, being a public figure, needed to be kept under a watch. Hence, the deliberate attempt to change her coach and control her life. This, however, led to grave mental anxiety and depression for Nadia. She even consumed bleach and attempted suicide: something she admitted much later. This was around the same time when her parents got divorced and her coaches were separated from her.

Depression can often affect even the best of talent. It is important to have strong self-belief and faith in one's abilities.

---

[2] 'Romanian Gymnastic Federation Expresses Concern', GYMN, https://bit.ly/3xBI31i. Accessed on 20 September 2022.

Just as pure gold is extracted only after applying heat and pressure, our true character is shaped only when we face extreme adversities.

> **Learning Tip:** Giving up on life is never a solution. Regardless of the adversities, one should always maintain high self-esteem and self-belief.

In the 1978 World Championships, Nadia was seven inches taller and 21 pounds heavier than she had been in the 1976 Olympics, when she had weighed only 86 pounds. Her performance was a bit lacklustre. She won the world title in beam event and silver in the vault event, but she lost her balance in the uneven bars, managing only to secure the fourth position. As a result of the debacle at the 1978 World Championships, Nadia was allowed to train at Károlyi's school. The following year, she won her third consecutive European all-around title, becoming the first gymnast in the history of the sport to do so.

Nadia's will and dedication towards the sport was for all to see in the 1979 World Championships. Before the commencement of the games, she was hospitalized for blood poisoning from a cut on her wrist. In spite of her doctors advising against it, she got herself discharged from the hospital and competed in the games. Not just that, she managed a score of 9.95, which ensured her team its first gold medal. Post her performance, she spent several days recovering in the hospital and also had to undergo a minor surgery for the infected hand. At such a young age, she risked her health to pursue her dream of bringing glory to her country. It speaks volumes of her commitment as an individual and athlete.

Nadia's fighting spirit is similar to that of entrepreneurs who refuse to give up on their dream. They toil harder each time an investor refutes their idea and continue till they succeed.

Learning Tip: Dreams can turn into reality if we are willing to work hard towards achieving them.

THE TURNING POINT

The 1980 Summer Olympics was a challenging point in Nadia's career. The Olympics were being held in Moscow. Owing to the Soviet invasion of Afghanistan, several countries, led by the US, boycotted the games. On the other hand, the Romanian government looked at it as an opportunity to participate in the 'first all-Communist games,' as most of the western democracies (62 countries in total) were boycotting the games. Nadia's major competitors in gymnastics were all from the Soviet Union and it was a new challenge for her to compete on their home turf. In her memoir, *Letters to a Young Gymnast*, she compares the games to walking into the lion's den.[3] She won two gold medals (balance beam and floor exercise) and two silver medals in team and individual all-around. However, once again, scoring discrepancies cropped up, which resulted in public protests led by her coach, Károlyi. These were captured on television, which the Romanian government considered humiliating.

Just as Nadia was able to perform well in Moscow regardless of the adverse situation, we too should also strive hard to give our best performance each time we are presented with an opportunity.

In 1981, the Romanian Gymnastics Federation informed Nadia that she would be part of a US tour named 'Nadia 81'.

---

[3]Comăneci, Nadia, *Letters to a Young Gymnast*, Basic Books, 2011, p. 98.

It was during this trip that she again met fellow American gymnast Conner. However, during this tour, her coaches Béla and Marta Károlyi defected to the US. They wanted her to join them, but she preferred to stay back in Romania.

THE 1984 SUMMER OLYMPICS

Nadia could not participate in the 1984 Olympics, as the government did not allow her to. In her memoir *Letters to a Young Gymnast*, she writes that an agreement was reached between the US and the Romanian government that the former would not allow any more defectors going ahead. She was not allowed to speak to her former coaches and was kept under strict surveillance by the Romanian authorities.

Whenever we face any adverse situation in life, we should remember that good times are not far away. This will motivate us to strive harder and prepare ourselves. Instead of focussing our energy on things we cannot control, we should try to make the most of things that are under our control. Nadia could have competed and won in the 1984 Olympics, yet she was forced to retire owing to the prevalent political situation in her country.

After the event, she was banned from travelling outside the country except for few selected trips to Russia and Cuba. This eventually led to her official retirement at the age of 23. One of the primary reasons for this was her inability to lead a normal life in Romania. In her memoir, she mentions the following: 'It was also insulting that a normal person in Romania had the chance to travel, whereas I could not [...] when my gymnastics career was over, there was no longer any need to keep me happy.'[4]

---

[4]Salen, Erika, 'Nadia Comăneci- Romania's National Treasure', *Herald Weekly*, 30 July 2022, https://bit.ly/3f315Yf. Accessed on 20 September 2022.

On 27 November 1989, she, along with a group of other Romanians, defected to the US via Hungary and Austria. While many may question her loyalty to her country, it could be argued that if she had actually wanted to defect, she could have easily done so in 1981, with her coaches.

She faced several hardships, yet she loved her country. She survived an authoritarian regime and managed to leave an indelible mark on the world of gymnastics. Each time she fell, she picked herself up and tried to score a perfect 10. It is the same spirit with which all of us should strive for excellence in our personal and professional lives. How we respond to a situation defines who we truly are.

PERSONAL LIFE

After defecting to the US, Nadia decided to help Conner, who was an Olympic gold medallist, in setting up his gymnastics school. The couple were together for four years before they got married in Romania. The wedding took place in 1996 and was telecast live on television across the country. Even her reception was held in the former presidential palace in the capital city of Bucharest. By that time, Romania was a very different country compared to the one she had left behind. Communism had ceased to exist and Romania was an independent country without Soviet influence.

Post her retirement and marriage, she has been serving as the honorary president of the Romanian Gymnastics Federation, the honorary president of the Romanian Olympic Committee, the sports ambassador of Romania and a member of the International Gymnastics Federation Foundation. Along with her husband, she manages as many as five ventures along with a sports equipment company. She has been actively involved in raising funds for children's clinics in Bucharest and, along with her husband, is also involved with Special Olympics. Despite her age, she has continued her passion towards the sport in whichever way she can.

Regardless of the adversities she faced in her life, Nadia is known for her indomitable spirit and for always striving to give her best in a competition. She is reputed for her clean technique and her ability to remain calm and stoic in the face of competition. This is an important lesson that all of us should try to emulate and adopt in our lives.

Nadia Comăneci's Major Recognitions over the Years

- 1975: The United Press International Athlete of the Year Award
- 1976: The United Press International Athlete of the Year Award Hero of Socialist Labour, Associated Press Athlete of the Year and BBC Overseas Sports Personality of the Year
- 1983: The Olympic Order
- 1990: International Women's Sports Hall of Fame
- 1993: International Gymnastics Hall of Fame
- 2004: The Olympic Order

20

Competing against Oneself

Sergey Bubka

I love the pole vault because it is a professor's sport. One must not only run and jump, but one must think. Which pole to use, which height to jump, which strategy to use. I love it because the results are immediate and the strongest is the winner. Everyone knows it. In everyday life that is difficult to prove.[1]

SERGEY BUBKA

Pole vaulting is an extremely challenging track and field event in which vaulting athletes choose the height at which they would like to enter the competition. They have three attempts to achieve that height, after which, they progress to the next height, which then becomes the next target to clear. On three successive missed attempts to achieve the target, the athlete is eliminated from the competition and the highest height attained is considered the result. In a sport like pole vaulting, where success is based on raising the bar each time the athlete takes the field, one man kept doing it over and over again, breaking his own world record

---

[1]Fernando, Shemal, 'Sergey Bubka Broke the World Record 35 Times', *Sunday Observer*, 12 December 2021, https://bit.ly/3BpghYo. Accessed on 8 September 2022.

35 times! That man is none other than Sergey Bubka, who is regarded as the greatest pole vaulter of all time. He is the only athlete in the world to have won six successive world championships.

EARLY LIFE

Bubka was born in the Soviet city of Voroshilovgrad (in modern-day Ukraine) in 1963. His father, Nazar Bubka, was a member of the Soviet Army, while his mother, Valentina, worked in a hospital. As his father was part of the military, he believed in instilling strict discipline in his children from an early age. This went on to play an important role in shaping young Bubka's discipline and focus. He started his sporting career as a sprinter and long jumper before being introduced to pole vaulting at the age of nine by a friend when he joined a vaulting club. The coaches at the club were initially reluctant to have him and felt that he should start training after he was 12 years of age. However, his friend kept insisting till Bubka was given the opportunity to start his training. It was there that he discovered his love for the sport. In his own words, 'It sort of happened by accident but I was comfortable, and once I had started I never considered giving up.'[2]

Even though his father wanted him to quit the club, Bubka continued to pursue his interest. It is important to stand your ground for something that you love and not cave in under pressure. In fact, being passionate about our goal coupled with our commitment can be described as the perfect recipe for success. In short, passion plus commitment equals to excellence.

---

[2]Satish, A.K.S., et al., 'Kohli, Frankel, Serena ... The Untouchables', *Gulf News*, 26 October 2018, https://bit.ly/3xGEWp0. Accessed on 21 September 2022.

During his stint at the club, several coaches recognized Bubka's talent for pole vaulting. It was there that he first met his coach Vitaly Petrov and started training with him from the age of 11. When he was 15 years of age, his parents got divorced. So, he went to live with Petrov in the city of Donetsk. The duo formed a formidable partnership that lasted 16 years, till 1990, when Petrov moved to Italy. During this period, Bubka rose from being a virtually unknown athlete to a world champion. Petrov later went on to coach other world champions such as Yelena Isinbayeva, Giuseppe Gibilisco and Fabiana Murer.

If we consider the circumstances Bubka was under as a 15-year-old, it is commendable what he managed to achieve. Under such circumstances, anyone would have given up hope and lost focus, but they only made Bubka mentally stronger and more resilient. The role Petrov played in Bubka's life was immensely instrumental, particularly towards the later years of his career. Petrov was more than a coach to Bubka, he was a mentor, and above all, family. Coaching and mentoring are very similar, as they both encourage communication, honest feedback and self-improvement. However, the role of a coach is more important, as he guides an individual to achieve his potential and is not limited to sharing experiences as in mentoring. However, the best coaches are the ones who combine both coaching and mentoring.

Learning Tip: Find a life coach who can guide you to achieve your goals.

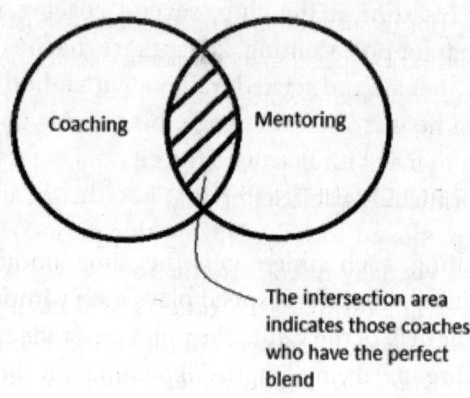

Importance of Being a Mentor as a Coach

Apart from Petrov's guidance, it was a strong sporting culture in the former Soviet Union that aided Bubka's phenomenal success. Achievement in sports was a matter of national pride and upon creating world records, athletes were given recognition by the government. Moreover, owing to the ongoing Cold War with the US, sports, and particularly performance at the Olympics, were seen as a matter of superiority and victory for the nation. According to Bubka, he even went to military camps to practise, as there were proper sports facilities available there. Although military camps are highly restrictive, he was willing to take the risk. Risk and rewards are always proportional to each other. The more the risk, the higher the reward. It was those additional hours of practice that made all the difference. From being a good sprinter, Bubka became a world champion.

Every entrepreneur's story too is about taking risks and about stepping out of the comfort zone of a stable job. One must take calculated risks that are necessary for success.

> **Learning Tip:** To succeed in your career, you must look at developing a risk appetite and evaluate each opportunity in terms of risk and rewards.

THE ART OF POLE VAULTING

In pole vaulting, each athlete gets the same amount of time to take the jump. Therefore, speed plays a very important role along with the grip of the vault. The poles are made of fibreglass or carbon fibre in varying lengths depending on the stature of the athlete. However, as a safety precaution, it is recommended that the athletes not use poles with ratings below their weight. This is to prevent the breakage of the pole when it bends to create vertical propulsion. In terms of the science behind the sport, it aims at converting the energy produced by the run ($E=0.5mv^2$, where m is the mass of the athlete and v refers to the velocity) into vertical propulsion ($E=mgh$, where m is the mass of the athlete, g the gravitational pull and h is the height jumped by the athlete). Assuming that there is no loss of energy, the height that a pole vaulter can jump is equal to $v^2/2g$, thereby implying that speed remains the most critical aspect. There are six steps that the athlete takes in order to execute the jump perfectly:

- **Approach:** During this stage, the athlete sprints so as to maximize the speed and to get into the right position for take-off.
- **Plant and take-off:** Approximately three steps from the final step, the vaulter has to lower the pole and get ready for vertical propulsion by planting his pole in a metallic pit known as the box. The goal is to convert the kinetic energy from the run to the potential energy

of the jump with minimal loss of energy.
- **Swing up:** This step involves the athlete swinging the trail leg forward and rowing the pole.
- **Extension:** This refers to the extension of the hips upwards with outstretched legs. Once this step is executed, the pole begins to recoil and pushes the vaulter upwards.
- **Turn:** In this phase, the athlete turns their body 180 degrees towards the pole and angles their body towards the bar.
- **Fly-away:** In this stage, the athlete releases the pole and executes their jump.

If we consider the dynamics of the steps involved, it requires tremendous coordination and skill, such as holding the pole in the right place, ensuring the correct thrust and initiating the jump at the correct moment. It is as much a sport of speed and physical strength as it is of timing. Bubka started his career as a sprinter and a long jumper and was able to combine those skill sets to emerge successful in pole vaulting.

In many ways, it is similar to how cross-functional teams work in an organization with employees combining multiple skills to excel at work. In today's work environment, most of us combine multiple skills to arrive at the desired result. This sport as a discipline is no different.

It is worth noting here that one of the main reasons for Bubka's success was his ability to grip the pole higher than most athletes. The technique came to be known as the Petrov-Bubka Pole Vault Model. It helped Bubka continuously put energy into the pole while rising towards the bar which, in turn, enabled him to exploit the recoil of the pole and exert more energy during the jump. Their experimentation, challenging the limits of the sport, was based on smart innovation, which resulted in significant dividends. Just as Petrov and Bubka developed this technique to improve the height of the jump, we too should focus on innovation.

It plays an important role in every aspect of our lives today. In order to stay relevant and ahead in an ever-changing world, we need to innovate and do things differently. The same methods and execution will only yield the same results.

Innovating at our workplace is not just about improving profit margins but also about delivering greater value to the end customers. This, in turn, helps build a differentiated product. For example, Domino's Pizza differentiates itself not just in terms of taste but also in their service delivery model of 30 minutes or free.

MANY FIRSTS

Bubka's career graph is a clear marker of self-development and continuous improvement. He broke the world record 35 times, which included 17 outdoor and 18 indoor world records, during his career.[3] He pushed the bar higher each time and created new benchmarks for others to emulate. He set his first world record of 5.85 metres on 26 May 1984 which he bettered to 5.88 metres just a week later, and then to 5.90 metres a month later. He cleared 6 metres for the first time on 13 July 1985 in Paris. Most athletes considered this height unattainable, but Bubka did not let such negative thoughts deter his ambition. In 1994, he clinched the outdoor world record of 6.14 metres, which had been unchallenged and unsurpassed for a period of 26 years (approximately 19 years

---

[3]Gibson, Paul, 'The Strange Evolution of the Pole Vault World Record: From Bubka to Lavillenie', *The Guardian*, 16 February 2015, https://bit.ly/3xa4YRd. Accessed on 9 September 2022.

after his official retirement, before it was eventually broken by Swedish pole vaulter Armand Duplantis in 2020)!

The benchmarks we set are important tools to measure success with. They help analyse how we measure up to competition and if our goals are realistic. It tells us if we are good enough to compete with others having similar skill sets. However, competing against oneself requires tremendous passion and motivation to continue the journey towards self-improvement. If we analyse Bubka's appetite for creating his own benchmarks, the same can be replicated by each one of us by following these six key steps:

- Determine: Analyse your strengths by introspecting and start working upon them by following a defined routine.
- Understand: Try to get insight on your competition by observing what they do better and how you can improve.
- Aim: Start aiming for a target in your mind and visualize how you can achieve it.
- Communicate: Start preparing yourself and seek guidance from your friends and family.
- Improve: Focus on principles of continuous self-improvement.
- Evaluate: Check if you are on the right path and whether you will achieve your goal.

Bubka revolutionized the game of pole vaulting. He was faster and stronger than any of his peers. His technique, first used by the Swede Kjell Isaksson, allowed him to load the pole with more energy than his rivals. This helped him to efficiently use the recoil action to swing his body up and over the bar. According to Belarussian–Australian pole vaulter Dmitriy

Markov, 'Bubka does not jump, he flies. Everyone else jumps but if you want to match him you must be prepared to fly.'[4] Bubka's contract with Nike which offered him pay-outs in the range of $40,000 (according to estimates) each time he broke his record provided him the necessary financial incentive to keep excelling.[5] His dominance in the sport was so significant that no sponsor was willing to offer the traditional win bonuses, as he was expected to win each time he competed.

Our true competition is only with ourselves. We can fail sometimes, but as long as we have tried our best, failures should not impact us. Bubka, despite his dominance, could only win one Olympic gold medal in the 1988 Seoul Olympics. He had to miss the 1984 Olympics, as the Soviet Union boycotted the games. In 1992, he was considered a favourite but could not clear a single bar in the final competition. During the 1996 Atlanta Olympics, he was forced to pull out owing to an injury to his right Achilles tendon. In the 2000 Sydney Olympics, he did not qualify for the finals. He even lamented after the injury in 1996 that the Olympics are not meant for him.

If we look at his failures in the Olympics, we see a struggling athlete. Yet, behind this struggle lies a person who won six consecutive World Championships (1983–97) and created the world record of 6.14 metres when most critics had written him off. In the 1997 World Championships, he created a new championship record of 6.01 metres at the age of 34 when most people believed that he was past his prime.

Bubka could have easily given up after the 1992 Olympics or when he was unable to participate in the 1996 Olympics, but he carried on building a legacy. He believed in himself.

---

[4]"Bubka, Sergei', Encyclopedia.com, https://bit.ly/3qplvgl. Accessed on 9 September 2022.
[5]Ibid.

In a similar manner, as individuals, we too should believe in our own abilities. Our resilience in the face of adversity is what truly defines our character. We must not be afraid to embrace failure, as only then can we learn the true value of success and how to handle it. We should challenge ourselves continuously to keep improving and focus on our long-term goals. If we consider Bubka's failure in the Olympic Games, he was candid enough to admit while also expressing gratitude for the success that he achieved. In his own words, 'I cannot complain, I had a wonderful career, but there should have been more Olympic gold medals than one.'[6] We should have a positive outlook even when things are not going our way. This helps us focus and deliver optimum results in the long run. It is important to be mentally strong, resilient and never give up.

> **Learning Tip:** Have strong self-belief. This helps us focus on our long-term goals and not be disappointed with short-term setbacks.

When, in 2014, Bubka's record was finally broken by French pole vaulter Renaud Lavillenie at the Pole Vault Stars meeting in Donetsk, the former, who was in the audience, got to his feet to greet his successor. The indoor world record of 6.15 metres had been unbroken 21 years. Although it was only the indoor record that was broken, owing to the rule change in 2000 by the International Association of Athletics Federations (IAAF, now known as World Athletics; Rule 260.18a), the world records can be set in facilities with or without roof. Thus, Lavillenie's achievement was considered the official record for both outdoor and indoor. The duo shares an excellent relationship, and Bubka, in an interview, had this to say about his record

---

[6]'Academy Member: Sergey Bubka', Laureus, https://bit.ly/3TPoADQ. Accessed on 9 September 2022.

being broken: 'When you are an athlete and competing, when you lose the record it's different. You work and try to get it back. But when you retire, it's something you cannot control. It's not yours honestly. I would say this belongs to [the] sport.'[7]

Bubka could have argued that his outdoor record was still intact, but he was gracious enough to look at the bigger picture and how it will benefit the sport. In a similar manner, we should always respect those who are talented, even if they are competing with us. There should be healthy competition based on mutual respect.

LIFE BEYOND POLE VAULTING

At the age of 21, Bubka married gymnast Lilia Tutunik. They have two sons Vitaliy (named after his coach) and Sergey Jr (a professional tennis player). According to him, 'My family is a reflection of my life and they make me very proud. My wonderful wife, a former athlete as well, is strong and wise and provides great support for us all. She shares my passion about the importance of sport for society.'[8] There is no doubt that without a supportive life partner, he would not have been able to focus on his sporting career. One of the most important decisions in life is choosing the right life partner, as we need mental and moral support at all times.

One can only become a true champion in any sport if there is strong passion towards the game. Post-retirement as well, Bubka continued pursuing his passion. His association with the

---

[7] Alvares, Rohan, 'The World Record Is Not Yours, It Belongs to Sport: Sergey Bubka', *The Times of India*, 19 January 2018, https://bit.ly/3FYUCc9. Accessed on 10 November 2022.

[8] John, G., 'Dil Mange More – the Magis', G. Jon's Page, https://bit.ly/3S2TMy2. Accessed on 21 September 2022.

International Olympic Committee dates back to 1996, when he was elected member of the Athletes' Commission. He has served as the president of the National Olympic Committee in Ukraine. He has been involved with the IAAF since 2001 and is presently its senior vice president. He has also served as a member of the Ukrainian parliament and as the prime minister's advisor for youth, culture and sports. He founded the Sergey Bubka Sports Club, which provides training and support to hundreds of young athletes.

Bubka is actively involved in several social causes through his association with the World Health Organization, including providing support to child victims of the Chernobyl nuclear disaster and promoting the fight against tuberculosis. He received the 'UNESCO Champion for Sport' in 2003 for his role in promoting sports and encouraging disadvantaged children through sports.

There are very few sports personalities who have not only excelled in sports but also led a model life outside it, and Bubka is one of them. We should always prioritize our family in spite of leading a hectic lifestyle. Furthermore, we should always try to give back to society in whichever manner possible. It is not the size of our contribution that matters but rather our willingness to make it. Just like Bubka, all of us can improve our skills and work towards creating benchmarks for others to emulate, defying age and adversities. It is our passion and willingness to work hard that eventually makes our dreams a reality.

Sergey Bubka's Performance in World Championships

Year	Venue	Position	Winning height (metres)
1983	Helsinki	1st	5.70
1987	Rome	1st	5.85
1991	Tokyo	1st	5.95
1993	Stuttgart	1st	6.00
1995	Gothenburg	1st	5.92
1997	Athens	1st	6.01

21

Leading from the Front

M.S. Dhoni

If you don't really have a dream, you can't really push yourself; you don't really know what the target is.

M.S. DHONI

Leadership is about inspiring others to reach their goals. In the world of sports, and in particular in a team sport, it involves driving a team towards a shared goal—victory. In many ways, it is identical to running a business, as it also involves motivating employees towards achieving a common target. Now imagine the leader himself is as young and novice as his team members and has been tasked with bringing in success for the team. It will be quite an uphill task, you have to admit. Yet, it was under similar circumstances that M.S. Dhoni took over the reins of the Indian cricket team and built it into a powerhouse of world cricket.

Cricket is not just a game in our country; it is a religion of sorts and cricketers are worshipped like gods. To his credit, it was Dhoni who started the trend of small-town boys making it big on the world stage of cricket. In the 2007 ICC T20 World Cup, the Indian team comprised many young and inexperienced players. Dhoni was the pioneer behind leading this young team to victory. He knew when to capitalize on whose strength and use it to the team's advantage. This victory came on the heels of India exiting the 50-over World Cup in the group stages earlier that same year. Later on, Dhoni led the team to victory in the 2011 World Cup thus ending a 28-year World Cup drought. Today, Dhoni is regarded as one of the best finishers of the game and one of the finest captains the sport has seen. So, what is it that makes him so unique and different? Let us find out.

EARLY LIFE

Mahendra Singh Dhoni was born in Ranchi in the Indian state of Jharkhand. His father Pan Singh Dhoni worked in a junior management position in MECON Limited (formerly known as Metallurgical & Engineering Consultants Limited), and his mother Devaki Devi was a homemaker. He is the youngest among his siblings. Dhoni's simple upbringing played a major role in shaping his humble and down-to-earth nature. From his early childhood, he admired Australian wicketkeeper Adam Gilchrist and former Indian captain Sachin Tendulkar. As a sportsperson, his initial interest was in football and tennis, and he represented at the club and district levels in both the sports. It was during a practice session for goalkeeping at his school that his coach noticed his skills and felt he had the potential to be an excellent wicketkeeper. Even though Dhoni had not played much cricket prior to this and used to play football, he excelled with his skills and became the regular wicketkeeper for the local club. From Class 10 onwards, Dhoni started focussing more on cricket, pursuing it wholeheartedly.

If we look at his initial trajectory, he was able to adapt quickly to the new role and excel at it. He made use of his skills as a goalkeeper to master wicketkeeping. In a similar manner, we too should look at adapting our skill sets to suit new opportunities. Adaptability, which combines the elements of flexibility and versatility, is a key component in succeeding. Flexibility is the ability accept changes, whereas versatility is our ability to execute the task.

Learning Tip: Be open to change and willing to accept new challenges to grow in your career.

One of the most significant influences in Dhoni's early career was Deval Sahay, who selected him to play for Central Coalfields Limited (CCL). He was also instrumental in Dhoni's selection to the Bihar team. In fact, his experience of playing with the public-sector unit (PSU) played an important role in shaping him as a better cricketer. In 2006, Dhoni himself remarked in an interview: '...my innings with Central Coalfields Limited (CCL) in Ranchi taught me the importance of discipline [...] I played for them from 1998-2002 and punctuality, for example, was a feature of that experience... I'm thankful to the PSU and the organisation's Mr Debal [*sic*] Sahay.'[1] During this time, Dhoni also worked with the Indian Railways as a travelling ticket examiner at the Kharagpur station, West Bengal. Ironically, it was the same time that India made it to the finals of the 2003 World Cup and lost to Australia. It would have definitely made a significant difference, had Dhoni been a part of that team.

Dhoni's consistent performance in the Ranji Trophy, Deodhar Trophy and Duleep Trophy resulted in his selection to India A Team's tour of Zimbabwe and Kenya in 2004. In the tri-nation tournament in Kenya comprising India A, Pakistan A and Kenya, Dhoni scored a massive 362 runs in six innings,

---

[1]'Dhoni's Appeal to Corporates, PSUs–India "Keeper Seeks Support for Emerging Cricketers"', *The Telegraph Online*, 23 September 2006, https://bit.ly/3x5BIv3. Accessed on 8 September 2022.

including two centuries. This performance caught the attention of the then Indian captain Sourav Ganguly, who ensured his selection to the Indian team.

The Indian cricket team has always been somewhat lacking in its wicketkeeping. While other teams boasted of talented wicketkeeper-batters, such as Gilchrist (Australia) and Mark Boucher (South Africa), India was in need of a talented wicketkeeper who was also useful with the bat. During the 2003 World Cup, Rahul Dravid had to wear gloves to lend balance to the side.[2] India also experimented with the likes of Parthiv Patel, Dinesh Karthik and Syed Saba Karim to find a viable alternative to Dravid. It was eventually Dhoni who filled this void.

In 2005, during the six-match ODI series (Pepsi Cup) against Pakistan, Dhoni scored 148 runs off only 123 deliveries in Vishakhapatnam, making it the highest score by an Indian wicketkeeper. The same year, he bettered this record against Sri Lanka while chasing 299 runs in a bilateral series by scoring an unbeaten 183 runs off 148 deliveries. This was also the record highest score at that time by any batter in the second innings. Dhoni's overall performance in the series earned him his first 'Man of the Series' award. He also played a critical knock in the final ODI during India's tour of Pakistan in 2006 and was briefly ranked as the No. 1 player in ODI cricket.

> **Learning Tip:** Focus on upgrading your skills so that when the right opportunity knocks at your door, you are prepared.

---

[2] Adhikari, Somak 'Here's Why Rahul Dravid Was Wicketkeeper in the 2003 World Cup: It Was the Only Way He Could Be in the Team!' *Indiatimes*, 11 August 2017, https://bit.ly/3RNNQZc. Accessed on 8 September 2022.

TRYST WITH CAPTAINCY

In 2007, the Indian team made an early exit from the World Cup after a shock defeat at the hands of Bangladesh in the group stage. This led to wide-scale protests and some protestors even vandalized Dhoni's farmhouse near Ranchi.[3] In the midst of this, it was decided that seniors, like Tendulkar, Dravid and Ganguly, would not be a part of the inaugural 2007 T20 World Cup and Dhoni was declared the captain of the Indian team.

One can't help but admire the maturity with which Dhoni led an inexperienced team to victory. His calm and composed nature on the field was exactly what the Indian team needed. According to the manager of the Indian team during the T20 World Cup, Lalchand Rajput, Dhoni's mantra was very simple: don't take tension, give tension.[4] This helped in ensuring a pleasant atmosphere in the dressing room and players could concentrate on the game rather than the negative comments in the media. Another significant feature of the tournament was how Dhoni inspired his teammates R.P. Singh, Yuvraj Singh, Yusuf Pathan, Piyush Chawla, Joginder Sharma and Robin Uthappa to play to their full potential and deliver match-winning performances.

One of the most important league matches was against Pakistan when the scores of both the teams were tied, leading to a super over, which is similar to a penalty shootout in soccer where each team has to nominate five players to aim at the stumps. Surprisingly, India chose part-time bowlers

---

[3]Saeed, Umaima, 'SK Flashback: When India Were Knocked Out of the 2007 World Cup', Sportskeeda, 23 March 2017, https://bit.ly/3Rt6O7N. Accessed on 8 September 2022.

[4]Malu, Jatin, 'MS Dhoni's Advice for Players in T20 World Cup 2007 Revealed by Lalchand Rajput', Republic World, 30 June 2020, https://bit.ly/3qlUOcq. Accessed on 8 September 2022.

and spinners for the bowl-out, whereas Pakistan went ahead with their regular bowlers. The Indian team managed to hit the stumps in each of the deliveries, whereas Pakistan missed theirs. It was revealed later that Dhoni had already made his players practise at the nets, anticipating a bowl-out. After he analysed the movement of the pitch, he decided to go against the pacers. It was this critical and effective thinking that made the difference. In the T20 World Cup final against Pakistan, Dhoni kept his nerve when S. Sreesanth held on to Misbah-ul-Haq's catch in the final over to give India a crucial victory. If we look at the Indian team's T20 experience prior to the World Cup, there were seven players, including Dhoni, who had played just one T20I prior to the tournament and eight players who made their debut during the cup. The Indian players had very little experience of playing T20 cricket matches and there was much negative press owing to the team's dismal 50-over World Cup performance. Also, the Australian and South African players were far more experienced. This was a real challenge for Dhoni. He had to keep the morale of the players high as well as ensure a sure-shot victory.

Learning Tip: It is important to be calm and composed and be prepared for all scenarios.

Good leaders make successful teams. Consider the example of Microsoft, where Steve Ballmer and Paul Allen played a pivotal role during the initial period alongside Bill Gates. Similarly, Sheryl Sandberg's role was as important in running Meta as is Mark Zuckerberg's. Dhoni was instrumental in building the core of Team India comprising senior cricketers, such as Harbhajan Singh, Virender Sehwag, Yuvraj Singh and Zaheer Khan, around whom youngsters blossomed in their respective roles.

One of the key aspects of Dhoni's leadership is his ability to back talent if he is convinced of it yielding results. A few of the notable youngsters who were groomed during Dhoni's tenure as captain include Virat Kohli, Suresh Raina, Ravindra Jadeja and Bhuvneshwar Kumar. Former Indian cricketer Zaheer Khan acknowledged that Dhoni played a significant role in mentoring youngsters. In an interview, he brought out the similarities in the captaincy styles of Dhoni and Ganguly. Praising Dhoni, he said, 'When MS got the team, he had a lot of senior players who were experienced at the international level. So he didn't have to do much in terms of getting them up to speed. But once all those guys started retiring, when the young batch came in, he played a similar kind of role, did similar kind of things to what Dada was doing with the young lot.'[5] Indian wicketkeeper Rishabh Pant too has acknowledged the role Dhoni played in shaping his career, 'He (Dhoni) has been like a mentor to me, on and off the field. I can approach him freely with any problem I may be facing, and he will never give me the entire solution for it.'[6] Though Dhoni acted as a mentor, he never spoon-fed the players by giving the complete solution himself. Individual players had to discover the solution themselves. This in turn boosted their self-belief and made them self-reliant.

> **Learning Tip:** A mentor will help you learn from their experience and give valuable feedback.

---

[5] "Zaheer Khan Recalls How MS Dhoni and Sourav Ganguly Mentored Youngsters and Turned Them into World Beaters', *Latestly*, 16 April 2020, https://bit.ly/3fQdr6L. Accessed on 10 November 2022.

[6] "Rishabh Pant Reveals How "Mentor" MS Dhoni Helps Him Solve Issues without Giving Full Solution', NDTV, 2 May 2020, https://bit.ly/3D4HJvJ. Accessed on 8 September 2022.

In the 2011 World Cup final against Sri Lanka, Dhoni promoted himself up the batting order instead of Yuvraj to keep a left hand–right hand combination at the batting crease. Gautam Gambhir and Dhoni stitched together a winning partnership, with the latter scoring an unbeaten 91 runs and finishing the match with a towering 6 at the Wankhede Stadium. Prior to the match, Dhoni was not among the runs in the tournament, yet he took up the challenge and led from the front. He subsequently led India to the semifinal of the 2015 World Cup as well, which included a seven-match unbeaten streak (11 overall including the 2011 World Cup).

In the Indian Premier League (IPL) as well, Dhoni always led from the front, making Chennai Super Kings one of the most successful teams. Leading a team in the IPL proves to be an interesting challenge, as it entails playing with cricketers you are pitted against in international cricket as well as a bunch of youngsters. Dhoni executed this challenge beautifully and has even been acknowledged by former Australian cricketer Michael 'Mike' Hussey as the best captain in the world.[7] Dhoni's captaining style allows his players to be themselves, as he has faith in their abilities.

A leader should apply the same principle to a corporate set-up and the results will take care of themselves. Just as players come from different backgrounds and cultures, workplace environments are equally diverse. To lead such a team effectively, one must be patient and approachable. These are skills that are equally important to become an effective leader along with proper communication skills.

---

[7] 'He's the Greatest Finisher of All Time: Michael Hussey Reveals MS Dhoni's Philosophy', *Outlook*, 14 April 2020, https://bit.ly/3E8cekl. Accessed on 7 November 2022.

> **Learning Tip:** To be an effective leader, one must be willing to listen and build an atmosphere of mutual respect and trust.

While critics often criticized Dhoni's batting performance as being dismal along with having a low strike rate, there is another side to the story. Dhoni had sacrificed his No. 3 batting position, taking into account the winning chances of his team rather than himself. He could have continued to play at No. 3 in the ODI team and amassed significantly more runs while batting, but he felt that if he played lower down, it would lend stability to the team. Moreover, when there was a promising youngster like Kohli in the side, Dhoni was willing to sacrifice his slot. At positions No. 6 and No. 7, Dhoni often got less than 10 overs to bat, where the focus was on quickly accelerating the score without much time to settle in the middle.[8] Despite these odds, Dhoni has managed to score more than 10,000 runs in ODI cricket and is regarded as one of the best finishers of world cricket. He adapted his role from hitting big shots to lending crucial support in the middle overs. He gave more emphasis on winning matches rather than on achieving personal milestones.

When his first child was born, Dhoni was in Australia as the captain of the Indian team for the 2015 World Cup. He decided not to fly back, as the tournament was just a week away. For him, his sense of national duty was top priority. By being a team player, Dhoni also ensured that the team always comes first. Just as a captain is the last person to jump ship in times of distress, a true leader needs to first ensure the well-being of his team members. Another significant characteristic of Dhoni as leader is his ability to give credit to other players

---

[8] Kumar, Sashwant, 'Could MS Dhoni Have Been an All-Time Great No. 3?' *Wisden*, 6 April 2022, https://bit.ly/3hplA2l. Accessed on 10 November 2022.

while accepting more than his share of responsibility in post-match press conferences.

> *True leaders lead from the front. In the midst of the Covid-19 crisis, many CEOs offered to work with a reduced pay or even a token sum of money. Such leaders are inspiring, as they put the interests of the organization and people before theirs. For example, the Tata group did not lay off anyone despite incurring losses during the pandemic.[9] This, in turn, promotes loyalty among the workforce and also helps in building a better brand equity for the firm.*

Learning Tip: To be a true leader, one should be bold enough to accept responsibility and generous enough to give credit to others.

Succession planning is an important part of any organization's mandate. It defines the direction in which the company has to move in the years ahead after the leader's retirement. This is often a long-drawn process, with committees appointed to pick the next leader.

In this aspect too Dhoni provides us a few lessons. He relinquished his captaincy in Test cricket by announcing his retirement during India's tour of Australia in 2014. Virat Kohli was handed over the baton. He never failed to acknowledge Dhoni's role in grooming him as a future leader. 'I think a large portion of me becoming captain was also to do with him (MSD) observing me for a long period of time. It just can't happen like he goes and selectors say you become captain,'

---

[9]Chatterjee, Dev, 'Covid-19 Crisis: Ratan Tata Says Layoffs Show India Inc's Lack of Empathy', *Business Standard*, 24 July 2020, https://bit.ly/3FPH6aL. Accessed on 7 November 2022.

Virat said in an interview.[10] Dhoni later also gave up the ODI and T20 captaincy, appointing Kohli the Indian captain in all the three formats. Normally, a player does not want to give up captaincy, unless specifically told to do so by the selectors. This is normally followed by much speculation on who will be the successor. On the other hand, Dhoni planned and executed his captaincy to perfection, leaving no room for such rumours. While on the field, Dhoni guided Kohli, which kept the pressure off his shoulders during critical moments of the game. This was achieved through field placements and bowling changes at critical junctures of the match.

> **Learning Tip:** It is important for leaders to have a proper succession plan in place to ensure stable and sustainable growth.

Another striking feature of Dhoni's leadership is his stoic demeanour and self-control. He does not show his emotions and rarely loses his cool both on and off the field. In fact, it is passion for the sport that drives him, not money or fame. He rarely criticizes players publicly and believes in giving personalized feedback. He is always empathetic. In his last Test match at Nagpur, Dhoni offered Ganguly to captain the side for the final few overs of the game as India inched closer to a series-clinching victory. Such gestures speak volumes about his leadership style.

Dhoni's leadership style is a combination of Theory Y and Situational Leadership. In 1960, a social psychologist, Douglas McGregor developed two theories explaining how the management styles of managers are dependent on their

---

[10] 'A Large Portion of Me Becoming Captain Was to Do with Dhoni Observing Me for Years', *The Times of India*, 30 May 2020, https://bit.ly/3BqeXDi. Accessed on 21 September 2022.

beliefs about what motivates their employees. The theories were called Theory X and Theory Y. Theory X managers have a pessimistic view of their employees, that they are naturally unmotivated. Theory Y managers have an optimistic view of their employees, that they are intrinsically motivated. Theory Y leaders go on to create a more collaborative and trust-based relationship. Situational Leadership Theory was a model created by Paul Hersey and Ken Banchard, which states that there is no single 'best' style of leadership. Leadership is task-relevant and every leader should adapt to the performance readiness of the team members. Effective leadership varies according to task, person and group. Dhoni has been both a Theory Y and a situational leader. As a Theory Y leader, Dhoni has faith in his players' abilities and trusts them to do their best. As a situational leader, he understands that it is up to him, how he responds to a situation. This makes him very composed. His risk-taking abilities also indicate his appetite for success. During the 2007 T20 World Cup final, he handed the ball to Joginder Sharma owing to his variation in pace, which might have troubled an in-form Misbah-ul-Haq. The move paid dividends as Haq misjudged a delivery leading to a catch by Sreesanth behind the stumps, making India the world champion.

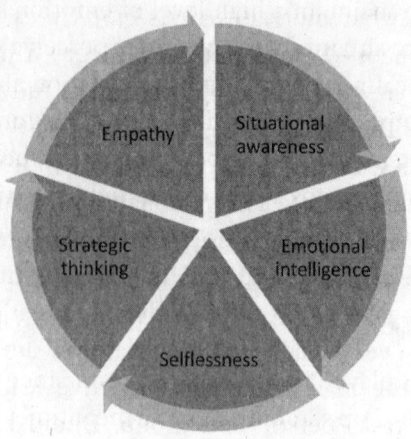

Elements of Dhoni's Leadership Style

If we analyse Dhoni's leadership style, it can be easily attributed to the following elements:

- **Empathy:** His ability to listen and guide his teammates on professional and personal issues.
- **Situational awareness:** Dhoni never loses control of the situation. He understands it well and makes his decision accordingly.
- **Emotional intelligence:** His face and body language do not reflect any pressure even in critical situations. This makes it difficult for the opposition players to read his mind, making him one of the best finishers.
- **Selflessness:** His ability to always put his team before himself earned him the respect and trust of his team members.
- **Strategic thinking:** His ability to read the game and place fielders in the perfect position makes him one of the best cricketing brains.

It is critical to maintain a high level of emotional intelligence. Our reaction to situations is how others perceive us. We should try to remain calm even in a stressful situation and respond by following a simple 30-second rule. Take a pause and think about the appropriate response for about 30 seconds before initiating it. Just as Dhoni keeps track of the field positions during a match, we too should be observant of our surroundings and make decisions accordingly.

Learning Tip: Always respond, not react, to situations.

Dhoni has not played international cricket since India's exit in the 2019 World Cup semifinals. In the meantime, he completed a two-week stint with the Indian Army in Jammu and Kashmir. Apart from this, he also operates a number of business ventures including restaurants, an entertainment company, sports teams, lifestyle brands and sports academies.

At 41, Dhoni knows he is not getting any younger. He knows there are new promising players in the team. He knew this was the right time to retire. Cricket fans all over the world were shocked when 'Captain Cool' announced his retirement from international cricket on 15 August 2020. Even his retirement announcement was a humble post on social media captioned 'from 1929 hrs consider me as Retired (*sic*)'. It was reminiscent of how he had once stepped down from his captaincy. Dhoni has led his life by example both on and off the field. Dhoni had been a mentor for the Indian team for the 2021 T20 World Cup. Fans across India hope to see Dhoni associate with cricket for a longer tenure, either as a mentor of the Indian Cricket Team or may be even as a coach in future matches.

M.S. Dhoni's Batting and Wicketkeeping Performance over the Years (till September 2022)

	Matches	Innings	Not Outs	Runs	Average	100s	50s	Catches	Stumpings
Tests	90	144	16	4876	38.09	6	33	256	38
ODIs	350	297	84	10,773	50.57	10	73	321	123
T20Is	98	85	42	1617	37.60	0	2	57	34
IPL	234	206	79	4978	39.2	0	24	207	84

22

Master of the Trade

Rafael Nadal

The only way of finding a solution is to fight back, to move, to run and to control that pressure.

RAFAEL NADAL

Rafael Nadal is one of the most electrifying tennis players of the modern era. If we consider his achievements, Nadal has the most clay court titles (63) and also holds the longest single-surface winning streak in matches (clay courts, 81) and in sets (clay courts, 50). As a result of his dominance, he is even referred to as 'The King of Clay'. However, his victories in grass courts and hard courts in recent years has established him as one of the best players of the game. Andre Agassi considers Nadal as one of the greatest player of all time, as he has had to compete with the likes of Roger Federer and Novak Djokovic to establish himself.[1]

Apart from Agassi, Nadal is the only other male tennis player to win the Olympic gold in singles and four Grand Slams in his career, thus completing a Career Golden Slam. He has been given the Sportsmanship Award thrice, named the

---

[1]Associated Press, 'Andre Agassi Tabs Nadal No. 1', ESPN, 8 May 2014, https://bit.ly/3qGjzjG. Accessed on 16 September 2022.

'ATP Player of the Year' five times and awarded the ITF World Champion four times. In 2011, he was named the Laureus World Sportsman of the Year. In addition to this, Nadal has held the World No. 1 ranking for a total of 209 weeks, including being the year-end No. 1 five times. Let us try to decode the secret behind his phenomenal career.

EARLY LIFE

Rafael Nadal was born in the Balearic Islands, Spain, to Sebastián Nadal Homar, a businessman by profession, and Ana María Parera Femenías. His family has a sports lineage, with one of his uncles Miguel Nadal, being a former professional footballer who represented the Spanish national team and FC Barcelona. It was under another one of his uncles, Toni Nadal, a former tennis coach, that Rafael initially started his training at the age of three. Nadal clearly had the advantage of being born in a family which had the means to support his career. However, it was his hard work that made him sustain. In his initial years, he pursued both soccer and tennis, and it was at the behest of his father that he chose the latter. This was largely done so that he had ample time for his studies.

The association with his uncle Toni as coach continued from 1990 to 2017, which was largely responsible for Nadal's transformation into a world champion. Toni was both assertive as a coach and supportive as a family member, and he had a great influence on Nadal. Toni instilled in him the lesson that excuses are never enough after losing a match. Imagine yourself in a sales role and you are unable to meet your target. Will your excuses be taken into account? No. One needs to identify the gaps and then work accordingly to fill those.

Learning Tip: Ask yourself what you can do today to improve yourself and create a better version of yourself than you were yesterday.

INITIAL CAREER

Nadal's first major victory was at the age of eight when he won the under-12 regional competition. He was one of the youngest participants in that age group. Following this, his uncle made him train harder and also encouraged him to play left-handed tennis to get a natural advantage on the court. Tennis is not just about speed and accuracy but also about strength and agility. It is as important that a shot has power as it is to place it in the right corner of the court.

Nadal adopted a three-step strategy to be successful:

- Hit the ball: This is a reflection of strength and will trouble the opponent with the amount of pace and bounce.
- Find the gaps: Analyse the opponent's gameplay and discover his weakness. Once that is done, try to score by hitting the ball in those areas.
- Exhibit dominance: Any sport is played as much in the mind as it is on the ground. By exhibiting his power and strength on the court, he will be able to impact his opponent psychologically and affect their morale.

His three-step strategy can easily be adopted in a corporate set-up too by any individual by upgrading one's skill sets, delivering high-quality work prior to schedule and always raising the bar. It is also similar to a corporate performing a need-gap analysis in determining the right product for the market. To excel in any profession, one needs to be aware of the environment, perform a SWOT (strengths, weaknesses, opportunities and threats) assessment and focus on a continuous path of self-improvement.

At the age of 12, Nadal won the Spanish and European tennis titles in his age group. Given his skills, the Royal Spanish Tennis Federation asked him to move to Barcelona for further training. However, his father advised against it, as that would impact his studies. So, he decided to sponsor his son's training but without having to relocate. Toni favoured this decision. The support Nadal received from his family was critical in shaping the champion athlete in the early years of his career. In his words: 'If my uncle had not introduced me to tennis or helped me decisively during practically my entire career, I would not be where I am. That if my father and my mother had not been willing to accompany me to a place every weekend and not doing the things that maybe they had other options to do, maybe they had more fun.'[2]

People who put in hard work are successful. Simple. There is no substitute to hard work. Having access to a large amount of resources is beneficial only if there is a desire to succeed.

In May 2001, the 14-year-old Nadal defeated Pat Cash, former World No. 4 and Grand Slam winner, in an exhibition match on a clay court. While one can argue that Cash was nearing the end of his career, yet to face defeat at the hands of such a young athlete speaks volumes about Nadal's skills on clay court which the world was yet to discover.

Nadal started playing professional tennis at the age of 15. His first victory was against Ramón Delgado, who was then World No. 81, on 29 April 2002. This was Nadal's first ATP

---

[2]'Rafael Nadal Claims He Was "Lucky" to Have Had Certain People by His Side, Pays Special Tribute to Uncle Toni and His Parents', Sportskeeda, 6 April 2021, https://bit.ly/3DWuoGc. Accessed on 28 September 2022.

match, when he was ranked 762 in the world. The victory came in straight sets (6-4, 6-4) in a match that lasted an hour and 23 minutes, making him the youngest player to secure an ATP victory.

One of the reasons why Nadal was successful at such an early age is his spirit of sacrifice for the sport. The harder you practise, the luckier you become, and Nadal epitomizes that.

The life story of any entrepreneur, from Jeff Bezos and Jack Ma to Dhirubhai Ambani, has one factor in common: success that has been the result of sacrifice, passion and dedication. Interestingly, the three components are always in sync with each other and the absence of one will lead to failure.

In 2002, Nadal managed to reach the semifinals of the boys' singles tournament at Wimbledon and also helped Spain defeat the US in the Junior Davis Cup. He finished the year with an ITF Futures record of 40-9 in singles and 10-9 in doubles with six victories, including five on the clay court and one on hard court. It is important to note that his first victory against Ramon was also on clay court in Mallorca, Spain.

STYLE OF PLAYING

There are normally two types of strategies that players employ on the court. They either play near the baseline or near the mid-court and the net. Nadal prefers the former, which leads him to use tremendous power in his shots, and is known for his athleticism and speed around the court. The one thing that sets him apart from other players is the amount of topspin he is able to generate owing to his forehand grip. He has the highest topspin rate in comparison to any professional player on tour, meaning he can hit the ball with extreme spin to wear down his opponents.

According to a study by San Francisco-based tennis researcher John Yandell, the number of revolutions per minute in a forehand shot by Nadal can be as high as 4,900 (with an average of 3,200) compared to about 2,700 for Federer and about 1,800–1,900 for former tennis greats like Pete Sampras and Andre Agassi.[3] The spin in the ball is important, as it confuses the opponent about the level of bounce and the pace they can expect. Another point to note is his focus on the consistency of his service rather than looking to hit winners. This helps him focus on accuracy without creating too many variations.

Tennis as a sport is physically demanding and takes a significant toll on the body. Nadal's aggressive playing style makes him susceptible to injury. In 2004, when Nadal was detected with Mueller-Weiss syndrome in his left foot, his doctors told him he would never be able to play professional tennis again. Yet, his self-belief kept him going and he defied all odds to make a comeback.

THE RISE OF RAFAEL NADAL

In 2003, Nadal won two challenger trophies and finished the year ranked No. 49. Within a year, his ATP ranking jumped from 762 to 49, and he also received the 'ATP Newcomer of the Year' award. The year also marked his Wimbledon debut, when he became the youngest player to qualify to round three since Boris Becker. The following year saw his first victory against Federer at the Miami Open, where he won in straight sets. Nadal, however, could not play in the French Open owing

---

[3]Fromal, Adam, 'U.S. Open Tennis 2010: 10 Reasons Rafael Nadal Is the Dominant Player in Tennis', Bleacher Report, 6 September 2010, https://bit.ly/3SHnUz9. Accessed on 30 September 2022.

to a stress fracture in his left ankle. In the same year, he also became the youngest player to register a singles victory in the Davis Cup final, beating the then World No. 2 Andy Roddick.

In 2005, Nadal dominated the clay court, winning 24 consecutive singles matches. He also won the French Open in his first appearance ever. He is the first teenager since Sampras to win a Grand Slam tournament. During the course of winning the French Open, he defeated Federer in the semifinals. The rivalry between the two continued the following year when Nadal defeated Federer again in the finals to clinch his second French Open title. The duo met again in the Wimbledon finals in 2006, where Federer won. Nadal finished the year as World No. 2.

Within a short span of four years, Nadal was able to transform himself from being a rookie to a world-class player. His dominance over the clay court continued in 2007, when he, once again, won the French Open finals defeating Federer. The two star players also played an exhibition match, which came to be known as 'Battle of the Surfaces'. This particular court was half clay and half grass and was meant to test their skills as Federer dominated on grass courts. Nadal won this exhibition match, once again proving his skill and talent.

The year 2008 was very significant for Nadal, as he not only won the French Open but also the Wimbledon finals, beating Federer in what became the longest game in terms of time spent on court. The match lasted four hours and 48 minutes because of rain delays. Nadal eventually won the match in the tie-breaker fifth set 9-7 in near-darkness. He became the third player to win both the French Open and Wimbledon in the same year and also ended Federer's streak of 65 consecutive wins on grass courts.

At the 2008 Olympics in Beijing, Nadal defeated Chile's

Fernando González in the final to win his first Olympic gold medal. In 2009, he defeated Federer in the Australian Open in a five-set final to become the first Spaniard to clinch the title. However, he lost in the fourth round of the French Open and had to withdraw from Wimbledon owing to tendinitis[4] in both his knees. Federer won the Wimbledon title and Nadal ended the year as World No. 2 despite his Davis Cup win.

The year 2010 was eventful for Nadal. He became the only male player in tennis history to win Grand Slam tournaments on three different surfaces (clay, grass and hard courts) in the same calendar year. He won the French Open without losing a set. He then won the Wimbledon and US Open to complete his Career Golden Slam. He finished the year as World No. 1. The year 2011 was a mixed year for Nadal, as he could not win a number of matches. He was able to retain the French Open by defeating Federer but lost the Wimbledon final to Djokovic. The Serbian player once again defeated Nadal in the US Open to become the World No. 1. In 2012, Nadal and Djokovic met again at the Australian Open final, which lasted five hours and 53 minutes and is the longest Grand Slam final in terms of duration. Djokovic eventually won the finals, but it spoke volumes about his opponent's tenacity, considering he had just recovered from a knee injury.

Nadal was finally able to end Djokovic's eight-match victory streak at the Monte Carlo trophy. This was followed by his victory over Djokovic at the Italian Open. In the 2012 French Open final, he once again clashed with Djokovic, whom he defeated in four sets, becoming the only tennis player ever to win seven French Open titles. Nadal lost in the second round

---

[4]Tendinitis is an inflammation or irritation of a tendon. The condition causes pain and tenderness just outside a joint.

of the Wimbledon and subsequently pulled out of the 2012 Olympics owing to tendinitis. He finished the year as World No. 4. It was after a period of eight years that he ended a season without being World No. 1 or No. 2.

His growth trajectory follows a pattern similar to an Elliot wave curve[5]. Each time, after a defeat, he has come back stronger and with a greater will to succeed. His health issues persisted in 2013, when he had to withdraw from the Australian Open because of a stomach infection. However, he once again won the French Open defeating Djokovic in the semifinal and David Ferrer in the finals. His semifinal match with Djokovic lasted four hours and 37 minutes, and Nadal came back from being a break point down in the fifth set to clinch victory. This was very soon followed by a surprise loss to unseeded Belgian Steve Darcis in the first round of the Wimbledon. Nadal later defeated Djokovic again in the US Open finals. However, Djokovic defeated him in the China Open and the ATP world tour finals, and the rivalry between the two continued. Nadal's consistent performance throughout the season ensured he was able to regain his World No. 1 rank.

In 2016, Nadal's campaign had a premature end in the French Open owing to a wrist injury. This also resulted in him withdrawing from the Wimbledon. At the Rio Olympics, he won the gold medal in men's doubles. The year 2016 was the first season since 2004 when Nadal failed to reach the quarterfinal of any Grand Slam, largely owing to his wrist injury. In 2018, he had to retire in the quarterfinal of the Australian Open owing to a hip injury.

A defining feature of Nadal's entire career has been his

---

[5] An Elliott wave is typically an impulsive wave that moves with the trend followed by a corrective wave that is counter-trend. This pattern is used by financial traders for technical analysis.

ability to understand and read the game properly. He carefully analyses his opponent's playing style and then plays his shot at angles and areas that make it difficult for them to match. It is actually no different from an enterprise doing a market study and then launching their product accordingly.

The year 2019 saw him losing to Djokovic in straight sets at the Australian Open final, even though he had not lost a set on the way to the finals. Nadal's hip injury caused him to withdraw from quite a few events, such as the Miami Open. During the same year, he also won his 12th Grand Slam title at the French Open and made it to the semifinals of the Wimbledon, where he lost to Federer. He followed this up with a victory in the US Open and finished the year as the ATP No. 1 player. It is quite a remarkable achievement for a tennis player with multiple injuries, who is in his thirties, to achieve this feat.

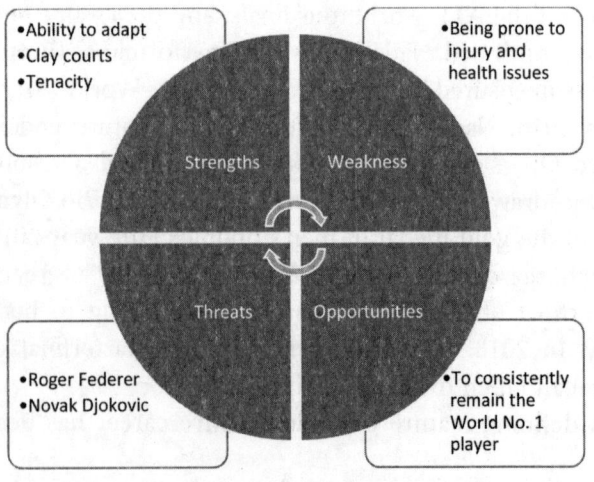

SWOT Analysis of Rafael Nadal

In terms of rivalries, Nadal has been clear to keep the competition only on the court. Throughout his career, his two major rivals have been Federer and Djokovic. With respect to the former, Nadal holds the edge with a 24-16 overall record and 10-4 in Grand Slam tournaments. However, his domination is largely on the clay court, where he holds a 14-2 advantage over Federer. Despite the rivalry on court, the duo enjoy mutual respect and often praise each other in public.

BUILDING BRAND 'RAFA'

Most of the brands that Nadal has been endorsing are the ones with which he has had a long-term association. Moreover, in the campaigns that he endorses, he has always focussed on bringing a personal touch. In short, the brands have become an extension of his real-world persona on the screen. For example, he has been associated with Kia Motors since 2006. Nike sponsors his signature sleeveless shirts and shoes, which are customized for him. He is also the brand ambassador of Quely, a family-run business from his native Mallorca which makes bakery products that Nadal has been a fan of since his childhood.

He owns and trains at the Rafal Nadal Sports Centre in his hometown of Manacor, Mallorca, which includes 26 tennis courts within its premises. During the Mallorca flood, he opened his academy to the flood victims and also donated €1 million to flood relief. He runs a tennis academy for underprivileged children in Andhra Pradesh. He has been part of the 'Million Trees for the King' project in Thailand. In 2007, he founded the Rafa Nadal Foundation, which focusses on social work and development aid, particularly for children and youth.

Nadal's Major Achievements over the Years (till September 2022)

Tournament	Record accomplished
Grand Slam	13 men's singles titles at one major
	10 consecutive years of winning 1+ title (2005–14)
	Winning titles on three different surfaces in a calendar year (2010)
	3 consecutive titles on 3 different surfaces
French Open	13 men's singles titles
ATP Masters 1000	Most men's singles titles at a single event (Monte-Carlo Masters)
	36 titles overall
	10 consecutive seasons with 1+ men's singles titles (2005–14)
	21 consecutive quarterfinals (2008–10)
Monte Carlo Masters	11 men's singles titles
Barcelona Open	12 men's singles titles
Rome Masters	10 men's singles titles
Madrid Open	5 men's singles titles

Acknowledgements

This book would not have been possible without the blessings of our parents (Dr Lina and Vishwanath Bhattacharya and Simaand Amarnath Sen). We would also like to thank our brothers (Abhishek and Prateek) and our sister-in-law (Pamela), who have constantly supported us through every phase in our lives.

We would like to express our gratitude to our publisher Rupa Publications, the editorial team (Sandhya and Manali) and our commissioning editor Yamini Chowdhury, for giving us the opportunity to write this book.

Rupa
20/1/23